THICKER THAN WATER

THICKER THAN WATER

A Monika Paniatowski Mystery

Sally Spencer

This first world edition published 2015
in Great Britain and 2016 in the USA by
SEVERN HOUSE PUBLISHERS LTD of
19 Cedar Road, Sutton, Surrey, England, SM2 5DA.
Trade paperback edition first published
in Great Britain and the USA 2016 by
SEVERN HOUSE PUBLISHERS LTD

British Library Cataloguing in Publication Data

Spencer, Sally author.
  Thicker than water. – (The Monika Paniatowski mysteries)
  1. Paniatowski, Monika (Fictitious character)–Fiction.
  2. Police–England–Fiction. 3. Murder–Investigation–
  Fiction. 4. Detective and mystery stories.
  I. Title II. Series
  823.9'2-dc23

ISBN-13: 978-0-7278-8561-6 (cased)
ISBN-13: 978-1-84751-670-1 (trade paper)
ISBN-13: 978-1-78010-724-0 (e-book)

Typeset by Palimpsest Book Production Ltd.,
Falkirk, Stirlingshire, Scotland.

PROLOGUE

At first, Jane Danbury had no idea at all of what had just happened.

She knew where she was.

Of course she knew *that*!

She was in her own lounge.

She could see the expensive wallpaper on the far wall, though it was rather worrying that it was refusing to stay still, but instead insisted on jiggling up and down like a badly tuned television.

So – she knew where she was.

What else did she know?

She knew that she had been talking to someone, only moments earlier . . .

Why couldn't she remember who that *someone* was? she wondered.

Didn't matter.

Wasn't important.

Move on!

. . . and saying things she should have said a long time ago. She knew that she had turned her back on the someone – who *was* it, for God's sake? – though she could no longer remember why she'd done that.

And she knew that that was when it had happened.

Whatever *it* was.

Did she have any clues, from which she might build up a picture of what had occurred? she asked herself.

Well, her head was hurting.

That was for sure.

In fact, it was hurting one hell of a lot.

And she had a vague sensation that something was being pumped out from a spot midway between her ears and towards the back of her skull.

Blood! she thought.

I'm spurting blood!

What was left of her brain had been working in overdrive in the split second after the blow was struck, but now her body had caught up with it, and she felt herself falling forwards.

This is all my fault, she thought as she fell.

I've been very stupid, and it's all my fault.

Her face hit the floor, and as it did, her nose almost concertinaed. It should have been an agonising experience, but she was almost beyond pain now, and she hardly noticed it.

It surprised her – annoyed her, almost – that as she lay dying (and she was sure she *was* dying) her hearing seemed to be as acute as it had ever been.

But it was. It undoubtedly was.

She heard the squeak of leather shoes, as the someone squatted down beside her.

She heard harsh, irregular breathing.

And she heard the soft swishing sound made by the soles of the shoes on the thick rug, as the someone shifted slightly to get a better angle on the task in hand.

And then she heard *nothing* – nor ever would again.

ONE

Wednesday, 5th October 1977

The phone call came through at 9.12 p.m., and by 9.14 Monika Paniatowski was already backing her car down the driveway.

Once out on the street, she straightened the vehicle up, and, before pulling off, lit a cigarette.

Paniatowski sighed. She had stopped smoking the moment she'd learned she was pregnant, and had told herself, as the pregnancy progressed, that she would never take up the habit again. But it hadn't worked out quite like that, and within days of giving birth to the twins – and perhaps *because* she had given birth to the twins – she had submitted gratefully to the old craving.

The police radio crackled into life, and a metallic female voice said, 'DCI Paniatowski, are you receiving me? Over.'

Paniatowski's left hand reached instinctively for where the radio microphone *should have* been, and found itself cupping empty air.

Different car, she reminded herself – *different car, different layout.*

For just an instant, she mourned the loss of her little red MGA which her change in circumstances had forced her to trade in for the larger – and far less loveable – Ford Cortina.

'DCI Paniatowski?' the metallic voice repeated.

Paniatowski's reprogrammed hand unhooked the microphone and lifted it to her mouth.

'DCI Paniatowski receiving you,' she said. 'What's the current operational status?'

'Inspector Flowers and her team have reached the house and secured the crime scene,' the voice replied.

'Has *my* team been contacted yet?'

'We've called DS Meadows' beeper several times, ma'am, but she's still not got back to us.'

'Shit!' Paniatowski said.

She'd only been back from maternity leave for three days. Her investigative skills had probably been dulled through lack of use, so the last thing she wanted was to embark on a high-profile murder investigation without her trusted bagman firmly at her side. And this murder just *had to be* high profile – because it had taken place in Milliners' Row.

'Do you want me to try and contact DS Meadows again, ma'am?' the operator asked.

If Kate Meadows wasn't responding, it could only be because she'd put her detective sergeant persona on hold and become Zelda, a creature of the night, who recognised no responsibilities and played by no rules but her own.

'Ma'am?' the operator said.

'Yes, beep her again – and keep beeping her until she answers – but get hold of DI Beresford and DC Crane first.'

Milliners' Row was located near the northern tip of the Whitebridge municipal authority. Though it would have been strictly accurate to call it a private housing estate, it would have also been thoroughly misleading, since it differed, in so many ways, from the housing estates which flanked it – at a respectful distance – on its left and right.

There were twenty-four houses in the Row, and the twelve on the south side looked across at the twelve on the north side over a wide avenue, along the centre of which ran a line of evergreen trees of exotic varieties rarely seen in Lancashire. Each house sat on a half-acre plot, and the plots were each surrounded by high, imposing walls. It was commonly referred to by most people in Whitebridge (often enviously, and occasionally bitterly) as *Millionaire's* Row.

There was no need for Paniatowski to count off the houses as she went, in order to establish which one was No. 7 Milliners' Row – the half a dozen police cars parked in front of it provided ample indication.

As she drew level with No. 3, a middle-aged police constable stepped out into the road, and waved her down with his torch.

'I'm afraid I'm going to have to ask you to turn around, madam,' he said, politely but firmly.

Paniatowski held her warrant card out of the window, and the constable shone the torch on it.

'Sorry, ma'am, I didn't recognise you,' he said. 'Is this your car?'

Paniatowski grinned. 'Aren't you only supposed to ask that if you suspect it's been stolen?'

'No, what I meant was, where's your MGA?' the constable explained hurriedly. He paused. 'You've never got rid of it, have you?'

'I'm afraid I have,' Paniatowski admitted.

'But it was such a lovely little car, and you kept it immaculate,' the constable said, as if mourning the loss personally.

'Right on both counts,' Paniatowski agreed, edging the big, graceless Cortina forward.

The woman standing on the pavement in front of the large ornamental gates was in her early thirties, and had the wiry body of a dedicated hockey player. She wore an expression which said she was fairly confident she had handled the situation well, but that she also recognised, given her relative lack of experience, that there was always a slim chance she had made a colossal blunder.

'What have you got for me so far, Elizabeth?' Paniatowski asked, when they'd exchanged greetings.

'The victim hasn't been formally identified yet, but she's presumed to be Jane Danbury. She's been living here, with her husband and three children, for about four years.'

'Where did you get this information from?'

'The au pair, a girl called Gretchen Müller.'

'Is she the one who found the body?'

'Yes, ma'am.'

'Was she here at the time of the murder?'

'No, she gets Wednesdays off, and she's been out for most of the day. She only came back to change into her party clothes.'

'When was this?'

'About three-quarters of an hour ago.'

'And she was the one who called us?'

'Yes.'

A lot of young women wouldn't have the presence of mind

to do that, Paniatowski thought. A lot of young women would just have run round to the neighbours' house in a blue funk. But then, of course, running round to the neighbours' house was no simple matter in a place like Milliners' Row.

'Where's the girl now?' she asked.

'She's sitting in the back of one of the patrol cars. I gave her a blanket, and a cup of hot sweet tea.'

'Where did you get the tea from?' Paniatowski wondered. 'Did one of the neighbours send his butler round with it on a silver tray?'

Inspector Flowers grinned. 'No, ma'am. I always carry a thermos flask of tea with me. It's remarkable how often it comes in useful.'

It was a nice, thoughtful, domestic touch, Paniatowski thought – perhaps just a little too thoughtful and domestic for a woman trying to claw her way up the slippery slope of promotion, where all the short cuts were reserved for men.

'The flask of tea's a good idea,' she said, 'but, if I was in your shoes, I'd delegate the job to one of my lads in future.' She paused to light a cigarette. 'Apart from talking to the au pair, what other actions have you taken?'

'We searched both the grounds and the house, to establish whether or not the killer was still in the vicinity, and, of course, we checked on the children.'

'Where are they now?'

'They're still in their rooms. The boys share a room, the girl has one of her own. They're all sleeping peacefully.'

Unlike the twins, who seem to take it in turn to be on bawling duty, Paniatowski thought ruefully.

'The children's rooms have been thoroughly searched, like everywhere else, but I thought it best not to disturb the children themselves until social services arrive to deal with them,' Flowers continued.

'What if they wake up, and wander downstairs?'

'I've posted an officer at each of their bedroom doors to make sure that doesn't happen.'

Flowers seemed to have dealt with the situation rather well, Paniatowski decided.

'Where's the husband?' she asked.

'According to Gretchen, William Danbury is . . .'

'Wait a minute,' Paniatowski interrupted, 'when you say, "William Danbury", are we talking about Councillor Danbury?'

'That's right, ma'am,' Meadows said. 'Do you know him?'

Paniatowski shook her head. 'No, but I know *of* him. He runs one of the few remaining mills in this town, he was the youngest-ever president of Whitebridge Golf Club, and he's a big wheel in local politics.'

All of which made him the last person she wanted breathing down her neck when she was investigating a murder, she thought.

'Anyway, you were on the point of telling me where he is at the moment,' she continued.

'Gretchen says he's off on a business trip. He was expected back today, but it's not unusual for him to stay away longer than he's said he will.'

Another vehicle arrived on the scene – a battered Land Rover driven by Dr Shastri, the police surgeon and veteran of hundreds of grisly post-mortems.

Shastri parked behind Paniatowski's Cortina, switched off the engine, and climbed down from the cab – except that 'climbed down' was not really what she did at all. Instead, the graceful descent of her sari-clad figure made it seem as if she was almost floating to the pavement.

Shastri smiled at Paniatowski.

'My dear Monika,' she said. 'What a pleasant surprise to find you here. I had heard, of course, that you were back from your leave, but when I did not see your car in the street . . .'

'It's good to see you, Doc,' Paniatowski interrupted, before there could be any more wailing and gnashing of teeth over the departure of the bright red MGA. 'The body's inside. Would you like to take a look at it?'

'Most certainly,' Shastri agreed. 'After all, humble Indian doctor that I am, that is what I am here for.'

As Flowers swung the left gate slightly open, Paniatowski noticed that there was a large sign fastened to it which announced that the house was for sale, and advised anyone interested in buying it to contact Holgate, Jones and Hudson (Estate Agents).

Her first thought was that it was surprising that the inhabitants of somewhere like Milliners' Row should submit to the same process, when selling their houses, as mere mortals like herself did.

Her second thought – which quickly and brutally elbowed the first thought aside – was to wonder if the proposed sale of the house and the murder were in any way connected. That was improbable, she readily admitted, but if she had learned one thing about murders, it was that they were very often stuffed to the brim with improbabilities.

It was at least a hundred yards from the gate to the house. The driveway which connected the two was wide enough for two large cars to pass each other comfortably, and was cobbled with dressed stone, which Paniatowski guessed had probably been very expensive. At the far end of the driveway, there was a turning circle and a spur which, presumably, led around the side of the house to the garage.

The house itself was fairly new, but had been built in the style of a Georgian mansion. The ground floor was brilliantly – almost blindingly – illuminated, but the upper floor, where the children were sleeping, was in semi-darkness.

'I want the kids out of the house as soon as possible,' Paniatowski told Flowers as they approached the front door. 'The moment you've shown us where the body is, get on to social services again, and, if necessary, give them a hard kick up the arse from me.'

'Right, ma'am,' Flowers replied.

Detective Inspector Colin Beresford was in bed – enjoying a romp with Lillian, a divorcée who shared his cut-and-run attitude to sexual encounters – when his beeper made its unwelcome intrusion.

'Don't stop now,' Lillian told him throatily. 'Ignore it.'

'I can't,' he said.

'Ignore it,' Lillian repeated, locking her ankles tightly together in the small of his back.

'I really can't,' Beresford told her, gently pushing her thighs apart and slipping free.

Bloody idiot! he told himself as he dressed. If you hadn't been so keen to show off with your over-elaborate foreplay, you'd have reached the grand finale long before your beeper went off.

But by the time he reached his car, he was thinking neither of his missed opportunity in the bedroom nor of the killing in the posh part of town. He had, instead, turned his thoughts to Monika Paniatowski. They had been friends for a long time – since he was a fresh-faced constable and she was a very determined DS – and he loved her with a love that was only occasionally tinged by the fact that he also fancied the hell out of her. And because he loved her, he worried about her.

He did not know who the father of her twins was, and though he was dying to ask, he had always restrained himself. But their parentage was not really the main issue, he'd decided. What really mattered was Monika's attitude to Philip and Thomas. Most of the time, she seemed like a typical new mother – fussing over them, fretting about them. And if there were also times when she seemed to resent the fact they had taken much of her freedom away, well, that was normal, too. But what really – really – disturbed him was that, once or twice, he had caught her looking at the twins with a look in her eyes that could only be described as fearful – and why should anybody be afraid of two little babies?

The hallway of No. 7 Milliners' Row was large enough to throw a fairly impressive party in. It was tiled with granite, and there was a broad spiral staircase at the far end of it which led to the upper storey.

The lounge – though probably, in a mansion like this, they should call it the reception room – opened off the hallway. It was as large as the whole of Paniatowski's ground floor, and was laid with a polished hardwood which had probably cost as much as her entire house.

Jane Danbury was lying on a large Persian rug in the centre of the room, halfway between a four-seater leather sofa and the marble fireplace. Her face was buried in the rug, and her arms were stretched out in front of her. The upper part of her skull – which, inevitably, the eyes were drawn to first – was a scramble of brains and bone. The parts of the rug close to her head were soaked in blood. Looking up, Paniatowski could find no sign of bloodstains on the ceiling, but that was probably because it was much higher than the usual domestic ceiling.

'Oh dear, that really is rather unpleasant,' Dr Shastri said, slipping on her overall in the doorway.

Paniatowski ran her eyes up and down the rest of the dead woman's body. Jane Danbury had been wearing a loose brown skirt and a fluffy pink sweater when she died. Both articles must have been expensive, but neither of them looked new. In other words, Jane had been wearing the comfortable, casual clothes that anyone might choose in their own home, and if the murderer had been a guest, it wasn't a guest she'd been trying to impress.

She'd not had a bad figure, either, Paniatowski had decided. The legs were good, and though the waist was not as narrow as it might once have been, well, how many women's waists didn't start to thicken a little when they hit their thirties? Perhaps the best way to describe her figure would be to call it curvaceous – except that it didn't seem quite right to apply the term to a dead woman.

Looking around the room, she saw something glinting in the corner, and when she got closer to it, she could see it was a heavy bronze figure which had clearly been flung across the room, hit the wall (there were indents in the plaster), and fallen to the floor.

The statue was about twelve inches long, and had a square base. Paniatowski squatted down beside it. It was (she read on the base) a representation of Joe Louis, who had been world heavyweight boxing champion from 1937 to 1949. The base itself was heavily stained with blood.

It was the second time in a year that she'd investigated a case in which the murder weapon had been a statue, she thought. In the first case, it had been a statue of Oscar Wilde, the Irish playwright. In this case it was the American pugilist. But what the weapons of choice had in common was that both murderers had been so enraged that they'd grabbed the first thing that would serve their purpose.

She stood up again and walked over to the fireplace. On the mantelpiece were a number of other statues – the Duke of Wellington, Winston Churchill, Rocky Marciano, Joe DiMaggio . . .

Most of the figures were evenly spaced along the shelf, but there was a significant gap between Churchill and Marciano.

That, without a doubt, was where Joe Louis had stood until very recently.

'I doubt very much if one blow, even delivered from a very strong man, could have produced this much damage,' she heard Shastri say, from behind her.

She turned around and saw that the doctor was kneeling beside the body.

'So what happened?' she asked.

'I can tell you what I *think* happened, but I may have to contradict some of what I have said – or perhaps even all of it – once I have conducted the post-mortem,' Shastri cautioned.

'I'd still like to hear it.'

'This is where she was attacked, as is obvious from the blood spatter. The blow struck her on the back of the head, and she fell forward onto the rug.'

'Was she still conscious after the first blow?'

'The position of her arms would indicate that she was – that she did her best to try and break her fall. But I have seen corpses with a bullet through their brains in a similar position, and clearly, in their cases, they were dead before they even started to fall.'

'So she might have been dead and she might have been alive, but whichever it was, he hit her again, to make sure?'

'Exactly. And in order to deliver the other blows, he must have knelt down beside her.'

'*Other* blows? You think there was more than one?'

'As I told you, my dear Monika, until I have conducted a more detailed examination . . .'

'That *is* what you think, isn't it?'

'The human skull is very tough, and the damage is extensive. It is possible it took only two blows, but I would guess it required three or four.' Shastri paused. 'I would also speculate that it must have been obvious to anyone – even someone with no medical training – that she was dead after the second blow.'

'But he kept on hitting her.'

'Indeed.'

So what did she know? Paniatowski asked herself.

She knew that the dead woman had felt secure enough to turn her back on her killer. She knew that the killer had not brought a weapon with him, but had improvised. And she knew that such was his rage that he'd kept on hitting her even after she was clearly dead.

'Would he have got any blood on his clothes?' she asked.

'I can't see how he would have avoided it,' Shastri replied.

That would be a real break in most cases, because people out on the street noticed a man with blood on him. But in this case – on this road – he could have been soaked in blood from head to foot and the chances were that no one would have seen it.

Inspector Flowers appeared in the doorway. 'Dr Lucas is here, ma'am,' she said. 'He's the family doctor, and he'd like to see Gretchen Müller.'

'Does he know what's happened?' Paniatowski asked.

'No, ma'am.'

'Then why is he here?'

'I . . . er . . . rang him.'

'You did *what*?'

'I rang him. I said we needed his help in a police matter, and he wasn't to discuss it with anyone.'

'And why would you have done that?'

'Gretchen said she was feeling cold, and asked to see her doctor. She's entitled to request medical attention, and I thought it might complicate matters later if I refused.'

It could well have done, Paniatowski thought, picturing a possible future courtroom scenario in her mind.

Paniatowski is in the witness box, and the barrister for the defence is about to question her.

'Gretchen Müller's statement was crucial to the way you investigated this case, wasn't it, Chief Inspector?' he asked.

'It was one of several leads we followed, yes.'

'I put it to you it was your most important lead. I put it to you that without her statement you would never have embarked on the pursuit – and subsequent persecution – of my client.'

'As I said, we had several leads.'

'And this lead on which you built your case was provided by a woman who was not only confused, but actually unwell. Isn't that right?'

'She seemed rational enough, and clear enough in her own mind, when I questioned her.'

'Isn't it true, Chief Inspector, that Miss Müller was feeling so unwell that she asked to see a doctor?'

'I don't know exactly how unwell she was feeling, but yes, she did ask for a doctor.'

'And you refused that request.'

'Yes.'

'I don't like idea of the family doctor being involved,' Paniatowski said. 'Why didn't you arrange for her to be taken down to Whitebridge General?'

'I suggested that, and she was quite insistent that it was Dr Lucas – and only Dr Lucas – that she wanted to see. I can understand why she feels like that. He's my doctor, as well, and he's very sympathetic and understanding.'

'But can we trust him?'

'Definitely, ma'am. I'd stake my reputation on it.'

'You just have,' Paniatowski said. 'Where is he now?'

'Just outside the front door.'

'Then I suppose I'd better talk to him.' Paniatowski glanced down at her watch. 'And where are the bloody social services?' she demanded.

'I've rung them again, and they swear they're already on their way, ma'am,' Inspector Flowers replied.

Someone at the back of the room coughed, but the man standing at the front – and holding a sheaf of poems in his hand – decided to ignore it.

> 'It leaves a trail of slime across my soul,' he recited,
> 'Like some terrestrial gastropod mollusc,
> High on drugs, and out for mischief.'

DC Jack Crane paused, to give his audience in Rawtenstall Central Library's Reading Room the opportunity to soak up the image. There'd been a time when what he'd produced had been much more lyrical, he thought, but the kind of work he was involved in now made it almost impossible for his imagination to generate images of skylarks and gently flowing water courses.

'It chills my blood, it slows my heart . . .'

A sudden buzzing sound filled the library. The progressives in Crane's (admittedly small) audience nodded their heads in approval at this bold use of sound effects during a performance. The traditionalists, in contrast, exchanged glances which said they could remember a time when young poets hadn't felt the need to resort to gimmicks but had, instead, relied solely on the power of their words.

Both groups looked a little disappointed when Crane stopped reading and said, 'I'm sorry, that's my beeper. I have to ring headquarters immediately.'

'There's a phone in the office you can use,' the chairman said, 'and if it turns out to be not as urgent as you seem to think it is, Mr Crane, then we'll all be more than willing . . .'

'It will be,' Crane interrupted. 'Thank you for having me. I'm sorry to have cut the reading short.'

He left the room to a smattering of applause, which, given the circumstances, he thought was more than he deserved.

On his way back to Whitebridge, he flicked the mental switch in his head, sending the poet into temporary oblivion and allowing the policeman space in which to work.

It was good that the boss was back, he thought. The team needed her, because though it *was* a good team, it had its weaknesses, and those weaknesses had to be controlled.

Colin Beresford, though a solid, hard-working – sometimes even inspired – bobby, was not above occasionally letting his prejudice for old-fashioned ways and attitudes colour his interpretation of the facts.

Kate Meadows, who had a real flair for the work, could sometimes be a loose cannon, trampling on rules and regulations as if she thought they did not actually apply to her.

And what of Jack Crane, MA (Oxon.)? he asked himself with a rueful grin.

Well, he thought that Jack Crane was pretty near perfect, except for those times when the boss pointed out that he wasn't and – faced with the evidence – he felt obliged to agree with her.

Dr Lucas was of medium height, no more than a few pounds overweight, and in his middle-to-late thirties. Very few women would have called him a handsome man, but even fewer would have been willing to condemn him as ugly. He had intelligent brown eyes and a mouth which could probably deliver a caring, sympathetic smile, but now the eyes were troubled and the mouth had the downturn of a very worried man.

'Liz Flowers asked me to come, but she wouldn't tell me what it was about,' he said to Paniatowski. 'Has somebody been hurt? Is it Jane?'

'Now why would you ask that?' Paniatowski wondered.

'Isn't that obvious? The police are here, and I've been summoned, so there must be something wrong,' Lucas said.

'What I meant was, why did you automatically assume it was Mrs Danbury who'd been hurt? After all, five people live in this house.'

'I don't know why I assumed it – I just did,' Lucas said, unconvincingly.

'As a matter of fact, you're right, and it is Mrs Danbury who was hurt,' Paniatowski said.

'I'm sure it was an accident,' Lucas said.

'An accident?' Paniatowski repeated quizzically. 'And you can say that without even examining her, can you?'

'He won't have meant it,' Dr Lucas said in a rush. 'He just doesn't know his own . . .'

'Go on,' Paniatowski said.

'I think I've said more than enough,' Lucas replied, his voice turning into a mere mumble.

'Are you telling me that you know who might have *accidentally* hurt Mrs Danbury?'

'No, of course not. How could I know that?'

The time for verbal fencing was over, Paniatowski decided.

'So you've no idea who could have smashed in her skull with a bronze statuette?' she asked bluntly.

'Oh, my God,' Lucas moaned. 'Is she dead?'

'You're a doctor – what do you think?' Paniatowski asked.

'William would never have done *that*. I swear to God he wouldn't have.'

'And by William, you mean William Danbury, her husband, do you?' Paniatowski asked.

'Look, I don't think you're being fair,' Lucas said, evading the question. 'You asked me to come here in my capacity as the family doctor, and if there's nothing for me to do *as* the family doctor, then I think I'd like to leave.'

'But there is something for you to do as the family doctor,' Paniatowski said. 'One of your patients, Gretchen Müller, has asked to see you.'

'Is she the one who . . .?'

'Yes, she's the one who found the body.'

'Poor Gretchen,' Lucas said. 'That must have been terrible for a young woman like her. Where is she?'

'Before I let you see her, I want to be sure that you're capable of dealing with her in a professional manner.'

'Well, of course I am – I'm a doctor.'

'You're also a friend of the family, so Jane Danbury's death must have come as a great shock to you.'

'Death always comes as a shock, even in my business,' Lucas said. 'But Jane wasn't exactly a close friend. I knew her, of course – I quite liked her – but my friend, who I've known since primary school, is William.' He took a deep breath and squared his shoulders. 'I assure you, I'm perfectly capable of treating Gretchen. In fact, it is my duty to do so.'

'All right,' Paniatowski agreed. 'But you are not to discuss anything that has happened here with her, and if she requires anything more than a mild sedative, you are to consult me first. Understood?'

'Understood,' Dr Lucas said.

DS Kate Meadows was no snob. It didn't matter to her whether the man wielding the whip or receiving the lash himself was a coal miner (and there had been several of those) or a high-flying barrister (a breed who, she had found, seemed to be both particularly drawn to S and M and, despite her obvious lack of interest in it, keen to talk about their work). What *did* matter to her was how inventive those fleeting partners were, and whether they could accurately judge the thin line of pleasure that lay between mild enough to be positively dull and extreme enough to draw blood.

Her partner that night (who, like all the others, had been reached through an anonymous advertisement in a contact magazine), definitely belonged at the upper reaches of the social scale, and had been most unusually creative, possibly as a result of experiences he'd endured in one of England's finer public schools. But now it was all over, and it was time to leave both him and the Grand Hotel, Lancaster, well behind her.

The man, who claimed that his name was Robert – as if names mattered to her, one way or the other! – lay contentedly in the hotel bed, watching her getting dressed, and as she was about to go, he said, 'Well, that was jolly good, wasn't it?'

'Yes,' she agreed, 'it was.'

'So why don't we do it again?' he suggested.

'I don't think so,' Meadows said, adjusting her spiked purple Zelda wig in the mirror.

'Why not?' the man asked, with a slight edge of hurt creeping into his voice.

Meadows sighed.

'It was great tonight, but the next time it wouldn't be quite as good, and after that . . .'

She let her voice trail off, hoping he'd got the point.

'I'm not so sure you're right there,' he said. 'If we both worked at it – if we both *wanted* it to work . . .'

That was the trouble with some men, she thought. They simply couldn't be detached. They refused to see that sex, on the one hand, and real life and relationships, on the other, were entirely different things, and that if you mixed them together you were asking for trouble.

'It's best to leave it as it is,' she said, heading for the door.

'Wait a minute,' he called after her. 'I know you.'

She froze. 'A lot of people think they know me, but it turns out to have been someone else entirely,' she said.

'No, no,' persisted Robert – or Nigel, or whatever else his bloody name really was. 'It's been bothering me, on and off, all evening, and I've only just pinned it down. It was some years ago, I admit, but we were introduced in the Royal Enclosure at Ascot.'

She remembered him now – grey morning suit, top hat, surrounded by other equally insignificant members of his over-privileged, inbred tribe. He'd even tried to pick her up, she recalled, though at least he'd had the wit to hold off on his crude manoeuvring until Her Majesty the Queen had left the Enclosure.

'It wasn't me,' she said.

'I think I can even remember your name. Yes, I'm almost sure I can. Aren't you Lady . . .?'

'My real name's Colleen Beresford – and I've never been south of Stoke-on-Trent,' she interrupted him.

'Extraordinary,' he said. 'I could have sworn . . .'

'Well, you'd have been wrong.'

She stepped out of the room and walked quickly to the end of the corridor. She did not wait for the lift, but took the stairs.

Her car was in the hotel car park, and as she slid her key into the ignition she checked her beeper and saw that she had been called several times, the last of those calls being nearly an hour ago.

'Shit!' she said.

Then she slammed her car into gear and wondered where she could find a secluded lay-by in which she could consign Zelda to the leather bag in the boot of her car.

The ambulance had taken the mortal remains of Jane Danbury to the mortuary, and the houses the length and breadth of Milliners' Row were already being canvassed in the hopes that one of the neighbours had actually seen something that had occurred beyond the walls of his private fortress.

'Where are those bloody people from the social services?' Paniatowski demanded, as she, Flowers and Beresford stood in the hallway, close to the spiral staircase.

'I don't know, ma'am,' Flowers admitted.

Paniatowski turned to Beresford. 'When all this over, I want you to remind me to pay social services a visit – and when I do, I'll not be leaving again until I've got somebody's balls on a silver platter,' she said.

'You need to calm down, boss,' Beresford counselled.

'Those children should be being looked after by someone competent by now,' Paniatowski exploded. 'None of what's happened is their fault, and they need protecting.'

But she knew that Beresford was right, and she forced herself to take several deep breaths.

There was a sudden disturbance at the front door, and a large man in a smart blue suit burst in, followed by two uniformed officers.

'This is my house,' the man bellowed, 'and I'll enter it any time I bloody well feel like it.'

Paniatowski stepped into the centre of the hallway, blocking the access to the stairs.

'Councillor Danbury?' she asked.

'Yes – and who the hell are you?'

'DCI Paniatowski. I wonder if you could . . .'

'I want to see my boys,' Danbury said. 'Don't you understand that, you stupid bitch? I want to see them right now!'

'Given the state you're in at the moment, Councillor Danbury, I don't think that would be a very good idea,' Paniatowski said, ignoring the insult. 'Perhaps when you've had a little time to cool off . . .'

Danbury strode furiously towards her. 'Get out of my way,' he shouted. 'Get out of my way before I knock you out of my way.'

Paniatowski held her ground, and Danbury came to a reluctant halt, just a foot from her.

'I've told you to get out of my way,' he said – and now his voice was lower and much colder.

'I'm afraid I simply won't allow you to go up those stairs,' Paniatowski told him.

Danbury turned his attention to Beresford, and said in a tone which could almost have been described as reasonable, 'Do me a favour, old chap, and talk some sense into this cretinous woman.'

'Sorry, I can't,' Beresford said.

'Why not, for God's sake?'

'Because firstly, she's the boss, and secondly, she's right – you shouldn't see the kids the state you're in.'

Danbury snorted. 'She's the boss,' he repeated in disgust. 'She's the boss and so you let her lead you round by the nose. Just what kind of a man *are* you?'

'I'm going to have to insist that you leave the house immediately, Councillor Danbury,' Paniatowski said.

'You're going to have to do *what*?'

'You heard me.'

If Danbury had sent out any signal – physical *or* mental – of what was about to follow, she would have employed the considerable skills she'd acquired during her judo training to ward him off. But he gave no indication at all. Instead, he shrugged, and half-turned towards the door.

'Please believe me, Councillor Danbury, as soon as we judge it reasonable for you to see your children, we'll arrange it,' Paniatowski said.

Danbury swung round and slapped her across her face with the palm of his hand. He was a big man, the blow was delivered with some force, and Paniatowski might well have collapsed unaided if she'd been given the opportunity.

But Danbury wasn't prepared to wait for that. He took another step towards her, grasped her by the shoulder and pushed. For a second, she tottered unsteadily, then her legs gave way. As she hit the floor, she was conscious of Danbury stepping over her.

Danbury already had his foot on the first step when his chin came into contact with Colin Beresford's fist. He turned, his face blazing with anger and pain, and Beresford punched him again, this time in the stomach.

The two uniformed constables, who had been watching the whole scene in stunned disbelief, snapped out of their trance, stepped forward and grabbed Danbury before he joined Paniatowski on the floor.

With both his arms restrained and his belly on fire, Danbury looked up at Beresford.

'I'll have your job for this,' he said, speaking with difficulty. 'And as for you, bitch . . .' he inclined his head as far towards Paniatowski as the situation allowed him, '. . . you need taming – and I'm just the man to do it.'

'Lock him up in the back of one of the patrol cars,' Beresford said. He bent down next to Paniatowski. 'How are you, boss?' he asked, as the two constables half-assisted, half-dragged Danbury to the front door.

'I can't believe I let that happen,' Paniatowski groaned.

'You didn't *let* anything happen,' Beresford assured her. 'If I give you some help, do you think you can stand up?'

'I'd better be able to,' Paniatowski said. 'I've still got a murder to investigate.'

Beresford assisted her to her feet.

'You're going to have a prize-winning bruise in the morning,' he said, examining her cheek. 'I think we should get it checked out right away.'

'I'll be fine once I've had a cigarette,' Paniatowski insisted. She raised her hand and massaged her jaw. 'You shouldn't have hit him like that, you know.'

'I needed to subdue him, and I employed "reasonable force",' Beresford protested.

Paniatowski grinned.

A pain shot up her jawbone.

'Yes, reasonable force,' she repeated. 'And if it comes to it, I'll swear blind before the chief constable, the review board and God Almighty Himself that that's just what it was. But you and I both know that there were other – less violent – ways you could have done it.'

'He hurt you, Monika,' Beresford said, with feeling, 'and I wanted to hurt him back. In fact, he should count himself bloody lucky I didn't kill him.'

One of the constables who'd been posted outside the bedrooms came down the stairs, looking flustered.

'One of the little lads has woken up, ma'am,' he said. 'He's calling out for his mother. I don't know what to do with him.'

'Leave it to me,' Paniatowski said, wishing the ache in her jaw would go away.

Climbing the stairs was a real effort, and there was a moment on the landing when she thought she would faint, but somehow she made it to the bedroom. As she sank gratefully to her knees next to the bed, she told herself that getting up again might well present something of a problem, but she would worry about that later.

The boy in the bed had a roundish, concerned face and troubled eyes.

'Who are you?' he asked.

'I'm Monika,' she said. 'And who are you?'

'I'm Simon. Where's Mummy?'

'Mummy's not feeling very well, and has had to go to hospital,' Paniatowski said gently.

'Will she be all right?' Simon asked.

'We'll have to wait until we hear what the doctors have to say,' Paniatowski answered, dodging the bullet.

'I thought I heard Daddy's voice,' the boy said. 'He was shouting. Daddy shouts a lot, you know.'

'It was probably just a bad dream,' Paniatowski lied. 'Listen, Simon, we're going to have to talk about what happens next. How old are you?'

'Seven.'

'And how old are your brother and sister?'

'Charles is five and Melanie is two.'

'So that makes you the oldest, doesn't it? The responsible one? The one whose job it is to look after the other two?'

'I suppose so,' Simon said uncertainly.

'Well, in a few minutes, you're going to have to prove just how responsible you are, because some nice people will be coming to pick you up and take you somewhere else for the night.'

'Why?'

Paniatowski laughed. 'Well, silly, because your mummy is poorly and your daddy isn't here, and even a big boy like you can't be expected to stay in a house without any grown-ups, now can he?'

'I don't know,' Simon said.

'Anyway,' Paniatowski ploughed on, 'your little brother and sister will probably be quite upset, but they won't be half as upset if you tell them everything's going to be all right. Could you do that for me?'

'I . . . I think so.'

'Good boy,' Paniatowski said encouragingly.

'What happened to your face?' Simon asked.

'My face?'

'You've got a big mark on it.'

Paniatowski laughed again. 'Oh that. I'm such a silly that I wasn't looking where I was going, and I walked into a door.'

'Mummy's always walking into doors,' Simon said.

The senior social worker was called Mrs Atherton, and she was a thin, troubled-looking woman in her mid-forties, with nicotine-stained fingers and fingernails which had been chewed down to the quick. Paniatowski wondered whether the hands were testament to the fact that she couldn't handle her job, or if they were an indication that she took her job so seriously that it was slowly killing her. It was possible, she decided, that it was both.

Mrs Atherton was accompanied by two members of her staff, one male and one female, who were considerably younger – and far less careworn – than she was.

'I'm sorry we took so long,' Mrs Atherton said. 'It wasn't easy to find accommodation for *three* children – especially at this time of night.' She read the look of scepticism on Paniatowski's face, and added, 'I didn't want to split them up. I thought it was important that they stayed together as a family, so I had to look for a unit that would take all three.'

Paniatowski felt all the anger that had been building up inside her begin to drain away.

'I think that was the right approach to take,' she said. 'The children are upstairs. The oldest one woke up a while ago, but he's dropped off again now. We haven't had a peep out of the other two.'

'I'll take one of the boys, and you can take the other, Toby. Olivia, I'd like you to handle the little girl,' Mrs Atherton said to her team. She turned her attention back to Paniatowski. 'You said the children are still upstairs?'

'That's right. There's a constable posted outside each of their doors.'

'Then let's do it,' Mrs Atherton said.

As she watched them walk up the broad staircase, Paniatowski found her heart going out to little Simon, who, sooner or later, would have to be told that he didn't have a mother any more.

She wondered if her own twins were missing her, or if they had already accepted Elena Lopez, her new live-in nanny-cum-housekeeper, as a reasonable substitute. Half of her hoped they had, but the other half knew she would be devastated if the six months of care she had given them had meant so little to them.

No one had been expecting the scream.

And why would they have been expecting it?

There should have been *no need* for anybody to scream in a house full of police officers.

To those standing in the hall, it was quite faint at first – almost no more than the rumour of a scream – and then, suddenly, it was louder, like the wailing of a demented banshee.

There was no need to ask where it was coming from, Paniatowski thought, as she ran up the stairs, two at a time.

There was pandemonium on the landing.

Olivia, the younger social worker, was clinging to one of the constables for support. She had stopped screaming now, and was sobbing loudly into the officer's shoulder.

Mrs Atherton, holding Simon in her arms, was doing her best to comfort the boy.

And a second constable was standing in the doorway of Melanie's bedroom, visibly shaken.

'I think . . . I think you'd better see this, ma'am,' he said.

Someone – presumably Olivia the social worker – had turned back the bedclothes so that Melanie could be gently lifted out of the bed – which would have been a good plan, if the girl had actually been *in* the bed.

But she wasn't.

Instead, there were two pillows, placed in the centre of the bed to resemble the shape of a sleeping child. And one of those pillows was heavily stained with what looked like blood.

TWO

M elanie Danbury's disappearance created a tidal wave of activity that swept through Whitebridge police headquarters and would, by morning, have engulfed the whole community.

Knowledge of her disappearance was not ten minutes old when the first police check-point was set up on Preston Road.

Within fifteen minutes of the discovery, uniformed constables were knocking on doors, and off-duty officers had been rung up and told to report immediately to their stations.

It was less than twenty minutes before commanders of neighbouring divisions were examining their rosters to see how tightly they could be squeezed, and how many men they could liberate for the search for the little girl.

A mere twenty-five minutes after the social worker's scream had first alerted the people in the house on Milliners' Row that something had gone very badly wrong, the night-time producer at North Western Television was already putting together the news item which would inform the wider world of the potential tragedy, while the newsreader himself was down in the costumes department, selecting a more sombre tie.

And through the minds of all those involved in this process ran a single thought – the unthinkable had happened, and something had to be done.

Fred Southgate was one of the first civilians to feel the impact of this tidal wave, and it came in the form of a loud banging on his bedsit door as he was making his night-time cocoa.

'Who is it?' he asked, a tremble already evident in his voice.

'Police! Open up!'

Southgate padded over to the door, opened it, and saw a police sergeant and a constable standing in the hallway.

'What is it this time?' he asked wearily.

The sergeant, a family man, took a step backwards, in order to get a better look at him.

Southgate was wearing pyjamas and a dressing gown of artificial silk, he noted. He was a tall, almost gangly man, and though he couldn't have been much over fifty, he had silky white hair and watery eyes. He looked like a kindly bookkeeper, the sergeant decided, and though it was true that he had once been a bookkeeper, there was nothing in the least kindly about the bastard.

'Step back into your room,' the sergeant said.

'Have you got a warrant?' Southgate asked.

'Step back into the bloody room *now*!'

Reluctantly, Southgate did as he was told, and the sergeant followed.

The constable was about to do the same, when the sergeant said, 'You stay where you are, son,' and closed the door behind him.

The sound of the door clicking shut was one of the scariest sounds that Southgate had heard in a long time, and he started to tremble.

'I want that constable who's standing outside to come in here,' he said. 'I want him as a witness.'

'Well, tough,' the sergeant said unsympathetically. 'That's not going to happen.'

'I've got rights,' Southgate whined.

'No, you haven't,' the sergeant told him. 'You lost any rights you may once have had when you took that little girl into the woods.'

'I did my time for that,' Southgate said. 'I served fifteen years in Strangeways.'

'And then they made the big mistake of letting you out,' the sergeant said. 'Where were you tonight, you scumbag, you piece of filth?'

Southgate folded his arms across his chest. 'I don't have to answer your questions,' he said, weakly defiant.

The sergeant slapped him. It was an expertly judged slap – hard enough to hurt and make Southgate rock slightly, but not with enough force to knock him off his feet or leave a mark that would be visible an hour later.

'Where were you tonight?' the sergeant repeated.

'I was here,' Southgate said, starting to cry. 'Where else would I be? I'm not welcome in the pubs, and even if I was, I've got no money to spend because I haven't got a job.'

'And whose fault is that, you disgusting pervert?'

'It's mine. I know it's mine. But I've really been trying. I haven't been anywhere near a primary school since they let me out.'

'Tell me about Melanie Danbury,' the sergeant demanded.

'Who?'

'Melanie Danbury.'

'I've never heard of her.'

'And I suppose you're going to tell me you've never heard of Milliners' Row, either.'

'It's . . . it's a posh housing estate on the other side of town, isn't it?'

'You know it is.'

'But I've never been there – I swear I've never been there.'

'Turn around and put your hands behind your back.'

'Are you arresting me?'

'I most certainly am.'

'I haven't done anything,' Southgate said.

But he turned around anyway.

The sergeant clicked the handcuffs into place. It was more than likely that Southgate was innocent on this particular occasion, he thought, but that wasn't his call to make. He'd been told to bring the man in for questioning – just as other officers had been told to bring in other men – and that was what he was doing.

He turned his prisoner around, and looked into his watery eyes.

Nah, he thought, he definitely didn't do it.

But then he pictured his own two small daughters, and hit Southgate again, just for good measure.

Some days you got lucky, Alfie Clayton thought, as he lay back in his armchair and stretched out his legs. Some days, you took on one big load with a delivery point of up to a hundred miles away, so you had the pleasure of a nice bit of driving, and – more importantly – you only had to hump your load onto the trailer once, and off the trailer once. But there were other days – and this had been one of them – when you got a number of short-haul jobs, so you were denied a decent drive and you ended the day with aching muscles. Still, you had to take the rough with the smooth, and it was nice being your own boss.

His wife, Marjorie, appeared in the doorway. She had already taken off her apron, which, he knew from experience, signalled the end of her day.

'Are you coming up to bed, love?' she asked.

Alfie checked his watch. Given the heavy morning he'd got ahead of him, he should make a move soon, he thought.

'I'll be up in a minute,' he said, 'as soon as the news bulletin is over.'

Alfie liked the local news. It warmed his heart to feel part of a community. But such feelings were to be denied to him that night.

'The police have issued a statement that the body of an as-yet-unnamed woman has been discovered in a house in Milliners' Row, in the north of Whitebridge,' the grim-faced announcer said. 'Foul play is suspected.'

'Oh dear, oh dear,' Alfie murmured to himself.

'In a further statement, it has been announced that a child is missing,' the newsreader continued.

A picture of a small girl appeared on the screen. She had blonde fluffy hair and dimpled cheeks. Her blue eyes were wide and innocent, and she was grinning unselfconsciously at whoever was holding the camera.

'Melanie Danbury is two years old,' the newsreader continued, speaking from behind the girl's smile. 'She was last seen earlier today. If you have seen her – alone or with some other person – the police urge you to ring the number on the screen. They are also appealing for volunteers to help in their search for the child. If you feel able to offer assistance, please register at Whitebridge Police Headquarters tomorrow morning – the earlier the better.'

The girl's image faded from the screen, and was replaced with that of the newsreader.

'Sport,' the newsreader said, his expression of regret slowly melting away. 'Harry Morgan, the manager of Whitebridge Rovers, has announced team changes for Rovers' match against Manchester City later in the week. Striker Jim Smith will replace Terry Whalley, whose performance so far this season has been disappointing and . . .'

Alfie had always been a big fan of the Rovers – had followed them faithfully through thick and thin – but he had no interest in them in that moment, and as he stood up to switch off the television, he felt a solitary tear run down his cheek.

The brass nameplate on the gatepost of No. 9 Milliners' Row announced that this was the residence of Colonel and Mrs Cardew, and when Beresford pressed the bell, a very military-sounding voice barked 'Police?' at him through the loudspeaker.

'That's right, sir,' Beresford agreed.

'Then you'd better come in.'

The gate buzzed open, and Beresford and Meadows walked up the drive to the house. They were met at the front door by a bald man in his seventies, who, despite the fact it was now well after midnight, was immaculately turned out in blazer, cravat and cavalry twill trousers.

'My lady wife thought we might as well go to bed, but I told her that if you knew your business – as you damn well should – you'd be paying us a call well before morning.'

'That's right, sir, we like to . . .' Beresford began.

'Well, you'd better come into the Mess, then,' Cardew interrupted him, turning on his heel and striding back into the house.

'Mess?' Beresford mouthed at Meadows.

'Officers' Mess,' Meadows mouthed back.

The Mess turned out to be a large lounge, filled with objects which even the densest of detectives could not have failed to recognise as having been brought back from the Indian subcontinent. The room was already occupied by a woman with fluffy white hair, who was wearing a twinset and pearls.

'Mrs Colonel,' Cardew said, by way of introduction. 'Can I get you something to drink?'

'No thank you, sir,' said Meadows, who didn't drink.

'We're on duty,' added Beresford, who confined his drinking to best bitter, pulled by someone standing behind a bar who had had years of experience in the mystical art.

'Well, I hope you don't mind if I have one,' Cardew said, walking over to the bar in the corner. He poured himself a stiff whisky. 'Always used to have an orderly in attendance to pour my drinks for me, but times change, and I suppose we just have to learn to change with them.'

'You know why we're here, do you, sir?' Beresford asked.

'Yes, we heard the late news bulletin – Jane Danbury's been murdered and little Melanie's been kidnapped. Frightful business, but what else do you expect in a society which has turned its back on all its old values?'

'Did you hear anything unusual this evening?' Meadows asked.

'From next door, you mean?'

'Yes.'

'No, we didn't. But it was never likely we would, is it? The two houses are quite far apart, and there's a garden wall between them. We never hear a sound from the Danburys' house.'

'I heard something, but I'm not sure if you'd call it unusual,' Mrs Cardew said.

'You never mentioned that to me, my dear,' the Colonel said accusingly.

'I've only just remembered,' his wife replied mildly. 'It didn't seem very important at the time.'

'What did you hear – and where were you when you heard it?' Beresford asked.

'I was out working in the front garden.'

'What time was this?'

'It was around eight o'clock.'

'But it was dark by then.'

'That's right, it was. That's the best time for it.'

'The best time for what?'

'I'm engaged in a fight to the death with the snails,' Mrs Cardew explained, 'and happily, I seem to be on the winning side.'

'I don't quite see . . .' Beresford admitted.

'The best way to deal with snails is to wait until darkness has fallen, and then soak all your plants. Then you walk away, leave it a few minutes, and return with a torch and a plastic bag. Sometimes I can catch as many as a hundred of the little blighters.'

'So you were in the garden . . .' Beresford prompted.

'I was in the garden, and I heard this car drive by, slow down, and finally stop. I couldn't swear it pulled up in front of the Danbury house, but I'm *almost* certain it did.'

'Did you happen to see what make of car it was?'

'The walls are ten feet high – it's a community requirement. You can't see the street from downstairs, and even from upstairs you can only just about see the opposite side of the road through the trees.'

'When did the car leave again?'

'I don't know, but when I came inside at twenty-five past eight, it must still have been there.'

Even if it was the murderer's car – and given the timing, that was likely – it wasn't much use if they didn't have the make, Beresford thought.

Alfie Clayton had switched off his bedside light ten minutes earlier, but now he turned it on again, got out of bed, and walked over to the dressing table.

'What are you doing, Alfie?' his wife asked with sleepy irritation.

'I'm resetting the clock.'

'Whatever for?'

'I've been thinking about that little girl. I want to join the search party tomorrow.'

'But you're booked up with deliveries all day,' Marjorie pointed out.

It was true. And as a self-employed lorry driver, if he didn't work, he didn't get paid.

'I want to help find Melanie,' Alfie said.

'Your customers won't exactly be pleased at being left in the lurch like that,' Marjorie said. 'Some of them might even start thinking about taking their business to somebody else.'

'I know,' Alfie admitted, 'but I want to be involved.' And then, in fairness to his wife, he added, 'Listen, if you tell me not to do it, I won't.'

'No, it's the right thing to do,' Marjorie said. 'But you've still not told me what that has to do with resetting the clock.'

'I want to get there early, to make certain I'm one of the ones that they choose.'

'But surely, they'll want as many volunteers as they can get.'

'I don't think it works like that,' Alfie said. 'If you're searching a wood, for instance, you want a certain number of men involved in the search and no more. Get too many, and all they're doing is barging into each other. And besides, they'll want bobbies supervising the operation, and there's a limited number of them.'

'So what time *are* you setting the clock for?' Marjorie asked.

'Half-past five.'

'Good God above – that's a bit extreme, isn't it?'

'I don't want to make a token offer to help, just so I can feel good about myself – I really do want to be part of it.'

Marjorie sighed, and wished she could have given her husband the children she'd known he desperately wanted.

'You're a good man, Alfie Clayton,' she said.

'I'm a cantankerous bugger,' Alfie contradicted her awkwardly. 'But sometimes,' he admitted, 'just once in a while, I can quite surprise myself.'

*   *   *

Keith Pickering had been acting chief constable of the Mid Lancs Constabulary for over a year. He had not stepped into a dead man's shoes, as was often the case with such appointments, but rather stepped into the shoes of a man who, burdened with guilt over the part he believed that he had played in his wife's death, had had a nervous breakdown.

And the problem with George Baxter's illness, Pickering often thought, was that it was much more complicated than something like cancer. The Big C was usually fatal, but if you survived, it soon became apparent whether or not you'd ever return to active duty. Mental illness was a completely different matter. George Baxter might wake up one morning and be completely cured – or, at least, cured enough to pass himself off as normal. In which case, he would want his job back – and he would bloody well get it.

All of which made life difficult for the man deputising for him, because however exemplary he was in his role, he was never going to be confirmed in the post unless Baxter decided to opt for a disability pension. And the converse was also true – if he wasn't quite exemplary enough, he would, without the luxury of tenure, be easy to get rid of.

These black thoughts were his almost constant companions, and they were never blacker than in situations like this one, in which he found himself looking across his desk at DCI Monika Paniatowski and Chief Inspector Clive Barrington.

'If it's acceptable to you, sir, we thought we'd split this operation,' Paniatowski was saying. 'I'll concentrate on finding Jane Danbury's killer, and Clive will lead the search for Melanie. We will, of course, coordinate our efforts with each other.'

Pickering nodded his acceptance. 'Have you brought in everyone with a record for child molestation?' he asked.

'Yes, we have,' Paniatowski replied. 'They're all being questioned right now.'

'And do you think that's likely to provide us with a lead?'

No, Paniatowski thought, I don't. This doesn't feel like that kind of case at all.

But because Pickering had the look of a worried, expectant puppy on his face when he asked the question – and because she knew that giving him a negative answer was not the way to keep him off her back – she said, 'I think it's far too early to say, sir.'

'We need you to authorise the overtime, sir,' Barrington said.

Oh God, the overtime! Pickering thought despairingly.

'Do you have any idea of how much that is likely to be?' the chief constable asked. 'Just a global figure will do.'

'It's impossible to say,' Paniatowski told him. 'It all depends on how soon we find Melanie.'

'So what you're asking me for is carte blanche approval?' Pickering asked.

'I don't see how it can be any other way,' Paniatowski answered.

It would play havoc with his end of year figures, Pickering thought. It would completely demolish the careful budget he had so painstakingly constructed. And it would probably all be for nothing – because the chances were that the girl was already dead.

But what choice did he have? He didn't want to go down in the records as the chief constable who starved a child abduction investigation of resources.

'Draw on whatever manpower you need,' he said, 'but just bear in mind that the more money you spend now, the less you'll have available later in the year.'

Paniatowski and Barrington nodded, as if they really *did* intend to bear that in mind.

Pickering checked his watch. It was almost one o'clock in the morning.

'Thank you, Clive, you can go now,' he said, but when he saw Paniatowski start to stand up, he added, 'Not you, Monika. We still have some important matters to discuss.'

'How did you get on with Mr and Mrs Danbury?' Colin Beresford asked Colonel Cardew.

'To tell you the truth, we didn't have much to do with them,' the other man replied, rather off-handedly.

'You didn't socialise?'

'No.'

'Was that your choice – or theirs?'

'I remember an occasion in India, when the PMC – who was a nice chap but had no real idea of how the army should work – thought it might be a good idea to invite the SNCOs and their wives over to our mess for a social evening,' the colonel said.

'Could you run that by me again?' Beresford said.

'The PMC is the President of the Mess Committee, and the SNCOs are the Senior Non-Commissioned Officers,' Mrs Cardew explained.

'Ah,' Beresford said.

'The evening was terrible – an excruciating, embarrassing disaster – as most of us officers had realised in advance that it would be,' the colonel continued. 'It was like mixing chalk and cheese.'

'And you regard the Danburys as the SNCOs of Milliners' Row?' Meadows asked in her usual direct call-a-spade-a-bloody-shovel way.

'I suppose you could say that,' the colonel replied.

'Now you're not being very fair to Jane there, Colonel Dear,' Mrs Cardew said. 'She comes from a very good background. I know her father owned a factory, but he had very little to do with running it himself, and he was a real gentleman.'

'When was the last time you saw Melanie?' Meadows asked.

'I believe we've only ever seen her once,' Mrs Cardew replied. 'We went round to the Danburys' just after she was born. That was what we used to do in the old days, when one of the men who the colonel commanded had a child.'

'And you never run across mother and daughter out on the street?' Beresford asked.

'On the street?' the colonel snorted. 'Of course not! No one from Milliners' Row ever meets anyone else on the *street*. We're not living on a council housing estate, you know.'

'No one really comes along the street, except the cleaners and gardeners, who get off at the bus stop the other side of the dual carriageway and walk the rest of the way,' Mrs Cardew explained. 'You see, we're a good three miles from the nearest decent shop . . .'

'And a good four miles from a pub that any of us would consider drinking in,' the colonel interjected.

'. . . so whenever we leave the house, we're always in our cars.'

Great, Beresford thought. Really great! This was just the sort of thing a team of detectives trying to track down a murderer really needed to bloody hear.

'So you won't have seen much of Jane Danbury, either,' he said.

'Virtually nothing,' Mrs Cardew agreed. 'She has a car of her own, but she hardly ever uses it. Unless she goes out with William – and I think that's a rare enough occurrence – she doesn't really leave the house.'

'I wish we could say the same about that girl they've got living with them,' the colonel growled. 'She's forever roaring up and down the street on that noisy motorcycle of hers. She seems to be out of the house so much that I don't know when she finds the time to complete her household duties.'

'My husband doesn't like Germans very much,' Mrs Cardew said.

'You've got it wrong, as usual, Martha,' Cardew said. 'I don't like *foreigners* very much – I despise Germans.' He turned to Beresford for sympathy. 'They tried to kill me, you know.'

'It was the war, dear,' Mrs Cardew said. 'It wasn't personal.'

'When a shell lands next to you, and damn near blows your leg off, it certainly *feels* personal,' the colonel countered.

Mrs Cardew sighed, and it was plain to Meadows and Beresford that this conversation had been a regular feature of the Cardews' life for the previous thirty years.

'The colonel's quite right – Gretchen does go out quite a lot, but I'm sure that most of the time she's running errands,' Mrs Cardew said.

'I suppose that even if someone had been watching the Danbury house, you'd never have noticed them,' Beresford said fatalistically.

'You're wrong there. I most certainly would have noticed them,' the colonel said.

'But I thought with the high walls and . . .' Beresford began.

'The colonel drives around a lot,' Mrs Cardew said.

'I *patrol*,' the colonel corrected her. 'I do it twice a day. And if I happen to see gypsies, drug addicts, hippies or any of the other detritus which has crawled out from under its rock since the end of the war, I get on the phone to Reg Holmes, and he sends someone up to deal with it immediately.'

'Reg Holmes?' Beresford repeated. 'Chief Superintendent Holmes?'

* * *

'This whole thing is a bloody mess, Monika,' the chief constable said. 'As a force, we're not looking good at all.'

'With respect, sir, shouldn't we leave worrying about how good or bad we look until after we've found Melanie?' Paniatowski asked.

Pickering shook his head. 'That's easy for you to say, but put yourself in my shoes for a moment. It's my job to protect the public, but it's also – and equally importantly – my job to protect the force.'

And to protect himself, because he was only the *acting* chief constable, and that made his position very precarious indeed, Paniatowski thought.

'The fact is, there's been a serious error of judgement tonight, and we have to be seen to be taking some sort of action over it *before* the press start kicking up a stink,' Pickering continued.

Paniatowski felt her stomach tighten up. Pickering had already mentally laid out the sacrificial altar, and was beginning the ritual which would lead up to someone lying on it while he wielded the knife. She knew she had to stop him before he got that far, and she thought she knew *how* she could stop him. She didn't *want* to do it – God, she hated even the thought of doing it – but she didn't see that she had any choice.

'Tell me again just how long it took the uniforms to discover that Melanie Danbury had gone missing,' Pickering said.

Paniatowski sighed. 'Inspector Flowers' team arrived at the house at about ten past nine. It was ten forty-six when the discovery was made.'

Pickering groaned. 'That long! And did they not – at any point – think to check the children's rooms?'

'They did check the children's rooms,' Paniatowski said. 'Of course they did. They had to, to make sure the killer wasn't hiding there – but they didn't want to disturb the children . . .'

'Or, in the case of Melanie Danbury, two pillows left to represent her.'

'. . . because they didn't want to wake them.'

'Whichever way you look at it, somebody's head has got to roll for what happened tonight,' Pickering said. 'I want you to see that for yourself, Monika, and I want you to tell me that, as a valued member of my senior staff, you'll back me all the way.'

What he *really* wanted was for her to be the first person to suggest the possibility that Flowers should be hauled up in front of a disciplinary board, thought Paniatowski.

What he really wanted was for her to be the source of the complaint.

'As a matter of fact, I don't agree with you, sir,' she said, 'but, as you said, I'm not standing in your shoes, and if you think that someone's head must roll, then I bow to your judgement.'

'Good,' Pickering said, sounding relieved. 'In that case, we need to discuss exactly how we . . .'

'You'll have my resignation on your desk first thing in the morning,' Paniatowski interrupted.

'What?' Pickering said.

'I was in charge for the last hour before it was discovered that the child was missing. That makes it my responsibility.'

It was a gamble – a big gamble – because Pickering might just decide that however valuable she was as an investigator, she could be even more valuable as a scapegoat.

Pickering was silent for almost half a minute, then he said, 'As I see it, Monika, your only failing is that you trusted Inspector Flowers to have done her job properly.'

'We'll have to agree to disagree on that, sir,' Paniatowski said.

Pickering glared at her. 'You're really prepared to make this a resigning matter, are you?' he demanded.

She loved her job – Jesus, she loved her job.

'I don't see that I have any choice in the matter, sir,' she said.

'So what would you do with Flowers, if you were sitting behind this desk?' Pickering asked.

'If mistakes have been made . . .'

'*If* they've been made?'

'. . . it would be more productive to give Liz Flowers and her team the chance to redeem themselves by working to get Melanie back.'

'Are you, by any chance, a Catholic, Monika?' Pickering asked, as if he were suddenly getting a whole new perspective on the situation.

Paniatowski felt herself redden.

'With the greatest of respect, sir, that's not really any business of yours,' she said, 'but, as a matter of fact, I am.'

Pickering nodded. 'I thought so.' He paused again. 'All right, then, I'm prepared to postpone any decision on Inspector Flowers until after this investigation is over. If we get a satisfactory result, then I'll probably agree to overlook her error of judgement. If we don't, well, that will be another matter entirely. Does that satisfy you?'

No, but she realised that was the best deal she was going to get.

'Thank you, sir,' she said.

'There's one more matter that needs clearing up,' Pickering told her.

'And what might that be, sir?' Paniatowski asked – though she already knew exactly what he was going to say.

'I believe you've got William Danbury in the holding cells.'

'Yes, sir.'

'Has he been questioned?'

'Yes, sir. DC Crane spent nearly half an hour with him.'

Pickering frowned. 'Wouldn't it have been better to give the job to a more experienced officer?' he asked.

'He's a highly intelligent officer, and I've trained him well,' Paniatowski countered.

Besides, she thought, who else on her team could have done it? She and Meadows were ruled out by virtue of the fact that they were women, and Danbury wouldn't have been likely to talk to Colin Beresford, the man who'd floored him only an hour or so earlier.

'So what did Councillor Danbury tell young Crane during their session? Anything of value?' Pickering asked sceptically.

'He told him that he couldn't think of anyone who might want to kidnap his child. Then he told Crane he wasn't saying any more until he'd talked to George Fullbright, his lawyer.'

'And has he talked to Mr Fullbright?'

'Not yet. Mr Fullbright wasn't at home when I sent an officer round there to collect him.'

'Well, then . . .' Pickering said, making an expansive gesture with his hands.

'Well, then, what?' Paniatowski said.

'Since he's apparently helped you all, he can . . .'

Another sentence left dangling.

Another opportunity for her to say what the chief constable didn't want to say himself.

'You want me to let him go! Is that what you're suggesting?' Paniatowski demanded.

'Believe me, I am fully appreciative of the fact that the man assaulted you, Monika . . .'

'Assaulted me? I'd call it slightly more than that. I'd say he bloody near knocked my head off my shoulders.'

'. . . and he should certainly not go unpunished for that. But even so, we must take into account the fact that when he hit you, he'd just learned that his wife had been murdered.'

'To be honest with you, sir, he didn't appear very concerned about his wife's death. The only thing he actually seemed to be interested in was his sons.'

'His children, you mean.'

'No, I mean his *sons*. And they're the main reason that I'm keeping him locked up – because when I saw him, he was certainly in no state to give them the kind of attention they'll need tonight.'

'Are you sure you're not being unduly influenced by the fact that now you have sons of your own, you're assuming that there is only one way to handle small children – *your way*?'

'The man was out of control,' Paniatowski said, determined not to give an inch.

'Yes, William does have quite a temper – but it never lasts for long, and I was wondering if . . .'

'William?' Paniatowski interrupted. 'So you know Councillor Danbury socially, do you, sir?'

'Yes, but only in the way that I know many people socially,' said Pickering, clearly back-footed. 'I am the chief constable, and *as* chief constable, I am expected to attend the kinds of events that important businessmen like William Danbury also attend.'

'And do you play golf with him, as well?'

'I have done – occasionally.'

'I'm not prepared to release Danbury without a written order from you, sir,' Paniatowski said.

'You're so inflexible, aren't you?' Pickering said, with a hint of anger in his voice. 'You expect other people to jump through hoops for you, but you won't bend even a little for anyone else.'

'I'm perfectly willing to allow the charge against Danbury for assault to be withdrawn, if that will make life somewhat easier for you,' said Paniatowski.

'I never asked you to do that,' Pickering said defensively. 'I want to make that quite clear.'

'It is quite clear, sir,' Paniatowski agreed. 'But you must admit that by not insisting that Danbury's charged, I'm giving you much more manoeuvring space when you're dealing with him.'

It was the early hours of the morning when Paniatowski finally arrived home, and as she drew up outside, she saw that the house was in darkness.

She slipped her key into the lock, opened the door as quietly as she could, and tiptoed along the hall and up the stairs.

The first doorway, at the top of the stairs, was Louisa's bedroom. Paniatowski came to a halt in front of it, and wondered whether she dared go inside.

It was three years, she realised, counting back, since she'd last visited her adopted daughter just before going to bed herself.

It had been at Louisa's insistence that the visits ceased.

'Oh, for heaven's sake, Mum!' she'd said, with sleepy anger, when she'd woken up during one of Paniatowski's nightly inspections. 'I am fourteen years old, you know. I really don't need to be checked up on.'

'I know it's stupid, but you're so precious to me, and . . .' Paniatowski had begun to argue weakly.

'Promise me you won't do it any more,' Louisa had said firmly.

She had promised, and though it had been hard to keep that promise, she'd somehow managed it.

But after the evening she'd had – after what had happened in that big house on Milliners' Row – she had to break the promise that night.

She just had to.

She turned the door handle and crept into Louisa's bedroom. She could see a dim shape under the blankets, and for one insane moment she felt a strong urge to strip back the bedclothes and make sure that it was her daughter – and not just a couple of pillows – lying there.

Then she heard Louisa's calm, regular breathing, and the madness passed.

She retreated from Louisa's bedroom and entered her own. In the pale glow of the nightlight, she could see the two cots, side by side.

She walked over to them and looked down at her two sons.

They were starting to develop their own personalities, she thought. Philip was both curious and demanding, whereas Thomas took life as it came, and once his basic needs had been met, he seemed quite happy to be on his own.

It was perfectly normal for fraternal twins to develop in different ways, and at different speeds, she had read in the books on child development.

But *were they* fraternal twins?

There was a part of her that believed that, as a result of that night in the woods, they weren't – and she felt that belief growing stronger and stronger, deep inside her, like some malignant cancer.

As she stood there in the twins' bedroom, the bedroom walls, melting and swirling before her tired eyes, seemed to take the form of trees – broad elms and ancient oaks.

And suddenly she could smell the heavy, damp earth in her nostrils, and she knew she was back there in those woods, reliving the whole terrible nightmare yet again.

The last thing she remembers is watching the Devil's Disciples dividing up their money. Now, as she slowly regains conscious-ness, she realises that she is lying on the ground, that she has lost her shoes, that her skirt is around her waist, that her breasts hurt – and that she has been raped.

The Disciples start to talk to her. They tell her that if she goes to the police, they will not believe her, and even if she is believed, she will never be able to pin it on them.

'And let's be honest,' one of them says, 'you must have enjoyed being shagged by three real men for a change.'

As she listens to them retreating through the woods, she has already accepted that she won't report it – not because (and they are right about this) she will never be able to prove they did it, but because it will damage her credibility as a senior police officer beyond repair.

She climbs painfully to her feet, determined to bury the incident as deep in the back of her mind as she possibly can. It does not occur to her – at that moment – that the three animals who violated her have left her with something which will make it impossible to forget.

Paniatowski steadied herself, leant carefully forward, and placed one gentle hand on each of the sleeping babies.

'I'll try to learn to love you as much as I love Louisa,' she whispered. 'Honestly I will.'

THREE

Thursday, 6th October 1977

The dried leaves, carried along by the early morning wind, were all the company that Alfie Clayton had as he made his way down the empty street towards Whitebridge police headquarters. Sometimes a sudden gust would propel them ahead of him. Then the wind would drop again, and they would flutter to the pavement, as if waiting for him to catch up.

Alfie wondered why there were *so many* leaves in the largely treeless centre of town, and supposed it was because it had been the driest early autumn for years, and so, instead of turning into mulch once they reached the ground, they had simply lain there until the wind chose them as its playmates.

He turned the corner – and groaned at what he saw ahead of him.

He should have set his alarm clock to go off even earlier, he told himself, because even though it was not yet light, a substantial queue – two abreast – had already built up outside police headquarters.

Then he saw who was standing at the very back of that queue. Tony-bloody-Haynes!

He and Tony had once been best mates, and had been joint owners of a homing pigeon called Billy Blue. He'd been a cracking bird, Billy – a real potential champion – but they'd never had the chance to find out just how good he might be, because Tony had taken the pigeon out onto the moors one day, and, without checking whether or not there were any hawks in the vicinity, had released him.

Tony, informing Alfie of the sad demise of their bird, had said it could have happened to anyone. Alfie had disagreed. The discussion had turned into an argument, and the argument had turned into a fight on the George and Dragon car park in which both men had lost teeth (Alfie still got stabs of pain in his mouth whenever the weather turned unexpectedly cold), and would probably have lost more if their friends hadn't intervened.

That had been in 1967 (around the time that Muhammad Ali had been stripped of his world heavyweight boxing title for refusing to be drafted into the US army, and Frank and Nancy Sinatra were at the top of the hit parade with a song called 'Something Stupid'), and, ten years on, the matter had still not been resolved. In order to avoid further, almost inevitable clashes, the two men now drank at different pubs (though, in their hearts, they both yearned for the George and Dragon). And it went even further than that. If they met in the street, they pretended not to see each other, and though the two families had once been quite close, none of Alfie's relations spoke to any of Tony's, and vice versa.

And now here was Tony Haynes at the tail end of a queue which Alfie desperately wanted to join himself.

For a moment, Alfie considered holding back until a few more men had joined the queue, and thus provided a buffer between himself and Tony.

But what if Tony was the cut-off point?

What if everyone in the queue behind him was thanked for coming and told that they could go home?

Squaring his shoulders, Alfie took the place in the line right next to Tony Haynes.

Overnight, the basement of Whitebridge police headquarters had been transformed. Just a few hours earlier, it had been a repository for junk which had yet to be classified as such, and so could not be thrown out. Now, with its rows of desks, numerous telephone lines and two large blackboards, it was once again the major incident centre.

Where did all the junk go when the room became an incident centre? Beresford wondered. And more to the point, if there was somewhere else to store it, why did it always find its way back into the basement once the investigation was closed?

There were some things in life it was probably best not to think about, he decided.

Normally, he would mount the podium to address the team, but then normally there would be up to twenty detective constables to address. Not this time. This time, because most of the resources were being pumped into looking for Melanie Danbury, there were only six constables and a sergeant.

That situation would change as soon as they found Melanie, of course, because then they would be searching for a *double* killer, and that would merit a team maybe four or five times the size of the present one. But that was in the future. For the present, addressing the team from the podium would seem as absurd to them as it did to him.

He cleared his throat. 'We're at a very early stage in this investigation. We know this attack wasn't the work of any of the known perverts, because they've all been questioned overnight and ruled out,' he said. 'But that's about the full extent of our knowledge. What we *don't* know, for example, is who Jane Danbury's friends are. We don't know what clubs or societies she attended, either, or even where she shopped.'

The colonel had said she hardly ever left the house, he reminded himself, but he was not sure how much faith he should put in the words of a man whose mind lived mostly thirty years in the past and on another continent.

'We will have all this information later in the day,' he continued, 'but until it comes in, we'll have to work with what we've got. And what have we got? Well, we know where she was killed. We've already done a door-to-door in the area, last night, but I'd like a second – more thorough – one to be carried out this morning. We also have the name of the contract cleaning agency which the Danburys employed, and I'd like everyone who's worked at the Danbury house questioned. Workmen often see more than we think they do, and can often be the source of valuable information. Isn't that right, Sergeant Bagley?'

'It is, sir,' the sergeant agreed.

'There have even been cases in which one of the people who worked for the victim is actually the killer,' Beresford said. 'He develops a grudge over the way he's been treated, and, since he already knows the geography of the victim's home, as well as the victim's habits, he's in an ideal position to get his revenge. But I must stress that doesn't happen very often, so don't get carried away when you're interviewing the contract cleaners. Is that understood?'

'Yes, sir,' said the six detective constables obediently, though one of them, DC Green, was already getting carried away.

It was just after a quarter to eight that Councillor William Danbury, accompanied by George Fullbright, his solicitor, was ushered into Interview Room B by a uniformed constable. When he saw who was already sitting at the table, anger flashed across his eyes like a sudden, unexpected bolt of lightning, and then was gone, leaving the eyes as cold and inexpressive as a fish's.

Deciding to interview him personally had been a provocative act, Paniatowski thought – but then provocation often brought out information that treading carefully missed out on completely.

'I am Detective Chief Inspector Monika Paniatowski, and this is Detective Constable Jack Crane,' she said. 'Please sit down, gentlemen.'

The previous evening, Paniatowski hadn't really formed any impression of Danbury, apart, of course, from the obvious fact that he'd been enraged enough to assault her.

Now, in the cold light of day – and under the harsh lights of Interview Room B – she took the opportunity to study him at length.

He was a handsome man with blond hair and blue eyes. In fact, Paniatowski realised, he bore more than a passing resemblance to Paul Newman. And he exuded an air of confidence which bordered on arrogance, even after having spent a night in the cells.

'Have you found Melanie?' Danbury asked.

'I'm afraid that, for the moment, we haven't,' Paniatowski replied.

Danbury nodded fatalistically. 'Of course you haven't,' he said. 'You'd have told me immediately if you had.' He paused. 'Do you have any leads?'

'We have certain lines of enquiry that we're following, yes.'

It was a lie. Though a small army of detective constables, drafted in from all over Lancashire at short notice, had kept the residents of Milliners' Row up for most of the night, they had learned very little.

'You're following certain lines of enquiry?' Danbury repeated.

'That's right.'

'And could you tell me what they are?'

'No, I'm sorry, I can't.'

George Fullbright coughed discreetly, opened his expensive leather briefcase, and took out a single sheet of paper.

'Before you begin your questioning, I would like to read out my client's prepared statement,' he said.

'*I'll* make the statement, George,' Danbury interrupted.

'Very well,' his solicitor agreed, sliding the sheet of paper along the table to him.

'And I don't need that,' Danbury told him. 'I want to say what I need to say, not what you think it's safe for me to say.'

'I'm not sure . . .' the solicitor began.

'That's the way it's going to be,' Danbury said. He looked Paniatowski straight in the eye. 'I want to apologise for my behaviour last night. I know there are those who will excuse it on the grounds that I was under incredible stress, but as far as I am concerned, that's no excuse at all. By way of some compensation, I'd like to make a substantial contribution to your favourite charity.'

Meadows would have said, 'Good – make the cheque out to Women Against Male Chauvinist Mill-Managing Pigs.'

Paniatowski merely said, 'That won't be necessary.'

'I *want* to do it,' Danbury said firmly.

'Thank you very much. I'm sure Oxfam will appreciate whatever you can spare,' Paniatowski told him.

'I also want to say that Inspector Beresford was quite right to hit me,' Danbury continued. 'And if he used more force than was strictly necessary, well, it was no less than I deserved.'

'Having given the incident a great deal of thought, we have decided not to charge you with attacking me,' Paniatowski said neutrally.

'Thank you,' Danbury said humbly.

Paniatowski caught a hint of a twitch in his left eye. He wasn't sorry at all, she thought, but he was playing *the role* of a man who was sorry – and the effort was nearly killing him.

'However, before you're released, there are some questions I'd like to ask you,' she said.

'Of course.'

'Where were you yesterday?'

'I was at a trade fair for coloured fabrics in Newcastle. I'd been there since Monday.'

'What time did you leave Newcastle?'

'My last meeting finished at five, then, rather than try to cross Newcastle in rush hour, I went back to my hotel room to make some notes on the meeting. So I would estimate it was around seven when I finally got away.'

'Did you come straight back to Whitebridge?'

'Yes.'

'You didn't stop en route for a drink?'

'It's irresponsible to drink when you're driving. It shows a lack of concern – and that means a lack of respect – for your family.'

'You arrived home at ten past ten. That's right, isn't it?'

'I don't know – I didn't look at my watch – but I'm more than willing to take your word for it.'

'When you entered your house, you already knew that your wife was dead, didn't you?'

'Yes.'

'*How* did you know?'

'I'm not following you.'

'There had been no public announcement of her death at that point. All you *should* have known was that there were a lot of police cars parked in front of your house, and that therefore *something* was wrong. So how *did* you know your wife was dead?'

'One of the police officers outside told me.'

'Which officer?'

'I really don't remember. It was the message, not the messenger, which left an impression on me.'

'So you're saying that you knew your wife was dead when you entered the house?'

'Yes.'

'Yet you didn't ask me *how* she died.'

'You've lost me again.'

'If someone tells you a loved one has died, the first thing you want to know is *how* they died. But you never asked.'

'Why should I have asked? I knew she'd been murdered. I knew her skull had been smashed in. What else did I need to know?'

'*How* did you know? Did the officer outside the house give you details?'

'He must have done. Where else could I possibly have got the information from?'

'That's exactly what I was wondering.'

'But even if I hadn't known the actual cause of her death, I don't think I would have acted any differently. My wife was dead. However she'd died, there was nothing I could do about that. But my children needed me.'

'You didn't refer to them as your *children* last night.'

'Didn't I?'

'No, you said, "I want to see my boys. I want to see them right now."'

'Did I really say that?'

'Yes.'

'Maybe that was because I'd got used to referring to my children as my boys, since that's what they were until Melanie came along. I was, naturally, including her in what I said last night.'

'I'll be holding a press conference later this morning,' Paniatowski told him. 'Is there anything you think it's particularly important for me to say?'

'Won't I be at the press conference?' Danbury asked.

'No, I don't think that would serve any real purpose.'

'Isn't it usual for the parent to make a personal appeal?'

'Yes, but as I said . . .'

'Then why shouldn't I?'

'The point of making that kind of appeal, directly to the abductor, is to destroy the preconceptions that he holds about the child he's kidnapped. The problem is, you have to understand, that he doesn't see the child as a person at all. Instead, what he sees is . . .'

Paniatowski fell silent.

'Go on,' Danbury said.

'It's better if I don't.'

'I can take it. I can take whatever it is that you have to tell me.'

'The kidnapper sees the child as an object, which is only there to satisfy his craving. It's like an alcoholic with a bottle of wine. He's not concerned about the wine's feelings – it's there to make him happy, to give him relief. I'm sorry to be so blunt, Councillor Danbury, but you see . . .'

'So why couldn't I make an appeal like that?'

'Because, if you don't mind me saying so, you seem so remarkably calm, Councillor Danbury,' Paniatowski said.

Danbury smiled slightly. 'Do I?'

'Yes, in fact, you seem almost unnervingly calm.'

'I'm not at all happy about the aspersions you appear to be casting on my client, chief inspector,' the solicitor said.

'There's nothing to worry about, George – it's just that DCI Paniatowski hasn't quite figured me out yet,' Danbury said. 'I'm not a cold man, chief inspector, but I don't choose to wear my heart on my sleeve. A real man, in my opinion, should have too much self-respect to go sobbing on other people's shoulders. He should keep his grief to himself. A real man should remain rational and in control, even in the face of a crisis.'

'That's what you're doing, is it?' Paniatowski asked. 'Remaining rational and in control in the face of a crisis?'

Danbury sighed. 'Look, the reason I'm here is so that you can ask me questions which might help you to find my daughter. Is that correct?'

'And also so I can ask you questions which might help us to find your wife's killer.'

'And also so you can ask me questions which might help you to find my wife's killer,' Danbury agreed. 'So how much use to you would I be, to either of those lines of questioning, if I were to sit blubbering about how unfair the world is, and why did it have to be *my* daughter who was taken?'

Alfie Clayton and Tony Hayes had been standing next to each other in the line for more than five minutes – and in complete silence – when Alfie patted his pocket and discovered that he had left his cigarettes at home.

'Have one of mine,' Tony said, holding out his own packet.

'I'll pay you back,' Alfie promised.

'There's no need,' Tony countered.

They lit up their cigarettes and puffed away in what could almost have been called companionable silence.

Then Tony said, 'When you hear about something like this happening, it really cuts your own troubles down to size, doesn't it?'

'You're right there,' Alfie agreed.

Both men fell silent again, but it was a moodier – more pensive – silence this time.

Then Tony said, 'I should have been on the lookout for hawks that day – and I wasn't.'

Alfie shrugged. 'It's a mistake anybody might have made. And even if you'd been looking, there's no guarantee you would have seen them before it was too late, now is there?'

Tony sighed. 'Poor little lass,' he said.

'I do hope we find her,' Alfie said.

'I notice that your house is up for sale,' Paniatowski said to William Danbury.

'Is that relevant to your investigation, chief inspector?' Danbury's solicitor asked sharply.

'It might be,' Paniatowski replied.

'Yes, my house is up for sale,' Danbury confirmed.

'Why is that?'

'For the obvious reason – because we've been planning to move.'

'To some other part of town?'

'No – to Canada.'

'That's a long way.'

'Yes, it is.'

'Is there any particular reason for the move?'

'I want to bring my sons up in a place where men can still be men.'

'And can't men be men here?'

'Real men can – with effort – be men anywhere, but it's much harder in a country where the government seems to be determined to turn growing boys into sissies who will jump whenever any petty official tells them to jump.'

'How did your wife feel about the move?'

'My wife prefers – she *preferred* – to leave all the important decisions about the family to me.'

'Can you think of anyone who might have a grudge against her, Councillor Danbury?'

'No, I truly can't. Jane didn't actually *know* many people. She didn't go out much. She preferred to stay at home and look after the children.'

'She might not have known *many* people, but she must have *some* friends. Can you tell me their names?'

'I'm afraid I can't. You should talk to Gretchen about that. She spent more time with Jane than I did.'

'Perhaps the killer had a grudge against you, rather than against your wife. Perhaps he's punishing you by killing Jane and taking your daughter.'

'That's preposterous,' Danbury said. 'Yes, I have made enemies in my business dealings, but they're all civilised men, and I refuse to believe that any of them could have done these terrible things.'

'What I'm trying to understand, Mr Danbury, is why anyone would kill your wife and abduct your baby, unless, of course, he hated either you or Jane.'

'If I had an explanation to offer, I would offer it – but I don't,' Danbury said. 'Will this take much longer?' he asked, glancing down at his watch, and then remembering it had been removed when he'd been taken into custody.

'No, I think that's all for the present,' Paniatowski replied.

'So I'm free to go?'

'Yes, but we'd like to take a blood sample before you leave.'

'Why would you want to do that?' the solicitor asked, frowning.

'For elimination purposes,' Paniatowski said.

Fullbright's frown deepened.

He wasn't the sort of lawyer who dealt with criminal cases, Paniatowski thought – land transactions and deeds of covenant were more his style – and he was feeling completely out of his depth.

'It's standard police procedure in a case like this,' she amplified, to make it easier for him.

'Before we agree to any such procedure, I feel I must consult one of my colleagues,' the solicitor countered.

'I can see no harm at all in giving a sample of blood,' Danbury said.

'William . . .'

'No harm at all.'

'Very well, if that is your wish,' the solicitor agreed reluctantly.

'But I want the whole thing over as soon as possible, because I need to go and pick up my boys,' Danbury said. He turned to Paniatowski. 'Where are they, by the way?'

'They're in a temporary foster home,' Paniatowski told him. 'Social services have assured me that the couple looking after them have had a great deal of experience in handling traumatised children.'

'Which probably means they'll mollycoddle them,' Danbury said. 'My sons don't *need* mollycoddling. They need to be with me, so they can find their own strength by drawing on mine.' He drummed his fingers impatiently on the table. 'I need that address – and I need it now.'

'It really might be wiser to leave them where they are for the moment,' Paniatowski said. 'You see, though I said you were free to go, we may want to question you again – and next time, the session may be much more protracted.'

'How much more protracted? Two hours? Three?'

'It may, in fact, stretch over more than one day.'

'You're saying I'm your prime suspect, aren't you?' Danbury demanded, as the veneer of reasonableness he'd imposed on himself slowly peeled away.

'No, I'm not saying that at all,' Paniatowski told him.

'Then what are you saying?'

'I'm saying that you might well be holding information in

your head – information which, possibly, you may not even be aware of yourself – that could lead us to the killer. I'm saying that extracting that information could turn out be a lengthy process.'

'Bullshit!' Danbury countered. 'You're a typical woman – either too lazy or too stupid to think things through properly. So what do you do? You look for the easiest – least complicated – solution. In nine out of ten cases, if the wife is dead, then it's the husband who did it – so I *must* be guilty, mustn't I?'

'We don't base our investigations on statistics we've collected on other crimes, Councillor Danbury,' Paniatowski said calmly.

'No, you probably don't, 'Danbury agreed. 'That's more the sort of thing that a male detective would do. But I'm willing to bet your methods are even cruder than that. If a man's clearly weak, then he doesn't scare you, and so he couldn't possibly be the killer. But if he's strong – if you find him intimidating – then you want him banged up as soon as possible, because that way you'll feel a little bit safer in yourself.'

'That's ludicrous,' Paniatowski said.

'You're attempting to punish me because I didn't cry, aren't you?' Danbury ranted. 'If I'd had tears streaming down my face, you'd have ruled me out as a suspect by now.'

'It's not as simple as that.'

'It's *exactly* as simple as that. So let me make my position – and, if you like, my feelings – crystal clear.'

'William . . .' the solicitor said ineffectually.

'My wife's death came as a shock to me, particularly given the violent nature of that death,' Danbury said. 'I was very fond of her, and I will miss her a great deal. But I am not *devastated* by her death – because only the weak allow themselves to be that. My life will go on without her. It has to go on without her. I owe that to my boys. And unless you can find some devious legal way to stop me, I intend to pick up the boys and take them home as soon as I leave this police station.'

'You can't take them home – that's still being treated as a crime scene,' Paniatowski said.

'Very well, then, I'll book a suite at the Royal Victoria. But I will *be* with my boys – it's my right.'

She could fight him over this, Paniatowski thought, but

Danbury could appear rational enough when he wanted to, and he had his solicitor to back him up, so she would only be wasting valuable investigation time, and she would ultimately lose.

'In my opinion, the best thing you can do for your children is allow them a couple of days of stability and continuity in the foster home,' she said.

'Whatever were they thinking of – making a woman a chief inspector?' Danbury said sneeringly – but also sounding genuinely mystified.

Maggie Thorne had taken refuge in the staff toilets. She had been expecting the police to visit EasyClean, true enough, but that still didn't make it any easier when they did eventually turn up.

She examined herself in the mirror, and saw a woman of thirty-five who seemed slightly butch (no accident, that, it was the look she strived for), but was otherwise unexceptional.

She could do this, she told herself. She could come across as perfectly ordinary – perfectly innocent. The trick was not to lose her temper, because once she did that, she had no control over anything, and would go in whatever direction the red mist pushed her – and to hell with the consequences.

'Just keep calm,' she whispered – and there was a hint in that whisper that she was already worrying she might not. 'Just keep calm, and you'll be all right.'

She rolled up the right sleeve of her overall, and bent her arm. In the mirror, she saw her bicep bulge – and immediately felt better. She always felt better when she saw how well her hours of dedicated work in the gym had paid off.

There was a knock on the toilet door and a male voice said, 'Are you in there, Maggie?'

'Yes, Mr Clayton,' she called back.

'The police are ready for you now.'

And she was ready for them, she thought.

'Just coming,' she said.

Paniatowski glared at the woman standing in front of her desk.

'You're an experiment, DI Flowers,' she said angrily. 'You do know that, don't you? And even after all these years – even after all the cases I've closed – so am I. There are people who still don't believe women belong in the force and are watching every move we make, just waiting for us to screw up.'

'You couldn't make me feel worse about Melanie than I already do, ma'am . . .' Inspector Flowers began.

'I'm not talking about Melanie,' Paniatowski told her. 'It was a mistake not to check she was really in the bed, but I know *why* you didn't check – and I'd probably have made the same mistake myself. So forget all that – what I'm talking about now, inspector, is that you seem to have no control over your team.'

'With respect, ma'am, you're quite wrong about that, and I think it's unfair of you to even suggest it,' Flowers said.

'Do you. Well, how do you explain this? When William Danbury entered his home last night, he was already in a state because he knew that his wife had been murdered – and not only that, he knew exactly *how* she had been murdered. That meant that our first encounter didn't go quite as well as it might have done.'

'Ma'am . . .'

'I should have been able to break the news to him gently, and watch how he reacted to it. Then, maybe he'd have been able to tell us something useful in return. Then, maybe he'd have been calm enough to take charge of his kids for the night. Then maybe I wouldn't have got smashed in the face.'

'Are you saying one of my team gave him those details, ma'am?' Flowers asked.

'No, inspector, *he's* saying it – but *I* believe him.'

'I know the people I had with me last night. I've worked with them all before. I'm certain none of them would have told him anything.'

'Then how did he find out, when the only people who knew what had happened – and who could have spoken to him before he went into the house – were *your* people?'

'I don't know,' Flowers admitted.

'I want you to find out who the big mouth is, and I want his name on my desk by lunchtime at the latest,' Paniatowski said. 'Is that clear?'

'Yes, ma'am.'

Paniatowski waved her hand dismissively. 'Then you can go.'

*   *   *

Detective Constable Tom Green liked to be liked, which, he recognised, was something of a disadvantage when what you were striving to be was a hard-bitten bobby. The weakness showed in most aspects of his work, but it was at its worst when he was questioning witnesses or suspects, because he had this tendency to veer away from interrogation and end up with conversation.

This time, things would go differently, he promised himself. This time, he would manage to keep things on a purely professional level.

'So how long have you been working for Mrs Danbury?' he asked the woman opposite him.

'I don't – I didn't – work for her,' Maggie Thorne said.

'But I thought . . .'

'I work for EasyClean (Leaves your house like a shiny new pin) Limited.'

'Of course,' Green agreed. 'What I should have said was, how long have you been working at Mrs Danbury's house?'

'Must be around eighteen months.'

'How did you get on with Mrs Danbury?'

Maggie shrugged. 'She was all right. We didn't see much of her. She just left us to get on with it.'

'She didn't supervise you?'

'No.'

'There have even been cases in which one of the people who worked for the victim is actually the killer,' Shagger Beresford had said at the briefing. *'He develops a grudge over the way he's been treated, and, since he already knows the geography of the victim's home, as well as the victim's habits, he's in an ideal position to get his revenge.'*

'But she must have at least inspected your work and, at some point, criticised it,' Green said hopefully.

'She didn't,' Maggie Thorne replied.

'You see, Maggie . . .' Green paused. 'It is all right to call you Maggie, isn't it?'

'Yes.'

'You see, Maggie,' Green said, knowing he was exceeding his brief, and searching for the stars when his eyes should have been firmly on the ground, 'you see, what we always look for in a murder case is motive. Now it's possible – and I'll go no further than that – that Mrs Danbury might have been so rude – so insulting – to one of the EasyClean staff that that person couldn't rest until he or she had paid her back. Do you understand what I'm saying?'

'Yes.'

'Obviously, that person isn't you, but I'm wondering if you'd witnessed an altercation between Mrs Danbury and any of the other cleaners.'

A look of indecision came to Maggie Thorne's face.

She's going to give me a name, Green thought excitedly. She's going to hand me a suspect on a plate.

'No, I can't think of anyone,' Maggie Thorne said. 'Like I told you, Mrs Danbury left us pretty much alone.'

'You're holding out on me,' Green said, in a voice which he considered to be a perfect balance between kindly and determined. 'You don't want to get any of your friends in trouble, and I can understand that. But you must ask yourself this – do I want to see a murderer walk free?'

'The people I work with are not my friends, and if any of them had had a row with Mrs Danbury, I'd tell you,' Maggie said. 'But they didn't.'

Green sighed. 'Thank you, Miss Thorne. On your way out, could you please tell the next one I'll speak to her now.'

She had made mistakes – she should never have corrected him about her not working for Mrs Danbury, for example – but, on the whole, it had gone well, Maggie thought as she walked down the corridor away from the office.

She had been tempted to accept his invitation to shift the spotlight onto one of the other cleaners, but it had been wise to resist it. After all, they had nothing to hide, but one of them could well have noticed that *she* had, so the spotlight would soon have been back on her, much more glaringly than before.

Besides, the police were so obviously going in the wrong direction that it was best just to let them carry on.

Jane was no interfering busybody who would insult you if you didn't do the work to her exacting standards.

The truth was quite the opposite.

Jane was as timid as a mouse, and it was that very timidity

which could enrage you so much that you simply had to lash out.

Maggie Thorne felt a sudden wave of nausea hit her. It was just as well that she was close to the toilets when it happened, because she only just made it into the cubicle before she threw up.

Meadows wondered why a woman as young as Gretchen Müller would be so liberal with her use of foundation. It was always possible, of course, that she had a terrible complexion, but her bare arms suggested that she had a very good skin.

What else could be said about the way the au pair was turned out? Her blonde hair was heavily lacquered and was brushed forward, so it covered most of her cheeks like a ski mask. She was wearing a cream silk blouse, which complemented her mid-length green skirt nicely and clung to her small, but very well-formed, breasts.

The blouse suited her perfectly, Meadows decided, the hairstyle not at all. So had the blouse been nothing more than a lucky mistake, or had Gretchen deliberately chosen a hairstyle which would make her look less attractive?

'I would like to apologise for calling you into the station so shortly after your shocking experience, but given the circumstances, I'm sure you can see why it was necessary,' Meadows heard Beresford say.

And while his voice was both sympathetic and professional, she caught a subtle undertone to it which told her that, despite himself, he was imagining Gretchen in bed.

'I want to help in any way I can,' Gretchen said.

'Perhaps you could give us an outline of your movements yesterday,' Beresford suggested.

'I am sorry? Outline?'

'Tell us what you did yesterday,' Meadows said.

'Ah yes! It was my free day, so I took my motorbike for a – I think the word is "spin" – for a spin in the countryside.'

'And where did you go?' Beresford asked.

Gretchen looked puzzled. 'I have told you – to the countryside.'

Beresford tried again. 'But where *exactly*? Did you, perhaps, visit any particular town?'

Gretchen shook her head – but carefully, so as not to disturb her hair.

'No, I did not go to any towns,' she said. 'Towns are too slow for me. I prefer the open road.'

'But you must have ridden *past* towns.'

'Oh yes.'

'And what towns were they?'

Gretchen frowned in what looked like concentration.

'When I decided it was time to turn around and come back, I was not far from a place called Dundee,' she said finally.

'But that's in Scotland!' Beresford explained. 'It's in another country!'

Gretchen smiled. 'Is it? I did not see any border posts.'

'And it must be at least two hundred and fifty miles from here. Are you telling me you drove five hundred miles in one day?'

'I did not go all the way to Dundee, so perhaps it was, after all, only four hundred.'

'Even so, that's at least eight hours' driving.'

Gretchen laughed. 'It was much less than that. I have a very big motorcycle, and I am a very fast driver. Sometimes, perhaps, I break the speeding laws.'

'And it must have been very cold.'

Gretchen shrugged. 'The cold does not bother me. At home, I swim in the river every day of the year.'

'Tell us about what happened when you returned,' Meadows said, cutting Beresford off before he could start to delve further into the life of this highly beddable Amazon.

'What actually happened? Or what I was planning to happen?'

'Let's start with what you were planning to happen.'

'I was planning to go to a public house in Whitebridge. It is called the Rising Sun.'

'Had you arranged to meet someone there?' Meadows asked.

'No.'

'So what made you choose that particular pub?'

'Many boys go there.'

'And . . .?'

'And I thought perhaps I might sleep with one of them.'

Beresford did his best to suppress a gasp. 'Is that what you always do on your day off?' he asked.

'Mostly it is what I do. Of course, if all the boys are ugly – or if there are only old men in the pub – then I will go back to my room and satisfy my urges myself.'

Beresford's tongue was now hanging out so far he was in danger of stepping on it, Meadows thought. But perhaps all that might change when she asked her next question.

'Who would you regard as an old man, Gretchen?' she said.

The au pair shrugged again. 'I do not know. I have never really thought about it – someone who is perhaps twenty-nine or thirty. Old like that.'

Meadows inwardly chuckled when she heard a rush of air from the thirty-three-year-old man sitting next to her, then, serious again, she said, 'So when you got back to Whitebridge, you went straight to the house?'

'Yes, I wished to shower before I had my sex.'

'And that was when you found Mrs Danbury?'

'Yes.'

'Did you phone the police immediately?'

'No, first I went into the garden and was sick.'

'But then you phoned?'

'Yes.'

'What did you do next?'

'I waited by the gate for the police to arrive.'

'You didn't check on the children?'

'No.'

'Isn't that strange? After all, you are the au pair, and looking after the children is surely part of your duties.'

'I looked after them when I first arrived, but I do not like children, and perhaps I did not make a good job of it, because Mrs Jane said that in future she would find me other things to do, and look after the children herself.'

'How did you get on with the Danburys?'

'I did not see much of Mr William.'

'And his wife?'

'We did not talk much. She had only two interests – her children and her health. When she was not fussing over the children, she was bothering the doctor with her latest illness.'

'So you didn't like her?'

'I didn't *dislike* her.'

'Tell me about her friends.'

'She did not have any.'

'Or enemies, either?'

'It is hard to make enemies when you don't leave the house.'

'So you have no idea who might have wanted to kill her?'

'Perhaps no one wanted to kill her,' Gretchen suggested. 'Perhaps she was just in the way of a man who wanted to satisfy his unnatural desires – and those of his friends – with a baby girl.'

'What kind of motorbike do you ride?' Meadows asked.

'It is a BMW R 75/6.'

'That's a very expensive bike.'

'Yes, it is,' Gretchen agreed.

'Did your father buy it for you?'

'No, my father has been dead since many years.'

'Then who . . .?'

'I have known many boys who have wanted very much to keep me happy,' Gretchen said. 'The motorbike was a gift from one of them.'

'The reason I've asked to see you, Monika, is so we can decide beforehand exactly how we're going to handle this bloody press conference,' Chief Superintendent Holmes said.

'You've been sending patrol cars to Milliners' Row every time that mad old colonel asked you to,' Paniatowski said accusingly.

'I beg your pardon?'

'Is he a golfing friend of yours, or something?'

'If patrol cars have paid more visits to Milliners' Row than they have to other parts of Whitebridge – and I'm not saying that they *have* – then perhaps it is because it is one of the more prosperous areas of the town, and therefore a prime target for burglars.'

'I've just been looking through the patrol car logs,' Paniatowski countered. 'It wasn't criminals they moved on – it was just people who happen to be considerably poorer than the ones who live on Milliners' Row.'

Holmes sighed. 'What's your point, chief inspector?'

'If we'd known, last night, what we know now, we wouldn't

have wasted our time asking questions there was no need to ask – so why didn't you simply tell us back then?'

Holmes turned to gaze out of the window. 'I didn't want it to appear as if the area was getting special treatment,' he said.

'But that's precisely what it *was* getting.'

'Instead of acting so self-righteously, chief inspector,' Holmes said, his eyes still firmly on the street below, 'you should be expressing your gratitude that I've been authorising random checks as part of the new policing programme I've been developing, because, thanks to that, you now know that no one's been watching the Danbury house, don't you?'

First he'd claimed Milliners' Row had been afforded no special attention, now, in complete contradiction of that initial statement, he was saying it was all part of an experiment. And if he felt it was necessary, Paniatowski thought, he would shift his ground again – and that would be acceptable, too, because he was a chief superintendent, and she was merely a detective chief inspector.

'Am I right?' Holmes demanded. 'Has my monitoring programme provided you with useful information?'

'Yes, sir,' Paniatowski said, forcing the words out, and hating herself for doing it. 'Thank you very much, sir.'

'You're welcome,' Holmes told her.

No one on the force called the two civilian scene-of-crime officers by their surnames, because no one on the force actually knew what those surnames were. Instead, the two men were simply referred to as Bill and Eddie.

Bill was tall and thin, Eddie was small and round. Bill had recently grown a moustache, and Eddie – perhaps in retaliation – was cultivating a small beard. Bill dressed little better than a tramp, and Eddie fell slightly short of his partner's high standards of sartorial excellence, but together, they were the best SOCO team that anyone on the Whitebridge force could ever remember working with.

It was Eddie who Meadows saw waiting at the gate, as she negotiated the police roadblock which had isolated the house on Milliners' Row from the rest of the world.

Eddie looked a little disappointed when he realised that it was the sergeant who was getting out of the car.

'Where's your boss?' he asked. 'She usually comes round to check things for herself.'

'She's giving a press conference,' Meadows told him.

'Oh, that's a pity,' Eddie said, 'because, you see, her and me have got a bit of a thing going between us.'

Meadows laughed.

'Do you find that funny?' Eddie demanded, aggrieved.

'Well, of course it's funny,' Meadows said, bending her knees slightly so she could look the small fat man straight in the eye. 'She's not a bad-looking woman, I'll admit that . . .'

'She certainly isn't!'

'. . . but let's face it, she's simply not classy enough to ever pull a man like you.'

Eddie beamed with pleasure. 'You should go far in your chosen career, sergeant,' he said.

'I intend to,' Meadows replied. 'So what have you got for me?'

'Fingerprints, as you would imagine – positively sackfuls of them.'

'But none of them, I take it, that you've lifted from the murder weapon?'

'Sadly not. That had been wiped clean.'

'Anything else?'

'Bill and me have been thinking about how the killer got into the place. We've checked the lock on this gate, and it's our professional opinion that it hasn't been tampered with in any way, shape or form.'

'But surely a professional cracksman can open a lock without you even knowing it,' Meadows said.

'Most locks, yes,' Eddie agreed. 'But this *isn't* most locks. It's a Handley and Chase. It was made in London by a locksmith who wouldn't even have been given the job until he'd had at least ten years' experience. Now there are men who could pick this lock – not many, but a few – but none of them could have done it without leaving a trace.'

'I see,' Meadows said.

'So how *did* the killer get in?' Eddie continued. 'Well, there are three possible ways. The first is he came over the wall. Do you think you could scale that wall, DS Meadows?'

Meadows turned and studied the wall.

'Yes, if I took a good run at it,' she said, after she'd made a few calculations in her head.

Eddie ran his eyes up and down her athletic frame.

'Yes, you probably could, at that,' he admitted, 'but most people would find it rather difficult – even quite strong men. Besides, we mustn't forget that though the killer came in on his own, he left with the baby.'

'No, we mustn't forget that,' Meadows agreed. 'Even I couldn't do it if I had a baby with me. Perhaps he brought some climbing equipment with him.'

'Grappling irons and things like that?' Eddie asked.

'Yes.'

'They'd leave marks on the wall that you'd spot if you looked carefully – and we *have* looked carefully. Anyway, even if he could get over the wall, that would solve only half his problem. Once he was in the grounds, he had to get into the house. The locks on the house were made by the same company that made the locks for the gate, and there's no evidence of forced entry there, either. So either . . .?'

'So either he had a key of his own, or somebody let him in.'

'Exactly.'

And given that Jane Danbury had turned her back on whoever had killed her, it was likely that she had known him, so either of those two theories was possible.

'I'd like to have a look around the house now, Eddie,' Meadows said.

'Be my guest,' the SOCO man told her. 'And if you do find anything you'd like a second opinion on, you won't forget to ask DCI Paniatowski to come and take a look at it herself, will you?'

Meadows laughed. 'I won't forget.'

They walked up the driveway towards the house that was *almost* as grand as the one that Meadows had once called home.

'Have you found any vomit, Eddie?' Meadows asked, as they approached the front door.

'As a matter of fact, we did.'

'Was it recent?'

'I would say so.'

'And was it in the garden?'

'Yes.'

Well, there was at least *one* part of *one* witness statement that she could confirm, Meadows thought.

Before they'd set out just after dawn, the volunteers had been addressed by Chief Inspector Barrington.

'There are two possible pitfalls with an operation like this one,' he'd told them. 'The first is that you start out dead keen, but after a couple of hours of finding nothing, you get careless, and overlook what could turn out to be a vital clue. The second is you *do* find something, and you're so enthusiastic that you treat it so roughly that you render it useless. So those are the two key words – alertness and care. Have you all got that?'

The volunteers had nodded that they had.

'Then good luck, and God bless you,' Barrington had said. 'You've every right to feel proud of yourselves.'

That had been over three hours earlier, and the search was now well underway. As in all searches of that nature, the more obvious places – woods, parks and abandoned buildings – were being checked out first. If that brought no results, the search would be extended to the edge of the moorland which surrounded most of Whitebridge.

Day Two – if there *was* a Day Two – would be both more expensive and more extensive. A helicopter would be brought in from Manchester to fly over the moors and search for signs of recent digging. Sniffer dogs – trained to detect the smell of death – would be used, some of them on loan from bordering police authorities. The canals and rivers would be dragged, and frogmen would be on hand in case they were needed.

Nobody wanted there to be a Day Two. What everyone prayed for was that Melanie would be found in an old mill or in a playground, frightened but otherwise unhurt.

And sometimes it did happen that way.

Sometimes the miracle came about.

But if miracles were common, they would cease to be miracles – and everyone involved in the search knew that.

FOUR

The Whitebridge Mortuary – a grim, ugly structure of post-war prefabricated concrete – had never exactly been one of Monika Paniatowski's favourite places, but since that warm summer night in Backend Wood, she had truly loathed and feared it.

She had come to the mortuary the morning after her rape to find Shastri, the only doctor who she could trust not to insist on her reporting her humiliation. Now, the very act of entering the building brought that sunny morning right back to her mind.

She could have asked Shastri to meet her somewhere else, and Shastri would have understood and immediately agreed, but she had never made any such request, because she was a firm believer that instead of running away from your fears, you should confront them.

She had hoped, in the early days after her rape, that the mortuary would become more strongly associated in her mind with her current work, and that memories of the past – lying on the table and allowing Shastri to prod and probe her, while, outside, the birds cheerfully heralded a new day – would gradually fade away, until they were hardly there at all.

And maybe, in time, things would pan out like that – but it certainly hadn't happened yet.

Shastri was waiting in her office, her beautiful sari all-but hidden by her pristine white lab coat.

She greeted her old friend with her magic smile, then grew more serious and asked, 'How did the press conference go?'

Paniatowski shrugged. 'As well as could be expected,' she said. 'I've got you a sample of William Danbury's blood. The lab's analysing it right now.'

'Thank you, that was so sweet of you, Monika, but I do not really need it,' the doctor replied.

Sweet of you, Paniatowski repeated in her head. It was typical of Shastri to make a blood sample – or a severed finger, or even, on one occasion, an eye – seem like a thoughtful gift that one friend might give to another.

'What do you mean, you don't need it?' she asked.

'Dr Lucas, who says he is the family physician . . .'

'Yes, he is. I met him last night.'

'. . . Dr Lucas rang me up, and asked me if I would like to know the blood types of Melanie Danbury, Jane Danbury and William Danbury. He had, he said, already obtained Councillor Danbury's permission to release the information.'

'And what did that information tell you?' Paniatowski asked eagerly.

'Firstly, the blood on the pillow does not match Melanie's.'

'Thank God for that,' Paniatowski gasped.

'It does not match William's either. It is type O, which, as you know, is the most common blood type. Millions and millions of people in Britain are type O, and the blood could have come from any of them, but since Jane Danbury was one of those millions and millions, I think it is a fair assumption that the blood is hers.'

'How did the blood get onto the pillow?'

'I would speculate the killer took it upstairs on his hand. How it got *there* is no mystery at all – it was a very messy murder, and the killer was right beside his victim. Perhaps he felt he dare not take the time to wash his hand, or perhaps he did not even notice the blood until he was upstairs. Whatever the case, he used the pillow to wipe the blood off.'

'What can you tell me about the murder itself?'

'I can do little more than confirm what I told you yesterday. I do not think the first blow killed Jane Danbury, but the second would definitely have done so, yet the killer struck her two or three more times after that.' Shastri paused. 'What my examination also revealed, however, is that the body bore evidence of extensive physical abuse which had nothing to do with what happened to it last night.'

'She'd been attacked before?'

'Yes, and not just once. Jane Danbury had been beaten – if not systematically, then at least regularly – over a considerable period of time.'

'How *badly* had she been beaten?'

'Her left cheekbone has been fractured at some point, her collarbone and two of her toes have been broken. All those things could, I suppose, have been the result of accidents, but the bruising on her body – some of it old enough to have almost faded away, some which cannot be more than two or three days old – must have been inflicted deliberately.'

'So you're saying she was a battered wife?'

Shastri shrugged. 'I could not be specific about that, because anyone could have done it, could they not? But in cases like this, as we both know, it is almost always the husband.'

The architect who had designed the Danbury house had been bloody good at his job, Meadows decided. The rooms were elegantly proportioned, and the way the building had been constructed meant that one pleasing space flowed naturally into another. Yet the interior decorating choices made by the Danburys – or more specifically William, because it just *had to* be him – had spoiled the whole effect. The hunting prints, the stuffed animals, the heavy leather and oak furniture, all combined to make the house not so much a home as a shrine to clumsy masculinity.

The theme was present even in the master bedroom. There was not a touch of femininity about it. But perhaps the most interesting thing about this bedroom was that it did not contain a double bed, but twins – and twins, moreover, which were so far apart that it was impossible to reach over from one bed and touch the other.

The boys' bedroom was decorated with prints of explorers and boxers, military leaders and astronauts. It was clear from both the style and the expensive frames that the boys had not chosen the prints themselves, but they had probably been chosen with the boys in mind – a source of inspiration that they would see first thing in the morning and last thing at night.

It was Melanie's room that really surprised her. Most girls' bedrooms that she'd seen had been wallpapered with cosy themes – fairy princesses, Disney characters or the like – but Melanie's room was painted rather than papered, and the paintwork seemed to pre-date the girl's birth by at least three or four years. There were toys, it was true, but the dolls looked cheap and the teddy bear was of such poor quality that its stitching was coming undone. Melanie's cot was clearly second-hand, and her wardrobe was made of chipboard.

It was all very interesting, Meadows thought, and she had already half-formulated a theory even before she found the home movie in William Danbury's study.

Dr Lucas lived on the border – officially unacknowledged, but generally recognised – between a 1950s council estate and a 1960s lower middle-class housing development.

Lucas's house itself was older than either of the two estates. It was a late Victorian stone-built dwelling, and was rather over-elaborate for a structure of its size. Its original owner had likely been a successful shopkeeper who had more aspirations than he had capital, Paniatowski decided. He would have been the sort of man who would think that gargoyles would give the place a touch of class, would want extensive servants' quarters though he could afford to employ no more than two servants, and would order the construction of a large wine cellar which would remain largely empty through lack of funds to stock it properly.

There was ivy growing up the gable end of the house, but rather than being trained to enhance the shape of the building, it had clearly been given licence to go where it wished.

Dr Lucas looked both unsurprised and rather nervous when he saw Paniatowski at his door, but that was easily explained by the fact that, as an intelligent man, he would have worked out that she must have talked to Shastri by then.

'Do come in, chief inspector,' he said, leading Paniatowski into a living room which smelled of old leather and just a hint of damp.

Paniatowski looked around. The furniture – a dark, heavy sideboard, ugly leather armchairs and a truly hideous tiled coffee table – would already have started looking old-fashioned when Lucas was still a child.

'Take a seat, chief inspector,' Lucas invited, and once she was sitting in one of the overstuffed armchairs, he added, 'Would you prefer tea or coffee?'

It was a delaying tactic, she realised, but since refusal would give him even more scope for delay – 'Are you sure? Would you like a fruit juice instead? Or perhaps you'd prefer a glass of wine?' – she simply said, 'Coffee would be nice.'

Lucas walked over to the door which led into the corridor.

'Would it be possible for us to have two cups of coffee, Mrs Dale?' he called out.

He came back into the room and sat down in the armchair opposite Paniatowski.

'So what can I do for you, chief inspector?' he asked.

Oh no, Paniatowski thought, you don't get off as easily as that. Before we get down to the matter that we both know brought me here, you could do with a little more time stewing in your own juice.

'How long have you had this practice, doctor?' she asked.

'Six years,' Lucas said, 'although I've actually been working here for nine. I came as assistant to Dr Wilton – he was rather old, and was finding the practice too much on his own – and when he retired, I bought him out.'

'Including this house?'

'Yes – and the furniture. I could hardly restrain myself from laughing at the expression on your face when you came into the room. You couldn't imagine why I'd bought this stuff myself. Well, now that mystery is explained. It's Dr Wilton's furniture. I keep meaning to replace it, but somehow I can never find the time.'

He was babbling, she thought. He wanted to put the hard questions off as long as possible, although, in a way, he would be relieved when they finally got to them.

'You must have been – what – around thirty when you bought the practice?' Paniatowski said.

'Yes.'

'And only a few years out of medical school?'

'That's right.'

'So I'm assuming that in order to buy the practice, you must have had rich parents behind you.'

Lucas laughed. 'Far from it. I'm the original working-class boy made good – that is, if your definition of good is running a modest practice in a neighbourhood which is not always easy.'

'So you borrowed the money to buy it?'

'Yes, I did.'

'From a bank?'

'No, not from a bank.'

There was a tap on the door, and then a stocky woman in late middle age entered the room, carrying a tray.

'Ah, thank you, Mrs Dale – that smells delicious,' Dr Lucas said.

The woman nodded to Paniatowski, and laid the tray on the hideous coffee table.

'Will there be anything else, doctor?' she asked.

'No thank you, Mrs Dale,' Lucas replied, and once she had left the room, he said to Paniatowski, 'I'd be totally lost without my housekeeper. I simply wouldn't be able to keep the whole show afloat.'

'So you're not married, then?'

'I was.'

'Divorced?'

'That's right.' Dr Lucas picked up the silver-plated coffee pot and poured the dark liquid into the two cups. 'Cream?'

'I take it black. No sugar.'

'So do I,' Dr Lucas said, handing her the cup. 'My wife was never cut out to be a doctor's wife – or, at least, not the kind of doctor I am.'

'What do you mean?'

'She's a city girl, with a city girl's romantic view of the countryside. When we got married, I think she saw me running a small country practice in which I was second in importance only to the squire, and the locals doffed their caps to her as the doctor's lady. That kind of society doesn't exist any more, of course – if it ever did – and it came as a shock to her that instead of yokels queuing up deferentially to see me, we had women in dressing gowns and curlers banging on the door at midnight, and demanding I give them tranquillisers.'

'So what happened?'

'My wife gave me an ultimatum,' Lucas said, his eyes filled with sadness, his jaw wobbling slightly. 'Either I gave up the practice, or she would leave me. I loved her – I truly did. But I suppose I loved my work more – and so we parted.'

It was all true, Paniatowski thought. He really *did* feel the pain. But, at the same time, he was trying to use that pain to make her like him more.

'Did you hope that by sending the Danbury family's medical records to Dr Shastri you'd earn a few brownie points?' she asked.

'No, I . . .'

'Did you think you *needed* to earn a few brownie points?'

'I don't know what you're talking about,' Lucas protested.

'Of course you do!'

'You're here to ask me if I knew that William sometimes hit Jane,' Lucas said, defeatedly.

'No, I'm here to ask you if you knew William beat Jane – often quite savagely.'

'He didn't mean to hit as hard as he did. He doesn't know his own strength. He never has.'

'She came to your surgery for treatment, did she?'

'Yes, and sometimes I went to the house.'

'Was that because she was too weak to come and see you?'

'No, no, of course not,' Lucas said hastily. 'It was because it was easier for me to make a house call.'

'How long has this been going on?'

'For years.'

'And you never thought that it might be your duty to report it to the authorities?'

'She didn't want me to. She begged me not to.'

Just as she had begged Shastri not to report her rape, she thought.

But that was entirely different.

Or was it?

'You must have read about other cases like Jane Danbury's,' she said quickly, to avoid drowning in a sea of introspection. 'You must know that whatever she said, she was in no position to know her own mind.'

'And what would have happened if I had reported it?' Lucas asked, almost whining now. 'She would never have testified against William, because she knew that he was basically a good man and that he loved her.'

'If we could have proved that a criminal act had been committed, we wouldn't have needed her consent.'

'William was a rugby player, you know – a prop forward, and rather a good one,' Lucas said. 'There are those who think that if he'd turned professional, he could have played for England.'

'And why would that be of any interest to me?' Paniatowski wondered.

'No reason at all,' Lucas replied, and now he was clearly fighting back, 'but then, chief inspector, you're not a man, are you?'

'I'm sure you have a point to make, but if you go at this rate I'll be drawing my old age pension by the time you finally make it,' Paniatowski said.

'William is handsome, a fine athlete, an excellent businessman, and excccdingly good company. Almost every man who knows him admires him, and would like to be like him.'

'I'm still waiting for the point.'

'These men who admire him would have done everything they could to block any prosecution mounted against William, and since some of them are police officers, and several are members of the judiciary, the prosecution would have faltered and died before it even reached the first hurdle. And that would have done no one any good, now would it?'

'It might have done Jane Danbury some good,' Paniatowski said. 'It might at least have made her aware that she had options.'

'She already *knew* she had options,' Lucas argued exasperatedly. 'She's not like a lot of my patients – a downtrodden woman living on a council estate, dependent on her husband's pay packet. She had both the means and opportunity to leave William, but she didn't. Now why was that?'

'You tell me.'

'Because, despite it all, she loved him, and her life would have had no meaning without him. She not only loved him, you see. She – like the men I referred to earlier – admired him.'

'She admired a domestic tyrant who beat the shit out of her?'

'Yes, because apart from those moments of madness, he *was* a very good husband and he *is* a very good person. He's done wonderful work in Whitebridge. I could show you a long list of the charities he supports – the Boys' Brigade, the Outward Bound Association, the YMCA theatre group . . . And I could give you the names of scores of people he's helped – not because there was anything in it for him, but because that is his nature.'

'What hold does he have over you?'

'He is my oldest friend.'

'Did he lend you the money to buy this practice?'

'No, at that point, he couldn't have afforded to do that. But what he did do, you see, was to work tirelessly at getting *other* people to lend me the money. It wasn't easy, because if the bank wouldn't touch me, then why should they? I think what swung it was his promise that he'd be personally responsible for the debt – that if I defaulted, he'd make sure they got their money back. That's the kind of man he is – he would give you the shirt off his back.'

'And then go home and kick his wife.'

'It's been bad recently, I admit that,' Lucas confessed. 'I don't know why it's been *quite* so bad – perhaps he's been having business worries – but it's not something he's done on a day-in, day-out basis. He hardly laid a hand on her during her pregnancies.'

'*Hardly* laid a hand on her? During her *pregnancies*?'

'And I believed – I really did believe – that Canada would have been a new start for them, a real chance for him to turn over a new leaf.' He paused. 'I know you're starting to think that perhaps William might have killed Jane, but you're wrong.'

'Am I?'

'Yes.'

'How can you be so sure? Give me a reason for your certainty.'

'I just know he wouldn't have done it.'

Paniatowski shook her head despairingly. 'Dr Lucas,' she said, 'that really isn't good enough.' She stood up. 'Thank you for your time.'

'Are you going to report me, chief inspector?' Lucas asked anxiously. 'Will I be prosecuted?'

What would be the point of that? Paniatowski asked herself. Lucas was – according to Liz Flowers – a good, caring doctor, and dragging him through the courts on a negligence charge wasn't going to undo the damage that had been done to Jane Danbury.

Still, she saw no reason to let him think he was off the hook quite yet.

'*Will* I be prosecuted?' Lucas asked, in the voice of a school-boy who has been caught smoking behind the bike sheds.

'I don't know,' Paniatowski replied. 'I'll have to think about it.'

The meeting was scheduled to be held in Paniatowski's office at noon, but when Crane arrived at five minutes to twelve, Meadows was already there, setting up her equipment.

'Why have you brought a projector with you?' Crane asked.

'It's to help the boss – who's understandably feeling very maternal at the moment – to think the unthinkable,' Meadows said enigmatically.

'Would you like to explain that?' Crane said.

'No,' Meadows replied. 'Not yet. Not until the time is right.'

Paniatowski and Beresford arrived, and Paniatowski briefed the team on her meetings with Shastri and Dr Lucas.

Then it was Beresford's turn.

'I've never conducted an investigation in a place like Milliners' Row before,' the inspector said. 'It's a completely different world, and the normal rules simply don't apply. Neighbours don't pop in and out of each other's houses, and they don't notice what's going on in the street, partly because nothing *is* usually going on in the street, and partly because of those bloody high walls and the trees that run down the middle of the road. So while we know from the colonel's lady that a car did stop outside the Danburys' house shortly before Jane was killed, nobody has any idea what kind of car it was, or who was driving it.'

'If Melanie hadn't been abducted, I'd have put my money on William Danbury,' Paniatowski said. 'We know that he beat his wife regularly, and maybe, on this occasion, he just went too far. But Melanie *was* abducted, so there has to be a third party involved, and logic points towards it being that third party, not the husband, who killed Jane. Bearing that in mind, I'd like us to run through the pattern we should expect to find when we study a standard abduction.' She paused to light a cigarette. 'Would you like to kick us off on that, Kate?'

'If you don't mind, boss, I'd like to hear what the others have got to say first,' Meadows replied.

What game was Meadows playing? Crane wondered.

But when he glanced across at the sergeant, her face revealed nothing.

'All right, if Kate doesn't want to come in at this point, perhaps you'd like to begin, Colin,' Paniatowski said, and it was clear to Crane that she was as mystified by Meadows' comment as he was himself.

'The kidnapper will normally have been stalking the mother and baby for some time,' Beresford said. 'He will have followed them to the shops, and watched them in the playground. It will have been from observing their routine that he will have developed some kind of plan.'

'But the stalking isn't just to do with the planning,' Crane said. 'It's an integral part of the kidnapper's overall pleasure. He enjoys the thrill of the chase – I read somewhere that most stalkers have an almost permanent erection during this part of the process – and he can actually come to feel that he's developing a relationship with his intended victim.'

'But the classic pattern seems to have no relevance to this particular case,' Beresford pointed out. 'Jane and Melanie didn't have the kind of routine that our man could latch onto. In fact, they rarely seem to have left the house and grounds, so most of the perverts capable of carrying out the act probably weren't even aware of Melanie's existence.'

'So are you saying that what we have to look for is another pattern?' Paniatowski asked.

'There *is* no pattern, because there *is* no stalker,' Meadows said, judging her moment to have arrived. 'Danbury kills his wife in a blind rage, but once he's calmed down, he begins to realise what a mess he's in. He can't take her round to Dr Lucas to be patched up this time, can he? And suspicion is bound to fall on him, because he's a wife beater. But if his daughter went missing, he suddenly realises, that would immediately shift the focus of the investigation, and most of our resources would be devoted to searching for her. Plus, that will automatically rule William out, as far as most people are concerned – because while they're willing to accept that a man might kill his wife in a rage, they're very unwilling to believe that he'd kill his *own child* in cold blood.'

'Are you saying that Melanie is dead?' Paniatowski asked.

'Yes – she's dead – and we all know she's dead.'

But did they? Paniatowski wondered. She tried to picture picking one of the twins out of his cot, taking him into the garden and . . .

'I'm not a fool,' she said, with a hint of anger in her voice. 'I know that parents kill their own children. But I just can't see William Danbury . . .'

'Can I show you the film that I found in William's study, boss?' Meadows asked.

'Why not?' replied Paniatowski, who, like the other members of the team, had been wondering – on and off – why the projector was there.

Meadows dropped the blinds on the windows and switched the light off. Then she flicked the switch on the projector. A humming sound filled the room, and a circle of white light appeared on the screen that Meadows had erected next to Paniatowski's filing cabinet.

'According to Gretchen, William Danbury bought this camera to record his sons growing up,' Meadows said. 'Note the wording of that – his *sons*, not his *children*.'

The film started running, and it was immediately apparent that it had been shot in the garden of the Danburys' house.

William Danbury is playing a game of football with his two boys. The boys are screaming with excitement, and, even from a distance, it is plain to see that Danbury himself is ecstatically happy.

The camera moves round to reveal a close-up of Gretchen, sitting at a garden table. The au pair has a magazine on her lap, and flicks through the pages as if she finds the whole thing incredibly boring.

'Who's shooting the film?' Beresford said.

'Wait and see,' Meadows told him.

The camera sweeps across the lawn, to reveal a small child in a white dress. It is obvious that Melanie Danbury has not been walking long, and that while she still finds it technically complicated, it is a joyous and liberating experience for her.

'She's a beautiful kid,' said Beresford, with a catch in his throat.

Melanie totters across the lawn, and reaches the spot at which her father is standing. Though she is clearly enjoying having her independence, she is also feeling quite tired.

'Watch what happens next,' Meadows said.

Melanie wraps her thin arms around her father's leg – maybe through affection, or perhaps merely for support.

Danbury makes no move to pick her up. Instead, he turns his head, and gazes frozenly into the near distance.

'What the hell is the matter with him?' Crane asked.

Melanie looks up and says something. The microphone is close enough to pick up the sound but not to distinguish the words.

'She wants him to pay some attention to her,' Beresford said, though he need not have bothered, because that was clear to everyone in the room.

Danbury continues to stare at the wall.

Through tiredness or boredom, Melanie relinquishes her grip on the leg. Without either its support or forward momentum to help her maintain her balance, she starts to sway, then falls backwards.

She is probably not hurt by the fall, but she is scared, and as she hits the ground, she starts to cry.

Danbury takes a couple of steps away from her.

'For God's sake, Jane, do something about the kid's screaming!' he says angrily.

And it is at that point that the film ends.

Crane, Beresford and Paniatowski, who had not seen the film before, sat in stunned silence once it had ended.

Meadows gave them a few seconds to think about it, then said, 'You don't always have to hate someone to kill them – sometimes, all you need to be is indifferent. Danbury is indifferent to Melanie. And if he convinced himself, as I'm certain he did, that it was necessary to sacrifice his daughter in order that his boys would not lose the father they so obviously needed, he could have killed her in a heartbeat.'

Paniatowski said nothing, but she didn't need to – the horrified expression on her face said it all.

'We know that Danbury beat his wife,' Meadows ploughed on. 'We know that there can't have been a stalker, because Melanie hardly ever left the house. We know there were only three keys to the front door – and Danbury had one of them. And we know that whoever killed Jane was no stranger, because she turned her back on him. It *has to* be Danbury.'

'Yes,' Paniatowski said slowly. 'Yes, it does.'

'Do you want me to pick him up, boss?' Beresford asked, with almost puppy-like eagerness.

'No,' Paniatowski said.

'No?' Beresford repeated.

'Danbury has two things going for him. The first is that he's supposedly the grieving father, so public opinion will be on his side. The second is that he seems to have a lot of influence with a lot of powerful people in this town. So we'd be putting our necks on the line by pulling him in – and if we couldn't make it stick, there'd be consequences for all of us.'

She saw the look of amazement in the eyes of the other three.

'But putting our necks on the line is what we do,' the eyes said. 'It's what defines us – what makes us special. So why don't we hang the consequences, like we always have before?'

Yes, well, it was easy for them to have that attitude, Paniatowski reflected. They only had themselves to think about if things turned sour, but she had responsibilities – she had kids.

'All I'm saying is that when we've got some rock-solid evidence on William Danbury . . .' she continued.

'We already have rock-solid evidence on him,' Beresford interrupted her. 'You admitted as much yourself, not two minutes ago.'

'No, I didn't,' Paniatowski countered. 'What we've got is a rock-solid *personal conviction* that he did it. If we're ever going to get real evidence – evidence that will stand up in court – we're going to have to be very careful about the way we collect it, because if the press or Danbury's friends get a whiff of what we're doing, they'll crucify us.'

The other three nodded. She was right. They could see that that *was* the only way to play it.

'Sergeant Meadows, I want you to go up to Newcastle upon Tyne and find out if Danbury's alibi holds water. I want you, Inspector Beresford, to come up with as much on Danbury's background as you can, and you, DC Crane, to do a similar check on Jane Danbury. And I need all that information by nine o'clock tonight, at the latest. Is that clear?'

More nods.

'What will you be doing, boss?' Meadows asked.

'What *I'll* be doing is trying to cover your tracks, so that no else realises what *you'll* be doing,' Paniatowski said.

Generations of Whitebridgians had, like Pavlov's dogs, been conditioned by whistles and bells. Thus, when the klaxon in the mill had been sounded at midday, they had been ready for their dinners, and when the klaxon sounded again at five, their stomachs had told them that it was time for tea. And though it had been quite a while since most people in the town had actually been mill workers, the conditioning had become part of their genes, so that even without an external stimulus, they still knew when it was the right time – the proper time – to eat.

The ladies of the Whitebridge Women's Royal Voluntary Service were as aware of this fact as everyone else, and had been working hard all morning to ensure that sustenance reached the men in the search parties at the appropriate hour. So it was that Alfie Clayton and Tony Hayes found themselves sitting on a grassy embankment, eating corned beef sandwiches and sipping warm sweet tea, at just after a quarter past twelve.

'It was a stupid argument,' Tony said, between bites.

'Yes, it was,' Alfie agreed, feeling no need to ask Tony what argument he was referring to.

'We used to be such good mates,' Tony said.

In Alfie's mind, an ancient projector clicked into gear and played a flickering newsreel of the time they had spent together on the back of his skull.

Their first day at school – short trousers and grazed knees . . . fishing for sticklebacks, falling in the pond, and trying to light a fire to dry their clothes, in the vain hope that their mams wouldn't notice and give them hell . . . desperately sucking on cheap cigarettes, in order to look old enough to be admitted to X films . . . going out on their first dates together . . . each acting as best man at the other's wedding . . .

And suddenly Alfie felt a great loss for the ten years when they hadn't done things together – became aware of a vast, empty hole which could have been filled with memories.

'We must never let it happen again,' he said, with more passion than he'd intended.

'What do you mean?'

'We're best mates, and nothing is more important than that – not a pigeon, not money, not . . . anything.'

They would never have hugged each other – it was not the sort of thing that Northern men did – but each put a hand on the other's shoulder, and it felt right.

While she'd been talking to Gretchen Müller earlier in the day, Meadows had experienced something which had, hitherto, been almost entirely alien to her nature – a stab of envy.

It wasn't that she envied the au pair her youth.

It wasn't even the au pair's looks – Meadows had a good ten years on the girl, but was confident that in any competition to pull men, she would easily come out on top.

It was Gretchen's spontaneity which irked. On her day off, the girl had simply jumped on her bike and driven almost all the way to Dundee.

But so what? Meadows argued with herself. Her own night-time persona – Zelda – got up to some things that would have made even free-spirited Gretchen's hair stand on end.

Yes, but the daytime part of her – Detective Sergeant Katherine Meadows – was becoming staid and predictable, almost without her realising it. Well, she would soon put a stop to that. She had been intending to go by car to Newcastle upon Tyne, but instead she would take her bike out of mothballs, and see just how little time it would take her to burn up the odd couple of hundred miles.

Paniatowski sat at her desk, staring at the wall.

How was it possible that a man could be so calculating as to murder his own child in cold blood? she asked herself.

Just what kind of man did he have to be?

As a human being – as a woman – she found it shocking that such men could exist. But what was even worse was that as a mother, it scared the hell out of her.

She needed to go home for a while, she realised. There was simply no choice in the matter, because she *had to* see her boys.

Paniatowski was halfway across the car park when she heard a woman's voice calling after her.

'DCI Paniatowski! DCI Paniatowski!'

She turned, and saw Inspector Flowers striding towards her.

My boys, she thought, I really need to see my boys.

'Whatever it is you want to see me about, could it possibly wait for half an hour?' she asked Flowers.

'You told me to question my team about what happened last night, ma'am,' Flowers said in a steely voice. 'You wanted an answer as soon as possible. Well, I've got your answer now.'

Flowers was angry, Paniatowski thought. No, it was much stronger than that. She was enraged – in much the same way as a lioness would be enraged if her cubs were being threatened.

'Go on,' she said.

'I can't give you the name you asked me for this morning, because there is no name to give you,' Flowers said. 'And the reason there is no name to give you is because none of my team did what you've accused them of doing.'

Of course they hadn't, Paniatowski thought.

She saw that now.

But just to be certain – just to be sure, in her own mind, that Flowers wouldn't be torn apart on the witness stand when the case came to trial – it would be wise to go on with the ritual.

'Tell me how you can be so positive that none of your team told Councillor Danbury something they *shouldn't* have told him,' she said, almost wearily.

Any call reporting a murder is always taken seriously, however likely the possibility that it is a hoax, and DI Flowers, who is cruising in North Whitebridge when the alert comes over the police radio, takes the call from the German au pair girl very seriously indeed.

She and her driver arrive in Milliners' Row at almost exactly the same time as the patrol car which contains a constable and a WPC, and which has been dispatched by Whitebridge Central.

As they pull up, Flowers sees the blonde girl clutching the gatepost for support. She tells the WPC to take the girl to her car, and then she and the other constables walk quickly up the driveway and enter the house through the open front door.

They find the body almost immediately.

The blood around it is already dry.

Flowers puts the back of her hand against the dead woman's cheek, and then against her own. It seems to her that Jane Danbury is much colder than she is.

Neither the dried blood nor the victim's temperature prove anything conclusively, but Flowers' gut tells her that the other woman has been dead for at least an hour.

The chances that the murderer is still on the premises are slim, but there is just a possibility that he might be, and Flowers decides that she will not search the house until she has some back-up.

She radios through to headquarters that she will need at least ten additional officers to secure the scene, and asks for whatever details can be quickly dug up on the residents of this house.

Five more patrol cars arrive. Flowers tells two of the male officers to wait for her in the hallway, and tells the WPC from the original patrol car to do the same. She has eight men left to deploy. She dispatches four of them to search the grounds, and the remaining four to block off the street and keep an eye on the au pair, who is still in the patrol car.

Back in the house, she instructs the four male officers to search every room thoroughly.

By now, she has learned from headquarters that there should be three children in the house, and she tells the WPC to check on them.

'But try not to disturb them unless you absolutely have to,' she says.

'That was how I deployed my team, ma'am – and it was how they were still deployed when both you and Councillor Danbury arrived. Now, Danbury claims that one of the officers outside told him what had happened to his wife, doesn't he? Well, I've been going through it over and over again since we last talked, and I'm sure that all I told the officers outside was that there was a body in the house, and that foul play was suspected.'

'You didn't tell them that it was a woman?'

'No.'

'You're sure about that?'

'Yes.'

'You can never be totally certain, you know. You had a lot on your plate at that moment. And if you had let it slip, then one of your team might have let it slip, too. He didn't necessarily even have to have told Danbury that it was his wife – he only needed to say it was a woman, and the husband could have worked it out, since Gretchen is more a girl than a woman, that it had to be Jane.'

'I didn't tell them that it was a woman,' Flowers said stubbornly.

'Well, if you didn't tell them that, you certainly didn't tell them how she died.'

'Of course not. One of the first things you're taught in scene-of-crime leadership training is that you never pronounce on the cause of death, even when it looks completely bloody obvious. I think the exact quote is, "Until the medical examiner has looked at the body, death is officially from causes unknown",' Flowers said. 'I didn't say a word to any of the officers outside the house.'

She hadn't told them, so they hadn't – *couldn't have* – told William Danbury.

Yet Danbury had known.

'If someone tells you a loved one has died, the first thing you want to know is how they died. But you never asked,' she'd said to Danbury that morning.

'Why should I have asked?' he'd replied. *'I knew she'd been murdered. I knew her skull had been smashed in. What else did I need to know?'*

'I'm sorry I doubted you, Inspector Flowers,' Paniatowski said. 'And please apologise to the other officers, on my behalf.'

'I will do, ma'am,' Flowers said, with all the magnanimity that relief can bring.

Paniatowski turned and walked to her car.

Danbury had done it, she told herself. There could be no doubt about that now. He had murdered his wife and kidnapped (and almost certainly killed) his own daughter.

Her cheeks felt damp, and she realised she was crying. She didn't want to even start analysing why that might be.

FIVE

The constable's name was Percy Moore. He was thirty-six years old, and had been married for more than ten years. He had two young daughters, he owned a caravan which he kept permanently at a Lake District caravan park, and, when Beresford tracked him down to the police canteen, he was at the tail end of demolishing a meal consisting of fried eggs, sausage, baked beans, fried bread and chips.

Beresford waited until Moore had pushed his plate aside, then slid into the seat opposite him.

'You can't beat a well-balanced meal, can you?' the inspector said. 'And to round it off, what could be better than a smoke?'

'Nothing could be better,' Moore said, taking a cigarette from the packet that Beresford was holding in front of him.

'You went to St Cuthbert's Primary School, didn't you, Percy?' Beresford asked.

'That's right, sir, I did,' Moore agreed, lighting first Beresford's cigarette and then his own.

'You must have been there at the same time as William Danbury,' Beresford said.

'I was,' agreed Moore, though perhaps a little cautiously, since the Danbury case had been front page news that morning.

'Was he a mate of yours?'

'Well, you know how it is – we were in the same class, and we played together sometimes,' Moore said.

'And have you seen much of him since you left St Cuthbert's?'

'Not really. He went to the grammar school and I went to the sec. mod., and that was sort of the parting of the ways. We might have run into each other in the pub once or twice and said hello, but that's about the extent of it.'

Beresford had not been expecting much from this conversation – after all, Danbury and Moore now moved in two different worlds – but he could not help but feel a *little* disappointed.

'What's your impression of him?' he asked hopefully.

'Haven't really got one,' Moore said. 'As I told you, we've hardly seen each other since primary school.'

'All right, what was your impression of him when you were at school?'

Moore thought about it. 'Absolutely totally bloody fearless, and absolutely totally bloody determined,' he said finally.

Beresford whistled softly. 'Strong words,' he said.

'But right on the button,' Moore told him. He paused to take a drag of his cigarette. 'Shall I tell you a story of our schooldays?'

'If you like,' Beresford agreed.

'There's always one kid in every playground that gets picked on,' Moore said. 'Sometimes, it's because he's small. Sometimes, it's because he's got some kind of an impediment, like a stammer. But sometimes, there's no obvious reason at all – he just seems to carry around an invisible sign which says "Kick me!" You know what I mean?'

Beresford nodded. He knew what he meant.

'Well, the kid in our year at St Cuthbert's was called Roger Lucas,' Moore continued. 'Most of us ignored him most of the time, but, for some reason, William Danbury decided he was going to be his friend.'

'He still is,' Beresford said.

'Well, there you go,' Moore said philosophically. 'Anyway, when this particular incident I'm going to tell you about happened, we were in Miss Madderly's class . . .'

'Which would have made you how old?'

'Eight.'

'Go on.'

'There was this lad in the Gaffer's class – that was the top class, the ones that would be leaving at the end of the year – who took a particular dislike to Lucas. Phil Briggs, his name was. At first, he'd just give him the occasional poke or push him over, but things gradually escalated until William Danbury decided to step in.'

'What did he do?'

'He squared up to Phil Briggs in the playground one dinner-time, and said that if Briggs didn't leave Lucas alone, he'd answer to him.' Moore took another drag of his cigarette. 'I say "squared up", but it wasn't really squaring up at all. William was big for his age, but Briggs was two years older, and you know what a big difference in height and weight two years means when you're only in primary school.'

'Indeed,' Beresford agreed.

'So a fight started. It didn't last long. Briggs got in a couple of good punches, and Danbury was on the ground, rolling around in agony. But he didn't cry – he didn't shed so much as a single tear. As soon as he was able to, he got up and hobbled away, but at dinnertime the next day, he was back, telling Briggs he'd better leave Lucas alone if he knew what was good for him.'

'And did it end in the same way it had the day before?'

'Yes, but this time, Danbury didn't seem quite so easy to knock down, and when he did go down, he didn't look quite as much in pain as he did the time before. This was a Friday. On Monday it happened again, only this time, it was different. Maybe Danbury had learned a few new tricks over the weekend, or maybe Briggs had just got overconfident. It may even have been that Briggs just didn't have the heart to keep knocking him down. Anyway, it was Briggs that went down this time.' Moore paused again. 'You know what kids' fights are like – once one of them is on the ground, the other towers over him and says, "Have you had enough"?'

Beresford grinned. 'Oh, I remember that,' he said. 'I remember both having it said to me, and being the one saying it.'

'It wasn't like that with this fight,' Moore said. 'Once Briggs was down on the ground, Danbury kept kicking him, and while he was kicking him, he was chanting the same thing over and over – "If you touch my friend again, I'll kill you . . . if you touch my friend again, I'll kill you . . ." Of course, that's the kind of thing kids do say, but he really did seem to mean it, and just thinking about it now sends a shiver down my spine.'

'What happened next?'

'You know what it's like when something really shocks you? You just stand there gaping at it – hardly able to believe what you're seeing. I think we all expected it to stop at some point, but when it finally became clear that it wasn't going to – that William would have kicked Briggs to death if he could have – a couple of the lads pulled Danbury away.'

'Did Briggs get his revenge?'

Moore shook his head. 'No, we all expected him to, but he never did. What actually happened was quite the reverse – every time he saw Danbury after that, he made himself scarce. I used to see him round town until a couple of years ago, always drunk and usually disorderly. He was regularly getting banged up in the nick. In fact, I was the arresting officer on one occasion.'

'You say you *used to* see him. Has he moved to somewhere else? Or has he changed his ways?'

'Neither of those things. He's dead now. Fell off a railway bridge, right in front of an oncoming train. Some say it was a drunken accident, some say it was a case of suicide, but if you ask me,' Moore sighed, 'if you ask me, I'd say that whatever it was – accident *or* suicide – it had its roots in that Monday morning in the playground.'

It is a truth universally acknowledged that for two women to become best mates, one has to be considerably less attractive than the other, Jack Crane thought, looking across the table in the Copper Pot Café at Gillian Blake, who, according to the headmistress of the exclusive private school they'd both attended, had been Jane Danbury's best friend.

It wasn't that Jane had – from the photographs he'd seen – been ugly, he told himself. It might even have been slightly unfair to call her plain. But when the two girls were together, there was no question that it would have been Gillian who got the most male attention.

'I was so upset to hear about Jane's death,' the woman said, 'although I suppose that, in a way, I'd already lost her.' A look of horror came to her face. 'Oh, what a terrible thing for me to say,' she continued. 'And how utterly selfish! When I think of those poor children . . .'

'I know you didn't mean it how it came out,' Crane interrupted her. 'You've been friends with Jane Danbury for a long time, haven't you?'

'We met in primary school, and we grew up together. And when I say *together*, that's exactly what I mean. We didn't live in the same house, of course, but we were rarely apart. In some ways, it wasn't like we both had a childhood – it was more the case of us sharing one.' Gillian Blake paused. 'Am I making any sense?'

'Yes, you are,' Crane assured her. 'Did you see much of her after you both left school?'

'Not *as* much, obviously. Jane got a job at her father's mill – it was only a minor clerical job, but I think he had bigger plans for her – and I went away to Cambridge to read law, so there was a physical distance between us. But we talked on the phone almost every day, and we always went on a skiing holiday to Switzerland every Christmas.'

'Was it just the two of you who went?' Crane asked. 'Or did you take your boyfriends?'

Gillian laughcd. 'Take our boyfriends? Good heavens, no. I needed a break from my boyfriends. I know this might sound rather immodest, but I was quite popular, you know.'

'I can well believe it,' Crane said.

And he meant it, because apart from her looks, Gillian had a spark which would make most men want to be with her.

'What about Jane?' he asked. 'Did she want to get away from her boyfriends, too?'

'Oh, Jane didn't have any boyfriends,' Gillian said. 'The first person she was ever serious about was William.'

'Tell me about that,' Crane invited.

'William got a job at Bradshaw's Mill straight after he finished his degree at the polytechnic. He was one of the bright young men that Jane's father brought in to streamline the business and make it more competitive. He was, by all accounts, very smart and very hard-working, and it wasn't long before he had made himself indispensable to Mr Bradshaw.'

'And then he started going out with the boss's daughter,' Crane said.

'That's right, he did,' Gillian replied, in a flat, unemotional voice.

'I take it you didn't approve.'

'It was really none of my business.'

'Would it make you feel disloyal to her to talk about it?'

'Yes, I rather think it would.'

'We're trying to build up a picture of Jane which will help us to catch her murderer,' Crane reminded her. 'If she really was your friend, then the best thing you can do for her now is to paint as accurate a picture as possible.'

Gillian thought about it, and sighed.

'We went out on double dates a few times – me with my latest beau, and Jane with William,' she said finally. 'But you could see that William didn't like it – that he'd rather have been alone with her.'

'Well, you know what it's like when you're young and in love,' Crane said.

'I don't really think it had anything to do with love,' Gillian replied seriously. 'Oh, I'm not saying William didn't love her – in his way – but I think it was much more about control.'

'Control?'

'Before she started going out with William, Jane had had all kinds of opinions on all kinds of things, but once they'd got together, she didn't seem to want to say much about anything. And even when she did express a thought, you'd see her looking anxiously at William, to check that he approved.'

'Did you ever talk to her about it?'

'Just once.'

'And what happened?'

'She flew into a rage almost immediately. Well, I say it was a rage, but it might have been closer to hysteria. She said that my problem was that I was jealous because she'd hooked herself such a good-looking man. I said that she was right about him being handsome, but there were other qualities you should look for when you were selecting the person you'd probably live with for the rest of your life. Then she said that William *did* have other qualities – that he protected her. And *I* said that maybe he did, but that before she started going out with him, she hadn't seemed to need any protection.'

'How did it end?'

'She stormed off. I rang her the next day to apologise, and she said I should think no more about it, because I wasn't the first woman to be jealous of her, and I wouldn't be the last. And because I didn't want to abandon her, I swallowed my pride and said nothing.'

'So you kept on seeing her.'

'Yes, but less and less as time went by. She asked me to be

a bridesmaid at her wedding, but it was William – not Jane – who chose the dress I would be wearing. And once she was married, I hardly saw her at all. She said she wanted to make a home for William, and she couldn't do that if she was always gallivanting about, but if you ask me, it was what he'd said, and she was just quoting him.'

'Is her father still alive?' Crane asked.

'No, he died within a year of the wedding.'

'And how did he feel about the marriage?' Crane wondered. Then he shrugged. 'Silly question, that. I don't suppose you know. I don't suppose anybody *really* knows.'

Gillian laughed again. 'That's where you're wrong,' she said. 'I know *exactly* how he felt – because I was one of the solicitors who drafted his will for him.'

Archie and Ethel Danbury lived in a house which was much like the one Beresford had been brought up in – which was to say, the type of terraced house which proclaimed 'respectable working class' all the way from its carefully pointed brickwork to its immaculately polished sash windows.

It was Mrs Danbury who answered Beresford's knock. She was a small, thin, nervous-looking woman, and when Beresford showed her his warrant card, she looked as if she were about to faint.

'I've come to ask you a few questions about your daughter-in-law,' Beresford explained. 'Could I come in?'

'I . . . I don't know . . . I'm not sure . . . you'd better wait there,' Mrs Danbury said, before scuttling off down the hallway to the back parlour.

She returned a minute later, looking somewhat relieved.

'He says . . . he says you're to come through,' she told Beresford.

She led him into the back parlour. There was only one armchair in the room, and Mr Danbury was sitting in it.

He was a large man, with the florid face of a heavy drinker. He looked Beresford up and down.

'Now you're what I call a bobby,' he said, 'a big lad who knows how to take care of himself, unlike those weedy young lefties they're letting into the force now. Do you lift weights?'

'Yes, as a matter of fact, I do,' Beresford said.

Danbury nodded. 'I can always tell.' He gestured to one of the straight-backed chairs. 'Well, sit yourself down, son.'

'I'm sorry to bother you at what I know must be a distressing time, but there are certain questions that I need to ask you,' Beresford said.

Mr Danbury glanced at his watch. 'What time's my programme on, Mother?' he asked.

'In about twenty-five minutes,' his wife replied.

'You hear that, lad?' Danbury said to Beresford. 'You've got twenty-five minutes.'

'I'd like to ask you a few questions about your daughter-in-law,' Beresford said.

'Well, then, you won't need anything like that amount of time, because I don't know much,' Danbury replied. He turned to his wife. 'You can go back to the kitchen now, Mother.'

'I'd prefer Mrs Danbury to stay,' Beresford said.

'She won't be able to tell you anything I couldn't, and anyway, she's got the supper to make,' Danbury said.

'It won't take long, but I really must insist she's present,' Beresford said firmly.

'Insist?' Danbury repeated.

'Insist,' Beresford confirmed.

For a moment, it looked as if Danbury was about to tell him to go to hell. Then the older man nodded and said, 'All right, you'd better sit yourself down, Mother.'

Mrs Danbury shrank into one of the other chairs.

'As I was saying, there's not a great deal I can tell you about Jane. She wasn't the sociable sort, and we didn't see much of her,' Danbury told Beresford.

'You didn't go to her house?'

'We were invited round there a few times, but Archie said . . .' Mrs Danbury began.

'I'll handle this, Mother,' Danbury said. 'She did invite us a few times, but that big house on Milliners' Row just isn't our sort of place. We like our simple home comforts, don't we, Mother?'

'That's right, we like our simple home comforts,' Mrs Danbury repeated dutifully.

'So you didn't see much of her?'

'Very little.'

'Which meant you also saw very little of your son, did it?'

'Whatever gave you that idea?'

'I just assumed . . .'

'Me and William go out shooting on the moors at least twice a month. He's not as good a shot as I am – I don't think he ever will be – but at least he tries. And recently, he's started to bring his two lads with him, so it's been a real family occasion.'

'Did you go out with them, Mrs Danbury?' Beresford asked, though he already knew the answer.

Mrs Beresford shook her head. 'No, it's too noisy for me.'

'And then, occasionally, we'll go for a few drinks. William might have gone up in the world, but he's still not ashamed to be seen out on the piss with his old dad,' Danbury bragged. 'And that's just how it should be – because I made him the man he is today.'

'How did your son and daughter-in-law get on together?' Beresford asked.

'What do you mean?' Danbury asked, and now there was a hint of suspicion in his voice.

'Did they have arguments? And did those arguments, as far as you know, ever turn violent?'

Danbury turned to his wife. 'Kitchen, Mother!' he said. 'Now!'

This time, Beresford did not try to stop her.

'Are you saying that you think William might have killed his wife?' Danbury asked, when Mrs Danbury had gone.

'I'm saying that I know he beat her up, and that I strongly suspect you know about it, too.'

'She might have felt the back of his hand once in a while. That's only normal.'

'Is it?'

'Of course it is. Women sometimes need reminding of who the boss is. But it has nothing to do with the police, and it doesn't mean he killed her. What kind of man do you think he is?'

'I'll tell you what kind,' Beresford said. 'I think he's the kind of man who feels he has the perfect right to take out all his frustration on his wife – who regards her as nothing more than his own personal punching bag. He learned that from you, didn't he?'

'Get out of my house!' Danbury said.

'I'm going,' Beresford said, 'but before I leave, I'd like to give you a piece of advice.'

'I don't need any advice from you,' Danbury said.

'And that piece of advice is this,' Beresford said, ignoring him. 'Don't take your frustration with me out on your missus, because I'll be coming back to talk to her tomorrow, and if there's a mark on her, there'll be consequences.'

'What, you'll have me arrested?' Danbury sneered.

'No,' Beresford replied. 'I'll beat the shit out of you.'

'You really think you could do that, do you?' Danbury asked, the sneer still in place.

'I know I could, Mr Danbury,' Beresford said quietly. 'And, more to the point, so do you.'

The sneer dissolved and was replaced by a look which said that Danbury had realised that the thing that made him the man he was – the thing that truly defined him – was slipping away from him.

'Get out!' he croaked.

I should never have said that, Beresford thought, as he stepped out onto the street.

It was unprofessional, and while it might have saved Mrs Danbury a beating that night, it was not a long-term solution to her problem.

No, he should never have said it – and he would have hated himself if he hadn't.

The hotel was called the Newcastle upon Tyne Ambassador, but it was obvious that its target market was not diplomats, but salesmen and business executives. Granite had been used extensively – perhaps even extravagantly – in the construction of the lobby, and the reception desk had a gentle curve to it which the designers probably thought was elegant. Meadows didn't share that view – she thought it was merely pretentious.

A woman of around thirty was standing behind the reception desk. She was wearing a smart red jacket with white piping, and a red and white striped blouse. The identification tag on the lapel of her jacket said that her name was Julie, and that she was an assistant supervisor.

She smiled at Meadows. It wasn't one of those instant welcoming smiles that receptionists are taught to conjure up at will during in-house training sessions, but rather one that said that Meadows' arrival had really made her day.

Meadows first showed Julie her warrant card, and then produced a photograph, and said, 'Do you recognise this man?'

'Oh yes, that's Mr Danbury,' the receptionist said. An expression of concern crossed her face. 'Has he done something wrong?'

'Do you think he's *likely* to have done something wrong?' Meadows countered.

Julie looked confused. 'Well, no, not really.'

'So, that's all right then,' Meadows said cheerfully. 'What I'd like to know from you, Julie, is whether or not Mr Danbury was still in his room at seven o'clock last night.'

'Well, he certainly *kept* his room on for the night, which was quite unusual,' Julie said.

'What do you mean – unusual?'

'Most of these conferences and trade fairs finish at around five o'clock in the afternoon, but the people who are attending them usually check out before noon, because if they don't, they have to pay for the next night whether they use the room or not.'

'But he didn't do that?'

'No, he didn't. He paid his bill before noon, just like the rest of them did, but he said he'd be keeping it for the additional night. "I think I'll have a little lie-down after my last meeting, Julie," he said, "and if you should just happen to be in the neigh-bourhood . . ." He was only joking with me, of course. He didn't mean any harm by it.'

'So you didn't take offence?'

'No. I might have done if one of the others had said it, but, you know,' Julie waved her hands helplessly in the air, 'there are some men who can just get away with that kind of thing.'

'Good-looking men,' Meadows suggested.

'Well, he is rather dishy, don't you think?' Julie replied, a little guiltily. 'Anyway, as I was telling you, he paid for the extra night.'

'So you couldn't say – one way or the other – whether he was in his room or not?'

'There might be a way to check,' Julie said, sliding open the

drawer of a filing cabinet under the desk. She flicked through
the files with deft fingers, selected one and gave it a brief inspec-
tion. 'No, I'm afraid we're out of luck there.'

'Out of luck where?'

'The hotel garage. They keep a record of the period of time
that cars are parked down there, so we know how much to add
to the bill, but it seems that Mr Danbury checked his car out
early in the morning, and presumably parked it on the street.'

Which is just what I would do, if I didn't want the hotel to
know exactly when I left, Meadows thought.

But aloud, she said, 'I wonder why he would have done that?'

'No idea,' said Julie, who was already rifling through another
drawer. 'These are the room service records. Another dead end,
I'm afraid. Mr Danbury used room service on the previous two
days – but not yesterday.'

'So, basically, you really *can't* pin down exactly when he left?'
Meadows asked.

'There's one more chance,' Julie told her. She picked up the
phone, and made a quick call. 'He must have brought his own
suitcases down, so there's no record there, but housekeeping says
that when they turned the bed down – at around eight-thirty –
he'd definitely gone.'

The room was an alibi of sorts, but it wasn't a very good one,
Meadows thought. Perhaps Danbury had simply underestimated
the police – it was surprising how many people did.

If he hadn't been there, there were ways to prove it – and
prove it she would – but it could take a hell of a long time, and
it was just the sort of police work she hated.

Still, if it had to be done, it had to be done.

'Have you got a list of all the people who actually attended
the trade fair?' she asked.

'Yes, but I'll have to get it from the back office,' Julie said,
disappearing through a door behind her desk.

She would have to ring up everyone who had been at the trade
fair, and ask them when they last saw William Danbury, Meadows
thought gloomily. Then she would have to cross-reference their
responses, and maybe interview several of them. And even then,
she wouldn't know when Danbury actually left the hotel – only
when he'd last been seen there.

Julie returned with the list, and Meadows pocketed it.

'Thanks for your help, Julie, I really appreciate it,' she said, turning and heading for the door.

'Wait a minute,' Julie said.

'Yes?'

'I couldn't help notice that you're dressed in leathers . . .'

Meadows grinned. 'Yes, I suppose they are kind of hard to miss.'

'. . . so I guess you must have come here by motorbike.'

Meadows' grin widened. 'Very well deduced, Julie. You should have been a detective.'

'What sort of bike is it?'

'A Yamaha XS-1.'

A dreamy look came into the receptionist's eyes. 'Could you do me a favour, sergeant?' she asked.

'What kind of favour?'

'I get off duty in five minutes. Could you possibly wait around and show me your bike?'

'Of course. After you've been so helpful to me, I'd be more than glad to.'

Julie looked at the Yamaha with a yearning which would have been funny if it hadn't been so earnest, and when she reached out her hand and stroked the leather seat, it was if she were caressing her lover.

'I take it you're a bit of a bike fanatic,' Meadows said.

'Oh yes, I most certainly am,' Julie agreed enthusiastically. 'And so is my fiancé, Charlie. But he's a vicar, you see, and most of his parishioners are really rather conservative. They'd be shocked if he roared up on a bike.' She grimaced. 'They're much happier to see him pootling round in a boring family saloon.'

'Well, all you have to do is wait until he's been made a bishop, and then you can both do what the hell you like.'

'I'll be too old to enjoy it by then,' Julie said. She sighed. 'Why couldn't I have fallen in love with a lorry driver?'

Meadows risked a grin. 'Speaking personally, I'd rather have a good man than a good bike any day of the week,' she lied.

Julie smiled. 'You're right, of course,' she said. 'Isn't life funny, though? You never know what's going to happen next.'

'No, you don't.'

'Take you turning up, for example. I've worked in the Ambassador for three years, and in all that time, I've never seen a woman in leathers in the place. And then, suddenly, there are two.'

'Two?'

'Yes, you today, and the woman – or rather the girl – yesterday.'

Meadows felt a tingle run down her spine.

'A girl?' she said neutrally. 'What was she like?'

'She was rather good-looking. She had blonde hair and she couldn't have been older than nineteen or twenty. How she could have afforded a bike like that, at her age, is beyond me. Maybe she'd only borrowed it – but if I had one, I wouldn't lend it to anybody.'

'This bike,' Meadows said tentatively, 'you don't happen to remember what make it was, do you?'

Julie laughed. 'Well, of course I do. It's burned into my soul.' She grimaced again. 'Oh dear, I really shouldn't have said that – not with Charlie being a vicar and everything.'

'What make was it?' Meadows asked patiently.

'It was a BMW R 75/6.'

Driven nearly all the way to Dundee! Meadows thought. What a load of bollocks! The truth was that Gretchen Müller had never got further than Newcastle upon Tyne.

As the day had progressed, Tony Hayes had grown less and less enthusiastic about the search he'd so willingly signed up for that morning, and by three o'clock in the afternoon, as he and Alfie Clayton were checking their assigned section of Lower Mill Woods, he could almost have been described as grumpy.

'If you ask my opinion on the matter,' he said to the man who had once been his best mate and was now – tentatively, at least – his best mate again, 'this whole thing's been a complete waste of time.'

It was certainly a boring job, Alfie Clayton agreed. Before the volunteers had been allowed into the woods, the police had marked out long, thin strips of it with lengths of cord, and each two-man team had been given its own strip. The first task each team had was to sift through the fallen leaves for any small object which might be hidden there. Once it was established that there *was* nothing, the leaves which had been sifted had to be bagged, so that the ground that they had been covering could be properly examined.

Sift, bag, examine . . . sift, bag, examine. Christ, it was tedious.

But then, they weren't there for the excitement, were they? Alfie asked himself. They were there because some helpless little girl had gone missing.

'If the lass is dead, she's probably buried out somewhere on the moors,' Tony said. 'That's where they usually end up.'

As a matter of fact, they *didn't* usually end up there at all, Alfie thought. From the cases he'd read about in the newspapers, most of the poor little mites were eventually found close to home.

But he said nothing, because he was carefully rebuilding his friendship with Tony, and he didn't want to spoil everything now, by arguing just for the sake of arguing.

Once the light began to fade – and it was certain that the search would soon be called off – Tony's spirits began to rise again.

'I've really missed the George and Dragon these last ten years, old mate,' he said.

'So have I,' Alfie agreed.

'Can you imagine the look on everybody's face in the public bar when we walk in side by side?' Tony chuckled.

'They'll not be able to believe their eyes,' Alfie said, joining in with his old friend's amusement. 'They'll think they're dreaming.'

The sergeant in charge blew his whistle.

'That's it,' Tony said happily, 'everybody back to the bus.'

The men turned round, and, as they'd been instructed earlier, walked back towards the road, being careful to tread only on the strip of land that they personally had been assigned to search.

They'd almost reached the edge of the woods when Alfie came to a halt at the base of an oak tree and stared down at the ground.

'What's the matter?' Tony asked.

'I never noticed this before,' Alfie said.

'Noticed what?'

'This,' Alfie said, pointing down to a patch of ground just beyond the roots which looked as if it had been disturbed.

He wondered how he'd managed to miss it during the search. Possibly, it was because it was at the base of the tree. Possibly, he and Tony had been talking about old times at that moment, and got distracted. But it didn't really matter *why* he had missed it, did it? The point was, he had seen it *now*.

'That's nothing,' Tony said dismissively, looking towards the other men, who were almost clear of the woods.

'You must admit, the soil does look as if it's been dug up,' Alfie said dubiously.

The sound of the minibus engine firing up bounced noisily from tree to tree.

'It's not been dug up at all,' Tony argued. 'The topsoil's been scratched a bit – that's all. It was probably a bloody badger or something. Look, you can see the claw marks.'

Yes, there were claw marks, Alfie agreed, but they did not seem, to him, to extend across the entire patch of disturbed earth.

'That chief inspector feller did say that the big danger with this kind of search lay in us getting careless,' Alfie pointed out.

Tony sighed exasperatedly. 'Even if somebody had dug a hole there – and I'm not saying, for a minute, that anybody has – it would have been too small to put a body in.'

'It's a little girl that we're looking for,' Alfie reminded him.

'I see you've not lost your stubborn streak over the years,' Tony said – and now there was a definite edge to his voice which said that he wouldn't be holding in his temper for much longer.

Alfie gave in. It seemed the only thing to do.

'You're right,' he said, 'it was probably a badger.'

'It was *definitely* a badger,' Tony told him. 'And now that you've come to your senses, let's get on that bus and ask them to drop us off at the George.'

He had really been looking forward to their evening in the George and Dragon, Alfie thought, but somehow it didn't seem quite so appealing any more.

SIX

It was twenty-five past eleven in the evening, and Whitebridge – unlike New York, the city that never sleeps – was getting ready for bed.

In the pubs, the last few customers, having been reluctantly shepherded to the door, paused on the threshold to say what a pity it was about that little girl and to wish the landlords a final goodnight.

In the bus station, the conductors, having completed their last run, were bagging up the day's takings – one bag for pennies, one for five pence pieces, one for ten pence pieces . . .

The larger shops still had their window displays illuminated, but at the stroke of midnight these would be extinguished, plunging into darkness travel posters for places where there appeared to be a marked absence of moorland scrub but an abundance of golden sand and palm trees, and condemning stylish overcoats draped on stylish mannequins into overnight obscurity.

The town had had enough for one day, and was looking forward to embracing that sleep which would knit up the ravelled sleeve of care.

There was no thought of sleep in DCI Paniatowski's office, where the team had been discussing the case – first from this angle and then from that – for well over an hour.

Here, the ashtrays were overflowing, and the air was as thick with tension as it was with tobacco smoke.

Jane Danbury had been dead for less than thirty hours, yet all the team felt as though they had been working on the investigation into her murder for their entire lives.

'So, to sum it all up, what do we know?' Paniatowski asked.

'We know that William Danbury beat up his wife – sometimes quite badly – and that he was so disapproving of her friendships that she ended up without any friends at all,' Crane said.

'That was partly her own doing,' Colin Beresford pointed out. 'Gillian Blake tried her very best to hold their friendship together, but Jane simply wasn't having any of it.'

'Her own *doing*, but not her *fault*,' Meadows said. 'It's classic battered wife syndrome. In her eyes, it wasn't her husband who was responsible for the violence – it came about because of something *she* was doing wrong. And given that, the worst possible thing that Gillian could have done was to criticise William.'

'What can we say about William?' Paniatowski asked.

'His father's a bloody brute, and he's grown up to be just like him,' Beresford said.

'He's having an affair with Gretchen,' Meadows added.

'How difficult will it be to prove that?'

'It won't be difficult at all. In fact, it will be a piece of cake. If I'd had a picture of Gretchen with me at the time, I could have proved it then and there. But I didn't, so I did the next best thing, which was to talk to all the staff who might have come into contact with her.'

'And what did they say?' Paniatowski asked.

'Several of them remembered the striking girl in leathers very clearly, and I've no doubt that when the Newcastle police show them the photograph I've sent up there, they'll make positive identifications.'

'Another thing we know about William Danbury is that, for all his swagger, he's really nothing but a hired hand,' Jack Crane said. 'He may *run* the mill, but he doesn't *own* it. Jane's father – Joseph Bradshaw – made sure of that when he drew up his will.'

'Go through the details of that will again,' Paniatowski said.

'The mill is in a trust, and Jane was the only beneficiary of that trust. She was entitled to all the profits, but under the terms of the trust, she couldn't sell the mill – or even give it away.'

'So how does William fit into all this?'

'William, as the managing director, has considerable freedom of action. For instance, shortly after Joseph Bradshaw's death, he fired over half the workforce – most of those sacked were, you'll not be surprised to learn, women – and began importing cheap cotton from India. All the imported cotton passes through the mill, and while it's there, they do just enough to it to get away with the claim that it's made in England.'

'With each new thing that I learn about him, my admiration increases,' Meadows said, in a hiss which would have had the boldest rattlesnake slithering for cover.

'The thing is, he can't take any money out of the company, and all expenditure has to be scrutinised by a board of trustees that old Joseph set up,' Crane continued. 'My guess is Joseph Bradshaw decided, on the one hand, that William was absolutely the best person around to run the mill, and, on the other, that you couldn't trust him as far as you can throw him.'

'Can the board of trustees fire him, if they don't like the way he's running things?' Paniatowski asked.

'No,' Crane said, 'the only person who could have given him the boot was Jane.'

'Jane had both the means and opportunity to leave William, but she didn't,' Dr Lucas had told Paniatowski.

And it was starting to seem as if the doctor was right, because, on paper at least, Jane held all the power.

'I've got two possible scenarios in my head,' she said. 'I want you to listen to them, and then tear them apart. The first is that Jane learns that her husband is having an affair with Gretchen. Now she's put up with a lot over the years, but that's the straw that finally breaks the camel's back. She decides to fire him, and then divorce him. If she does that, he'll be broke and – even more significantly from his point of view – he'll probably lose the custody of his boys.'

'It would destroy him to lose the boys,' Meadows said.

'Either she tells him what she's going to do, or he guesses that's what she's going to do,' Paniatowski said. 'And once he knows about it, he doesn't see he has any choice *but* to kill her.' She paused. 'So what do you think?'

'It's plausible,' Beresford said. 'It's *more than* plausible.'

'Second scenario: Jane doesn't know anything at all about the affair, but Gretchen and William decide they want to make their relationship more permanent, and if they're to achieve that without pain – if they don't want to lose either the lifestyle or the kids – then Jane has to go.'

'If one of them is correct, it doesn't really matter which one it is,' Crane said. 'In both scenarios, the children inherit the mill, and William, as their sole guardian, gets his hands on the money.'

'William books his hotel room for an extra day, and goes out of his way to point out to the receptionist that he'll be there until seven,' Paniatowski continued. 'But what he *actually* does is leave Newcastle upon Tyne at five. Now, most people planning to kill their wives would try to *sneak* back into their home, but he knows – given the neighbourhood – that there's little chance of him being spotted, so he drives straight up to the front gate. And it was him driving up that Mrs Colonel heard when she was out in the garden, conducting her war on snails.'

'If he did that, he was running a risk, even allowing for the high walls and indifference of the neighbours,' Crane said.

'Murder is *always* a risk, but in this case it wasn't a *big* one,' Paniatowski countered. 'And anyway, he's arrogant. He's got away with beating his wife up for years – why shouldn't he get away with killing her?'

'Good point,' Crane agreed.

'He batters Jane to death with a statuette, which is a nice touch, because it makes it look like whoever killed Jane wasn't planning to, and simply grabs the most readily available blunt instrument.'

'Yes, that *was* a nice touch,' Beresford said grudgingly.

'The next bit is rather tenuous, but given what we now know about William Danbury, I think it's more than possible,' Paniatowski continued. 'He deliberately dips his hand in his wife's blood, goes upstairs and wipes the blood off on Melanie's pillow.'

'And the reason he does that is because the whole purpose of the kidnapping is to distract from the murder, and the more dramatic it is, the more distracting it becomes,' Crane said.

'Exactly,' Paniatowski agreed. 'He lifts Melanie from her bed – she doesn't make a fuss, because, after all, he *is* her father – and drives away with her.'

'And half an hour later – as arranged – Gretchen Müller turns up and "discovers" Jane's body,' Crane added.

'And the first thing Gretchen does after that is to rush outside and spew up,' Meadows said.

'Do you think that her throwing up suggests she's innocent?' Paniatowski asked.

Meadows shook her head. 'Far from it! What I'm suggesting is that she and Danbury had worked out that throwing up would make her *look* innocent – so she took something to make bloody sure that she did.'

Alfie Clayton is in the woods. He knows they are the same woods he was in that very afternoon, yet in some ways they look quite different now. For a start, the trees don't seem quite as substantial as they had earlier. It is almost, he thinks, as if rather than taking hundreds of years to mature, they have been hurriedly drawn by a second-rate artist.

He wonders what he is doing in the woods, and yet at the same time, there is a part of him which knows exactly *why he is there.*

He has come back to complete a task he didn't finish earlier. That much, he is sure of now.

The problem is, he has no idea what that task might be.

A figure emerges from between the badly drawn trees. It is a little blonde-haired girl. She has an angelic face, except for her eyes, which are huge and red and burning.

'Look at your hands, Alfie,' she says in a voice which seems to echo through the trees. 'Look at your hands . . . look at your hands . . .'

He does look. At first, he doesn't understand why they are so red, or why, when he touches his right hand with his left index finger, it seems so sticky.

And then he does understand, and with that understanding comes a scream which is so loud – so very, very deep – that he thinks it will tear out his lungs.

'For God's sake, Alfie, whatever's the matter with you?' asks a voice which doesn't belong in the woods at all.

Alfie opened his eyes. He was sitting up in bed, and he was soaked in sweat.

'What *is* the matter?' his wife, Marjorie, repeated. 'Is it all the boozing you did in the George that's upset you? Because if it is that, then you've only got yourself to blame.'

It wasn't the booze, he thought. He'd only had a couple of pints – and he hadn't really enjoyed them at all.

'*Well, you are a right misery-guts*,' Tony had said, when he'd announced, at half-past nine, that he was tired and was going home to bed. '*This is supposed to be a celebration, and you're acting like you're attending a funeral.*'

And he'd realised that what Tony had said to him had not been too far from the truth. It had felt like a funeral to him – or, at least, like something remarkably similar to one.

'Alfie?' Marjorie said.

'It's nothing,' he told her.

'Nothing?' Marjorie repeated. 'You're woken up by your husband's screams in the middle of the night, and he tells you it's nothing.' She placed her left hand – gently, oh so gently – on his shoulder. 'I'm worried about you, Alfie.'

'There's no need to be,' Alfie said, doing his best to sound reassuring. 'I think maybe that corned beef we had at dinnertime was a bit off, and that's given me nightmares. But I'm all right now, so you can go back to sleep.'

He doubted he would get much sleep himself. In fact, the thought of going to sleep absolutely terrified him.

Marjorie snuggled down under the bedclothes and pulled the sheet tight around her shoulder.

He would have to go back to the woods, Alfie told himself. He dreaded the idea – especially after the terrible nightmare – but knew that he would find no peace until he did.

Paniatowski lit up a cigarette and sucked in the acrid smoke.

'Danbury's not got much of an alibi as it stands, and if we can break it, he's got nothing at all,' she said. She turned to Meadows. 'How confident are you that the Newcastle police will do a good job of questioning the staff at the Ambassador Hotel, Kate?'

'Very confident,' Meadows replied.

And so she was, because the superintendent she'd talked to had been positively bursting to get into her knickers, and though she had not exactly put it into words, she'd made it very plain that his chances would be greatly enhanced if he came up with some results.

'What I'd like you to do, Colin,' Paniatowski said to Beresford, 'is to contact all the regional forces between here and Newcastle, and get them to show photos of Danbury and Gretchen at every petrol station along the route.'

'If they had any sense, they'd have filled up with juice before they left Newcastle,' Beresford said.

'Then we'll just have to hope they didn't have any sense, won't we?' Paniatowski asked tartly. 'I also want everyone who attended that trade fair interviewed on the telephone, and then face-to-face if they sound promising. Put as many DCs as can be spared on that.'

'Right, boss.'

'We can't do any of that till the morning,' Paniatowski said, 'which is unfortunate, because we could really have used the information tonight.'

Beresford looked up at the clock. It was after midnight.

'Tonight?' he repeated. 'How would it be useful tonight? What more could we possibly *do* tonight?'

'We could pull Danbury and Gretchen in for questioning – and that's exactly what we're *going* to do.'

'You're not serious, are you?' Beresford asked.

'Yes.'

'Don't you think we'd be better waiting until we've broken Danbury's alibi before do anything as dramatic as that?'

'Can I remind you that you were all in favour of arresting Danbury this morning – and we didn't even know about his affair with Gretchen then,' Paniatowski countered.

'We were wrong – and you were right,' Beresford said. 'We said we had rock-solid evidence, but we didn't. We were all letting our feelings race ahead of our brains. You saw that then – why won't you see it now?'

'There are two reasons I want to do it tonight,' Paniatowski said wearily. 'The first is that as soon as it becomes public knowledge that we've arrested him, all Danbury's important mates are going to get together and start putting pressure on the chief constable to make me release poor William, who's surely suffered enough. By pulling him in while they're asleep, we'll at least be giving ourselves a few hours' head start.'

'And what's the second reason, boss?' Meadows asked.

Paniatowski wished she'd never mentioned the fact that there *was* a second reason.

'It's not important,' she said. 'The first reason is reason enough.'

'We'd still like to hear it,' Meadows persisted.

Paniatowski sighed. 'I think there's a possibility that Melanie is still alive,' she confessed.

The entire team looked at her with expressions that were a mixture of embarrassment and disbelief.

'Danbury's a cold bastard, but he's also an intelligent and calculating one,' she ploughed on. 'He knows that even the most carefully planned murder can go wrong. And he also knows that he may have made mistakes he doesn't even realise he's made. So he must be willing to accept that there's a possibility that we'll arrest him, and that – even if most of the evidence *is* circumstantial – we might be able to put together a strong enough case to get him convicted.'

'Go on,' Meadows said.

But there was no real curiosity behind the words – no real interest. It was simply that, because she was the boss, Meadows was humouring her.

'If he's convicted of his wife's murder, he'll probably serve, with time off for good behaviour, ten to fifteen years, and when he's released he'll still be a comparatively young man. But if he's convicted of murdering his baby as well, they'll lock him up and throw away the key. So he may have decided that he won't kill Melanie until he's confident he's got away with Jane's murder.'

'If that is the case, then we can afford to wait, can't we?' Beresford said. 'Because there's no way he can already be confident that he's got away with it.'

'I'm worried he might change his mind, or that Gretchen might convince him that keeping Melanie alive is too big a risk,' Paniatowski said.

Shit! she thought, I should never have said 'worried' just then – 'worried' shouldn't have any part to play in this discussion.

'Listen,' she continued, 'it's more than likely that he *has* already killed her. I accept that. But there is still a slight possibility she's still alive, and I don't think that's a possibility we can ignore.'

She looked at each of her team in turn.

They thought she'd lost it, she told herself. They thought that having babies of her own had warped her judgement about the baby who had gone missing.

And maybe they were right.

'So we pull Danbury and Gretchen in for questioning,' she said firmly. 'Are we all agreed on that?'

'You're the boss,' Beresford said flatly – which was not exactly the ringing endorsement she'd been hoping for.

The badger made his way steadily through the darkness, in the direction of the big oak tree.

He had made his first visit the night before, but had been disturbed, in the middle of his labours, by a large brown dog which had been abandoned by its heartless owner some days earlier.

The badger had not known that the dog was a stray, nor that it was hungry. He had not even known it was called a dog. What he *had* known was that a large, fierce creature was bearing down on him.

If he had been cornered, he would have fought, and since he had powerful jaws and weighed nearly forty pounds, he might well have prevailed. But since he hadn't been cornered, he had decided that rather than risk injury and possible death, he would flee back to his sett.

Tonight, there was neither sound nor smell of the big brown creature, but nonetheless, the badger approached the tree with caution. At its base, he paused and listened. He could hear the buzzing of night insects, and the croak of frogs, both of which – under different circumstances – he would have considered a tasty snack, but there was still no heavy panting to indicate that his enemy of the previous evening had returned.

Satisfied, he assessed the job in hand like a true professional, and began to dig.

It was half-past twelve. All the pubs were closed and shuttered by now, but the Prince Albert bar of the Royal Victoria Hotel remained open for the few guests who still had business to discuss or who simply couldn't resist adding one last drink to their expense accounts.

The three unmarked police cars pulled up in the service lane behind the hotel, where the general manager – Ralph Mansfield – had been pacing nervously up and down for the previous five minutes.

Mansfield recognised two of the officers who emerged from the unmarked cars.

One was called DS Meadows, he remembered. He'd had dealings with her before – well, more of a clash, really – and had emerged from the process feeling as if he'd been fed into a car crusher.

The other was a DI Beresford, who seemed a nice enough chap, if perhaps a little uncouth.

On the whole, he thought, it might be best to address his concerns to Beresford.

'Are you sure that all this is absolutely necessary, inspector?' he asked.

No, thought Beresford, I'm bloody well not, but it's what Monika wants, so it's what Monika gets.

'Of course it's necessary,' he said aloud. 'We wouldn't be here at all if it wasn't.'

'Couldn't it wait until morning?'

'I'm afraid not.'

'Mr Danbury has two small children in his suite, you know. Who'll take care of them?'

Beresford flicked his thumb in the direction of a uniformed policewoman standing by one of the cars.

'They'll be looked after by WPC Chalmers,' he said. 'She's done a special course on handling distressed children.'

'Professionally, my hands are tied in this matter, since I must obey the law,' the manager said. 'But on a personal level, I want it noted that I strongly disapprove of what you are doing. Aside from the fact that he's just suffered the tragic loss of his wife, Mr Danbury deserves some consideration for all he's done for this town, and I think it's disgraceful that . . .'

'Fair enough,' Beresford interrupted. 'You've talked me round – we won't take him in for questioning after all.'

'What did you just say?' the manager asked, astounded.

'If you think that it's such a bad idea, Mr Mansfield, then we won't do it.'

'I never suggested . . .'

'Funny, I could have sworn that you did.'

'Look, I just want this over with as soon as possible,' the manager said, visibly sweating, despite the cool night air. 'Miss Müller is in room 107, on the first floor. Mr Danbury is in the Prince Alfred suite.'

'We'll be sending two teams in, and each one will need to be accompanied by a member of your staff, who should have a passkey available,' Beresford said. 'Of course,' he continued, turning slightly so that Mansfield couldn't see his grin, 'if you've changed your mind again, and would prefer us just to go away . . .'

'No, no, you must do your duty,' the manager said, in babbling, panicked haste. 'I'll go and organise it right away.'

Beresford watched him disappear into the hotel. It had been amusing to screw with the man's mind – Meadows-style – for a while, he thought, but the fact was that Mansfield's view of William Danbury and his situation would be shared by a great many people in Whitebridge, and if they didn't get a result soon, things could start turning very nasty indeed.

Meadows appeared by his side. 'So who does what?' she asked.

'You take Gretchen, and I'll take Danbury,' Beresford said.

'Why should you take Danbury?'

'Because if the way he behaved last night is any indication, he might well turn violent.'

'That's typical of you,' Meadows said.

'What is?'

'You always grab all the fun jobs for yourself.'

Meadows knocked on the door of room 107.

'This is the Whitebridge police, Miss Müller,' she said. 'Would you please open up?'

There was no response from the other side of the door.

Meadows knocked again, and repeated her request.

Still nothing.

Meadows turned to the assistant manager, who was standing, rather nervously, next to her.

'Open it,' she said.

The assistant manager fumbled the first two attempts, but succeeded in opening the door with his third.

Meadows stepped inside.

The room was in darkness.

She reached for the switch.

The room was suddenly flooded with light – and empty.

She went straight to the bathroom. No toothbrush, no hairbrush, none of the jars or tubes which most women considered a necessary part of their daily maintenance.

Had Gretchen sensed the jaws of the investigation tightening around her and decided to do a runner? she wondered. That was certainly a possibility.

'Shit!' she said to her own reflection in the bathroom mirror.

Beresford knocked on the door of the Prince Alfred suite.

'This is the Whitebridge police, Councillor Danbury,' he said loudly. 'Open the door, please.'

He counted slowly to ten, and was about to knock again when the door was flung open.

William Danbury – wearing a silk dressing gown – was framed in the doorway.

'Have you found my daughter?' he asked.

'No, Mr Danbury, I'm afraid we haven't.'

And you not only *know* we haven't – you know *why* we haven't, he added silently.

'Then, if it's not about my daughter, I demand to know what the hell you're doing disturbing me at this time of night,' Danbury said.

'We'd like you to come down to police headquarters and answer a few questions.'

'Now?'

'Now.'

'And if I refuse?'

'If you come voluntarily, we can both walk out of here like civilised people,' Beresford said. 'If you refuse, I'll be forced to arrest you on suspicion of the murder of your wife, Jane Danbury, in which case, I'll be required to handcuff you. The choice is yours.'

'What's going on?' said a sleepy voice from within the suite.

Danbury shifted position to block the policeman's view, but it was far too late.

'Good evening, Miss Müller,' Beresford said. 'How are you tonight?'

The Gilded Cage was Whitebridge's longest established and most popular gay and lesbian club, and the two women sitting on high stools at the bar were called Phileda and Elaine.

Phileda towered over Elaine, since, at five feet eleven, she was the tallest woman there, whilst Elaine, who didn't quite reach five feet, was probably the shortest.

Phileda had been talking enthusiastically – and increasingly desperately – for nearly half an hour, but suspected that Elaine had only been listening intermittently.

Any minute now, I'm going to lose her, she thought.

And that would be a real pity, because Elaine was just the petite, Christmas-tree-fairy kind of girl that she really liked.

'Listen, I didn't put you off by telling you about the man I beat up for calling me a dyke, did I?' she asked.

'What?' Elaine replied, and from the blank expression on her face, it was clear that she hadn't been listening when Phileda told that particular story.

A woman walked up to the bar and tapped Elaine on the shoulder. When Elaine turned, the woman said, 'You stood me up last Saturday.'

It was amazing the effect that the woman – who couldn't have been more than five feet five – had on Elaine, Phileda thought. The bored expression had disappeared from her face, and been replaced by what could almost be described as terror.

'Well, what have you got to say for yourself?' the woman, who was obviously drunk, demanded.

'I'd never do that, Maggie,' Elaine said – and she was almost babbling.

'We agreed to meet here at eight o'clock on Saturday,' Maggie Thorne said firmly.

'No, we didn't,' Elaine protested. 'I said I couldn't come because I was doing something else.'

'And when I asked you to change your plans so you could, you said you'd think about it.'

'I did think about it, but I wasn't . . . I just couldn't . . .'

'You stood me up – plain and simple.'

In most other situations, Phileda would probably have stepped in earlier, but she'd been deliberately holding back this time – letting Elaine get more and more frightened, and closer and closer to the point at which she'd do anything for (or to) the person who rescued her.

And that point had now been reached, she decided.

Phileda climbed down from her stool and slid into the space between Elaine and Maggie.

'Look, Elaine obviously doesn't want to talk to you – so why don't you just bugger off,' she said, with the easy assurance of a big woman who has proved on numerous occasions that she knows how to handle herself.

Maggie looked up at her through bleary eyes. 'This is none of your business,' she slurred, 'so just keep your big nose out of it.'

'My big nose is staying right where it is,' Phileda said.

Behind her, she felt the Christmas-tree fairy begin tugging desperately at her sleeve.

'Don't argue with her,' Elaine pleaded hysterically. 'You don't know what she's like.'

What she is, is average height and pissed, Phileda thought. I could handle her with one arm tied behind my back.

'This is your last chance,' Maggie growled.

All it would take would be a good hard push – one hand on each shoulder – Phileda decided.

That would probably be enough to make Maggie fall over, and even if it wasn't, it would make it obvious to the other woman that she was well out of her league.

She put her plan into action – both arms up, one on each shoulder, push.

Maggie didn't move for at least five seconds, and when she did, she was *stepping* back, rather than being *pushed* back. And then she was advancing again, regaining all the territory she had lost and more.

She didn't raise her arm until she was within striking distance, but when she did, it was so fast that it was almost a blur. Then her fist connected with the underside of Phileda's chin, and the bigger woman seemed – for an instant – to be lifted off the ground.

Phileda rocked from one side to the other, in an effort to maintain her balance. She might have made it if Maggie hadn't kicked her on the kneecap, but once that had happened – and God! it hurt when it did – she was down on the ground, wondering which of her injuries she should try to soothe first.

Maggie stepped back, examined her writhing victim carefully, then kicked her in the chest. She was just about to aim another blow when the bouncer – a gay body-builder from Clayton-le-Woods – wrapped both his massive arms around her, and pulled her clear.

'These two girls get free drinks all night,' he shouted to the barmaid, as he dragged the struggling Maggie towards the exit.

Once they were outside, he flung the woman so hard against the dustbins that it dented one of them.

Maggie lay there groaning, and making no attempt to get up.

'I warned you the last time I wasn't having no more of that kind of behaviour,' the bouncer said. 'Well, this time, you're barred for good.' He walked back to the club door. 'You want to be careful, Maggie, you really do, because if you carry on like this, you're going to end up killing somebody.'

SEVEN

Friday, 7th October 1977

The bruise on Gretchen Müller's jaw looked – from its colouring – to be at least a day or two old. Meadows hadn't noticed it during the interview she'd conducted with the German girl the previous morning, but then what she *had* noticed during that interview was that Gretchen had been wearing heavy make-up.

Meadows reached out and switched on the tape recorder.

'Interview with Miss Gretchen Müller, commencing at one-thirty a.m. on the seventh of October,' she said. 'Present in the room are Detective Sergeant Kate Meadows and Detective Constable Crane. It is my duty to inform you, Miss Müller, that you are entitled to have a solicitor present during this interview. If you do not have a solicitor of your own, one will be appointed for you. Is it your wish that a solicitor be summoned?'

Gretchen shook her head.

'You must say yes or no in answer,' Meadows told her. 'We need to have it on tape.'

'I do not need a solicitor,' Gretchen said. 'Why would I? I have done nothing wrong.'

'All right,' Meadows said. 'What were you doing in Mr Danbury's suite at the Royal Victoria Hotel tonight, Gretchen? Was there something wrong with your own room, in the same hotel?'

'No, there was nothing wrong with it.'

'So, I repeat, why did we find you in Mr Danbury's suite?'

'Mr William told me that he wanted me to be near the children, in case I was needed.'

'But didn't you say yesterday that you were no good at handling children? Didn't you say that was why Mrs Danbury had decided to give you other duties and take care of them herself?'

'Mrs Danbury is dead, and so someone had to look after the boys,' Gretchen said.

'Couldn't *Mr* Danbury have looked after them?'

'He is a man,' Gretchen said, as if that was all the explanation that was necessary.

'So he is,' Meadows agreed. 'I really should have thought of that myself, shouldn't I?'

'I do not understand. Is that a joke?'

'I once went out with a man who worked as a magician,' Meadows said, ignoring the question, 'and he told me that the real trick to doing magic is to make sure that your audience is always watching the wrong thing. You'd make a rather good magician yourself, wouldn't you?'

Gretchen frowned. 'Is that another joke?'

'Do you remember the last time I interviewed you, Gretchen?'
'Of course.'

'And do you also remember the detective inspector who was conducting the interview with me?'

'Yes.'

Meadows grinned. 'You told him that you considered any man over the age of twenty-nine to be too old for you. And wasn't the look on his face when you said those words a real picture?'

Gretchen laughed. 'He . . . what is the phrase? . . . he fancied his chances with me, didn't he?'

'He certainly did, and he was crushed when you said you could never be attracted to what you thought of as an old man. That's what I mean when I said you were a bit of a magician.'

'I'm sorry?'

'You said you'd been planning to go to the Rising Sun to pick up a boy for sex. Isn't that right?'

'No, not exactly.'

'Then what *did* you say?'

'I said that if I found a really nice boy there, I would *probably* have sex with him.'

'And you said that you'd done the same thing several times before. Is *that* right?'

'I do not remember saying those words.'

'OK, you gave us the *impression* that you had. Is that fair?'

Gretchen Müller hesitated. 'I am not sure.'

'I'm not a gambler by nature, Gretchen, but I'm prepared to bet a year's salary that when we show your picture to the landlords of all the most notorious pick-up pubs in Whitebridge – and we *will* show them your picture, you can bank on that – not one of them will recognise you.'

'The pubs that I go to are always crowded. It is possible that those serving behind the bar might not have noticed me.'

'They might not have noticed you? But you're a very good-looking girl, Gretchen. And you're a natural blonde. How could they have missed you?'

'It is possible.'

'Did you love your father?'

'My father is dead.'

'That's not what I asked.'

'Yes, I loved him.'

'And how old were you when he died?'

'I was seven.'

'And how old was he?'

'I cannot say, not without thinking about it.'

'Then, by all means, think about it. We've got plenty of time.'

Gretchen made a pretence of calculating, though it was obvious to Meadows that she had no need to.

'He was thirty-seven,' she said finally.

'That's very young to die.'

'Yes.'

'And wouldn't it be nice if you could have him back – or perhaps find someone who was rather like him?'

'I don't understand what you're saying,' Gretchen said.

But she clearly did.

She'd just about got the measure of Gretchen now, Meadows decided. A good liar would always pitch her lies as close to the truth as possible, but Gretchen was a bad liar who only *thought* she was good. The best way to deal with someone like her was to give her free range to say whatever she wished at first, and then, by chipping away at lies and pointing out the inconsistencies, to narrow her options until she discovered for herself that she had no room to manoeuvre, and might as well admit the truth.

'You didn't go to Dundee the day before yesterday, did you?' Meadows asked. 'You went to Newcastle upon Tyne.'

'No.'

'Your bike was spotted. It was parked outside the Ambassador Hotel in the centre of Newcastle.'

'It was not my machine. It must have been another BMW which belonged to someone else.'

'There can't be many R 75/6s in England, because they are so expensive. Speaking of which, you suggested that a *boy* bought it for you. Did you really mean that a *man* bought it – a man who might be roughly the same age as your father was when he died?'

'I bought it myself.'

'That's not what you said yesterday.'

'It's what I'm saying now.'

'Where did you get the money from?'

'I saved it up.'

'Very enterprising of you – especially on an au pair's wages,' Meadows said. 'Now where was I? Oh yes! By tomorrow afternoon,

we'll have accounted for the whereabouts of every other R 75/6
in Britain, and I can pretty much guarantee that not one of them
will have been anywhere near the centre of Newcastle on Wednesday
afternoon.'

'I have just remembered something. I did stop in one of the
towns that I was driving past.'

'Why?'

'I wanted a coffee. And that town, you see, might have been
Newcastle.'

'You wanted a coffee, and you went right into the centre of
Newcastle – in rush hour traffic – to get it.'

'I must have done.'

'And could the place where you stopped for coffee have been
the Ambassador Hotel?'

'I suppose so.'

'We have statements, taken from several staff in that hotel, in
which they say that they saw you with Mr Danbury,' Meadows
lied.

'That is impossible,' Gretchen said firmly. 'I . . .'

'You what?'

'Nothing.'

'You were never seen in public together, because when you
arrived, you went straight up to his room, where he was waiting
for you? Is that what you were going to say, Gretchen?'

'No.'

'I've been wondering why, given what you were planning to
do later, you went up to Newcastle at all,' Meadows said, 'and
now I think I've got the answer. You had to have sex in order to
remind yourselves of just how badly you needed and wanted
each other – because that was the only way you could bring
yourselves to kill Jane Danbury.'

'I did not kill Mrs Jane.'

'Of course you didn't. Her husband did. But you were part of
it. Did you do it voluntarily, or did he force you – because if he
forced you, you've a good chance of walking away from this
mess as a free woman.'

'I did not kill Mrs Jane.'

Meadows stood up, walked around the table and came to a
halt next to Gretchen.

'What are you doing?' the au pair asked nervously.

'I'm just looking at you,' Meadows told her. 'There are a lot of things I'm not allowed to do to a suspect, but there's absolutely nothing against doing that.'

The sergeant returned to her seat.

'When I interviewed you yesterday, you were very heavily made up, so I didn't see that bruise on your jaw,' she said. 'But tonight, you weren't expecting to be brought in for questioning, so you didn't have time to mask it. It is a rather *nasty* bruise, isn't it?'

'It is nothing.'

'How did you get it?'

'I walked into a door.'

Meadows nodded. 'That's how it starts, you know,' she said. 'The first time he hits you, he's full of remorse, and he promises he'll never do it again. And it's some time before he *does* hit you again, but this time, when he apologises, it's perhaps not quite as sincere as it was the time before. And so the pattern develops – the beatings become more regular, the apologies weaker, until it gets to a point where he never seems to stop hitting you, and he's not sorry at all any more.'

Tears had started to appear in the corners of Gretchen's eyes.

'Billy is not like that,' she said.

'So it's *Billy* now, is it? You think that if he can just get away with murdering his wife, you'll have a wonderful life together. But you won't. Living with him will be like living in the middle of a never-ending nightmare, until finally, perhaps, he kills you, too.'

'It's not true,' Gretchen sobbed. 'He's not like that at all.'

'If he's not like that, then why did he hit you?' Meadows demanded.

'It was my fault. I made a mistake.'

'What kind of mistake?'

Gretchen took a deep breath. 'I want a lawyer,' she said.

Ethel Danbury lay in bed next to her snoring husband. She was not asleep herself. Instead, she was thinking about the events of the previous evening.

Archie had been unusually quiet for about an hour after that policeman had left, but then he began muttering to himself, which – she knew from experience – signalled trouble.

He would hit her that night – she knew he would – and, in a way, she would welcome the blows, because that would at least mean that the waiting – which was often the worst part – would be over.

She'd been in the kitchen when he finally called her.

'Come in here, Mother.'

She'd dropped what she was doing immediately – Archie didn't like to be kept waiting – and walked meekly into the living room.

'What did you tell that bobby, Mother?' Danbury had demanded.

She'd looked down at the floor.

'I didn't tell him anything.'

'So if I say you did, that makes me a liar, does it?'

'No, but . . .'

'I told the bobby that Jane hadn't been a very sociable sort. And what did you say?'

'I said . . . I said that she'd invited us over to her house a few times.'

Danbury had stood up, so that he was towering over her.

'Exactly. I said she wasn't sociable, and you said she'd invited us round. You made me look a fool.'

Sometimes he would just slap her about a little, but at other times he would use his fists. It would be the fists that night, she'd thought, and maybe, once she was down on the floor, he'd kick her, as well.

'So what have you got to say for yourself?' Danbury had demanded.

She could have said that she'd done no more than speak the truth. Jane *had* kept inviting them round, until it had become plain to even her that Archie would never accept.

She could have said that, but she didn't, because it was not what Archie wanted to hear, and if Archie didn't hear what he wanted to hear, the beating would be even worse.

So all she said was, 'I'm sorry.'

'Look at me!' he'd said. 'Look at me!'

She'd raised her head slowly, her eyes first taking in the clenched fist at his side, and then the face that was filled with rage. It was going to be a bad one, she'd thought.

And then a miracle had occurred. The fist had stayed where it was – which seemed to surprise Archie almost as much as it surprised her. For a moment or two he'd gazed down at the fist with an expression of hurt and betrayal on his face. Then he'd barged past her and out into the hall.

'I'm going to the pub,' he'd called over his shoulder.

It was only a postponement of the beating, she'd thought.

But it hadn't been. When he'd returned from the boozer, he had barely looked at her, and had gone straight to bed.

So why had she been spared the beating? It could only be because of Inspector Beresford!

Though banished to the kitchen, she had heard him talking to Archie through the door.

Don't take your frustration with me out on your missus, because I'll be coming back to talk to her tomorrow, and if there's a mark on her, there'll be consequences.

What, you'll have me arrested?

No, I'll beat the shit out of you.

So what had she learned from that?

She had learned there was at least one person in the huge, hostile world which surrounded her who was prepared to make at least a token gesture in her defence.

But more importantly, she had learned that Archie could be frightened – that the angry god, who had ruled her life for so long, had feet of clay.

It wouldn't last.

Archie would go for her again.

He simply couldn't help himself.

But the big difference was that next time, she wouldn't just lie back and take it.

George Fullbright, William Danbury's solicitor, did not look happy, Paniatowski thought. Perhaps that was the result of having to leave his snug bed and put in an appearance at police head-quarters in the middle of the night, but it seemed more likely that it was his instructions which were bothering him.

'My client would like to be questioned by another officer,' he said.

'Another officer?' Paniatowski repeated.

'A *male* officer,' Fullbright elaborated.

'Request denied,' Paniatowski said firmly.

'He . . . er . . . has made it clear to me that he is much more likely to cooperate with a man,' Fullbright pressed on.

'You don't get to make the rules, Mr Danbury – that's my job,' Paniatowski said.

'If you know what's good for you,' Danbury said, speaking directly to Beresford, 'you'll make this so-called boss of yours see sense.'

'Did you kill your wife, Mr Danbury?' Paniatowski asked.

For a moment, it looked as if Danbury would not answer, then he seemed to decide that to keep silent would be almost like admitting his guilt.

'No, I did not kill my wife,' he said.

'Did you kidnap your daughter?'

Danbury sneered. 'Since she *is* my daughter, how is it legally possible for me to have kidnapped her?'

'Did you remove her from your home on Wednesday night?'

'No.'

'Have you, Mr Danbury, been conducting an affair with your au pair girl, Gretchen Müller?'

'No.'

'You were in Newcastle upon Tyne on Wednesday, and so was she.'

'So were a lot of other people.'

'But not a lot of people who ride a motorbike like hers.'

'If you say so. I wouldn't know.'

'Did you beat your wife?'

'No.'

'Then how do you account for the bruising on her body?'

'She did it to herself.'

'You surely can't expect me to believe that?'

'She despised herself for not living up to the standards I set her. Whenever she failed me – and she often did – she would punish herself. I believe the technical term for it is self-harm.'

'It would have been physically impossible for her to have inflicted some of her injuries on herself.'

'I only have your word for that.'

'Let's go back to Gretchen,' Paniatowski suggested. 'Did you buy that motorcycle for her?'

There was the slightest of hesitations, then Danbury said, 'Yes, I did.'

'Because she was your mistress?'

'Because good au pairs are hard to find, and when you have found one, you do your best to keep her happy.'

'It seems a very *expensive* way of keeping her happy.'

'It would – to you. But given the mill's turnover, it's a mere drop in the ocean to me.'

'Did you tell your wife you'd bought Gretchen the BMW?'

'Yes.'

'I don't believe you.'

'I don't care what you believe.'

'I'm beginning to think that the motorbike might have played a key role in the chain of events,' Paniatowski said. 'How does this sound to you? Gretchen insists you buy the bike, and since you're besotted with her, that's what you do. But then your wife finds out about it. She realises you're having an affair with the au pair, and says she's going to divorce you. And that's when you start making plans to kill her.'

'You really are pathetic,' Danbury told her. 'First of all, as I've already told you, Jane knew I'd bought the BMW for Gretchen. But let's just say for the moment that she didn't know. However would she have found out?'

'She could have noticed that the money was gone from the bank account.'

'I handle all the money in my house. Jane never even saw the bank statements. She had no idea what was in the account.'

'But if she'd had suspicions about Gretchen's expensive toy, might she not, just once, have decided to look through the accounts?'

Danbury shook his head. 'She wouldn't have dared.'

'Dared?' Paniatowski said, pouncing on the word. 'Dared!'

'Yes, *dared*,' Danbury answered. 'I make no apology for being the master of my house, and for demanding fear of my displeasure and respect for my authority from my wife and children. The men who built this town up from nothing knew all about fear and respect. I march with them, and if others choose not to, then it is those others who are out of step.'

It sounded like a speech he had worked on, and already used several times, Paniatowski thought – which was probably exactly what it was.

She understood him now, or rather, she understood how he understood himself. He was William Danbury – a hard man who kept himself pure in soft times, a beacon of traditional values managing to keep afloat on a sea of liberal laxity and weakness.

'I'm an intelligent man, don't you think?' Danbury asked.

He was trying to take control of the interview, Paniatowski realised, and if he'd been anyone else, she would have immediately reined him in. But in Danbury's case, the interview might prove to be much more productive if she let him feel he was in charge.

'I said, I'm an intelligent man, aren't I?'

'Are you?'

Danbury snorted. 'If you can't see for yourself how bright I am, then you're even stupider than I took you to be.'

'What's your point?'

'If I'd wanted to kill my wife, don't you think I'd have gone about it in a different way?'

'What do you mean by that?'

'Don't you think I'd have arranged it in such a manner that it would have been impossible for you to accuse me of the crime?'

'Since your opinion of the police is that we're incredibly stupid, perhaps you didn't think it was necessary to come up with a more elaborate scheme,' Paniatowski suggested.

'I never said that all the police were stupid – only that you were. You are a woman in a job which should plainly have been reserved for a man, and you are proving to be just as inadequate as might have been expected,' Danbury countered. He paused for a second. 'Let me ask you another question, my "brilliant" chief inspector – have you considered the possibility, even for a moment, that someone other than me might have killed Jane?'

'Of course I have, but you are our prime suspect, which is why it's you, rather than anyone else, sitting in that chair.'

'And what exactly is it that makes me the prime suspect?'

'You have the means, the motive and the opportunity to have committed the murder.'

'And so does Gretchen. The girl is besotted with me – and, *unlike* me, she is not particularly bright. Perhaps she thought, in her muddled female way, that with Jane out of the way, she could fall straight into my arms.'

'You really are scum, aren't you?' Paniatowski asked.

She had not meant to say the words aloud, but she was certainly not sorry that she had.

The strain of not knowing, one way or the other, was becoming unbearable, and despite having told himself that the only sensible thing would be to wait until it was light, Alfie Clayton found himself driving towards Lower Mill Woods nearly an hour before daybreak. Yet even as he approached the woods, he was still not sure he would stop and get out of the car.

There were two good – if opposing – reasons for simply driving on, he told himself.

The first was that if there was nothing under the oak tree, the expedition would have turned out to be a waste of time, and he would feel a complete bloody fool.

The second (and much more terrifying) reason was that what he feared could be under the tree might actually be there. And if it was, did he want to be the one to find it?

'No, of course I don't want to be the one to find it,' he said aloud, though there was only his steering wheel to hear him. 'Who, in their right mind, *would* want to find it?'

But someone had to take the responsibility, and if not the man who had the suspicion, then who?

He parked at the edge of the woods, and got his gardening spade and torch from the boot of his car. He had wondered how hard it would be to retrace his previous day's route – after all, it was still dark and unless you were an expert, one tree looked pretty like another – but his feet seemed to know the way, and without taking even one wrong turning, he found himself approaching the oak.

Even from a distance, his torch could pick out the small hole at the base of the oak, with soil heaped on either side of it. So perhaps Tony had been right after all, and it had been the work of a badger or fox, burrowing itself out a new home.

Then he reached the hole and looked down into it.

'Oh, my God,' he gasped.

He dropped his spade and torch, and even though he could no longer see into the hole, he turned away.

He was finding that standing up was too much of an effort, so he sank to his knees. He didn't know whether to throw up or burst into tears, and then realised that he was doing both.

Later, he would say that he had no idea how long he had been kneeling there, retching and sobbing. It could have been as little as one minute, it could have been as much as ten, but however long it had been, it had felt like an eternity.

But eventually the vomiting stopped, the tears dried up, and he climbed back to his feet.

If he had been thinking clearly, he would have realised that the best thing he could do in these circumstances would be to go back to his car, drive to Whitebridge, and stop at the first police station he came to – but he wasn't thinking clearly, and instead, he picked up first his torch and then his spade.

EIGHT

When her elbow slipped along the desk, thus denying her head the support of her outstretched palm, Paniatowski realised – with a sudden jolt – that she must have been asleep.

She groaned, and looked across at the desk clock with bleary eyes. It was more than twenty-four hours since she'd known the comfort of her bed, she realised. That couldn't be good for anyone, she thought, and it certainly wasn't good for a middle-aged woman who'd given birth to twins only a few months earlier.

Her hand reached automatically for her cigarettes. Even the thought of smoking was revolting, but she lit up anyway.

As she was contemplating drowning the taste of the cigarette with the equally loathsome taste of yet another black coffee, there was a knock on the door, and Chief Inspector Barrington walked in.

From the ashen look on his face, it was obvious to Paniatowski that he was not the bearer of good tidings.

'Fifteen minutes ago, a man turned up at Whitebridge General Hospital with a small child,' Barrington said. 'He wanted the doctors to do something for her – but there was nothing they could do, because she'd been dead for at least a day. We think it's Melanie Danbury.'

'What do you mean – you *think* it's Melanie?' Paniatowski demanded.

'The body was buried at the base of an oak tree. Some animal – probably a badger, though it could have been a fox – had partly dug it up, and had eaten most of the face.'

'Jesus!' Paniatowski gasped.

'The problem is, I don't know what to do next,' Barrington confessed. 'Do I assume it's her, and call off the search, or do we keep on looking?'

'How many more children of her age have been reported missing in the area in the last few days?' Paniatowski asked.

'Well, none.'

'So chances are, it is her.'

'I agree, but before we can stop looking, we really need to get some sort of formal identification. And who do we get to make that identification? The mother's dead. The grand-parents – from what I can gather – have hardly ever seen her. She was virtually never taken out of the house, so we can't rely on the neighbours, and Mrs Danbury seemed to have no social life, so we can't call in one of her friends. And as for Mr Danbury . . .'

'Yes?'

'If he didn't kill his daughter, I've no wish to put him through seeing her as she is now . . .'

'And if he *did* kill her, he's going to deny it's her anyway,' Paniatowski supplied.

'Well, exactly.'

'I think there might be one person who could make the iden-tification,' Paniatowski said.

'*A police spokesman has confirmed that a thirty-seven-year-old man has been taken into custody and is being questioned about the murder of Jane Danbury,'* the newsreader from Radio Whitebridge announced.

'Shit!' said Paniatowski, glaring at her car radio as if *it* was responsible for leaking the news.

She should have been expecting it, she supposed. Once one civilian knew about an arrest – and in this case there were three, the manager of the Royal Victoria and his two assistants – then it was not long before it became public knowledge. Still, it was a great pity that the bankers and businessmen and lawyers who made up William Danbury's circle of admirers couldn't have been kept in the dark about it for a few more hours.

The newsreader droned on – there had been a demonstration against the proposed site for a new electricity substation, a local actor had landed a part in an American comedy series, Whitebridge Rovers' gate was up ten percent over the previous year – but Paniatowski was only half-listening.

Then, as she pulled up in front of Dr Lucas' house, the announcer said, *'In breaking news, a dead child has been discovered in Lower Mills Woods by Mr Alfred Clayton, a local lorry driver. Mr Clayton took the child to Whitebridge General Hospital, where the death was confirmed. As yet, the Mid Lancs police have issued no statement.'*

'Shit!' Paniatowski said – and this time, it was almost a bellow.

That information should never have been broadcast, because everyone who heard it would automatically assume that the dead girl was Melanie Danbury.

Of course, it probably *was* Melanie, but that was still to be confirmed.

She got out of the car, walked to the front door and rang the bell.

It was Dr Lucas himself who opened the door. Though it was still early in the morning, he was fully dressed.

It was obvious he was angry, and the anger showed not just in his face, but in his whole body. He seemed much taller and more solid than the last time they'd met – and much more purposeful, too.

'What do you want?' he demanded.

'Can I come in?' Paniatowski asked.

'No, you bloody well can't come in. My best friend has just

lost his wife, and must be out of his mind worrying about what's happened to his little daughter. And what do you do – you arrest him! It was *him* you arrested, wasn't it? He *is* the thirty-seven-year-old man who it said on the radio just now was helping the police with their enquiries?'

'Yes, it's him,' Paniatowski admitted.

'Then you can go to hell!'

She could come straight out with the reason she was there, she thought, but even for a doctor, who was used to death, what she was about to ask him to do wouldn't be easy, and she'd much prefer to broach the matter more gently – and inside the house.

'Please let me come in,' she said. 'We really do need to talk, Dr Lucas. It's important.'

Perhaps it was the urgency in her tone that made his anger drain away, she thought, or maybe it was simply that he found the anger too exhausting to sustain for long.

Whatever the reason, his shoulders suddenly drooped, his mouth slackened, and he was once again the well-meaning and slightly weedy Dr Lucas she was getting to know.

'I've been under a lot of strain,' he said, in a tone she recognised as suitable for framing an apology. 'I spent most of the night with Pete Hutton, you see.'

'Who?'

'Oh, sorry, of course there's no reason why you should know. He's a patient of mine, and he's in the terminal stages of cancer.'

'I wouldn't have thought there was much you could do for him.'

'There isn't. I was there mostly for Betty's sake. She's his wife, and she has no relatives to turn to, so I thought she would appreciate the support. I sometimes think I'm more of a priest than a doctor.' Lucas laughed, though there was very little humour in it. 'But that's no excuse for laying into you. I'm sure you think you're doing the right thing, even if I know you're doing the wrong one.'

He led her down the hallway into the living room.

'Would you like a cup of tea or coffee?' he asked. 'It may take some time, because Mrs Dale isn't up yet, and I don't know where she keeps everything. Still, I expect I can manage.'

'I'm fine,' Paniatowski assured him. 'You didn't hear the end of the news bulletin, did you?'

'No,' Lucas admitted. 'As soon as I heard that William had been arrested, I switched it off.'

'Then I'm afraid I've got some bad news for you,' Paniatowski said.

'Bad news?'

'We think we've found Melanie Danbury's body.'

The colour drained from Dr Lucas' face, and he seemed to be fighting for breath. He looked around for something to grab hold of, and settled on the back of the nearest armchair.

'But . . . but you can't have found her!' he gasped. 'You simply can't have!'

'You must have known that it was always a possibility,' Paniatowski said softly.

'Yes, but just because something's possible doesn't mean you think it's going to actually happen,' Lucas said. There was a slightly hysterical note in his voice, but his colour was returning, and he was feeling confident enough to relinquish his grip on the armchair. 'I mean, it's William's daughter we're talking about here!'

And that, on its own, should have been enough to protect her, should it? Paniatowski wondered. That, alone, should have raised her above the dangers that mere ordinary mortals have to face?

'Poor William!' Lucas said.

Bugger poor William – what about poor *Melanie*? Paniatowski wanted to scream at him.

But instead, she said, 'We'd very much appreciate it if you would look at the body, and try to make a formal identification.'

'*Try* to make it?' Lucas said. 'Why should I need to *try*?'

She told him what the badger had done.

'That's just terrible,' Lucas moaned. 'William will be destroyed when he hears about it.'

'Since she was your patient, we thought you might be able to base your identification on something other than her face,' Paniatowski said. 'You might recognise a scar or a birthmark, for example, which other people wouldn't even know about, and . . .'

It was obvious that Lucas was not listening – or rather that he wasn't listening to *her*.

'Is something the matter?' she asked, in a much louder voice.

'What? No, nothing's the matter. I thought I heard the phone ring, that's all. I'm expecting Betty Hutton to call me any minute now. What were you saying, chief inspector?'

'I was asking you if Melanie had a scar or birthmark that might make identification easier.'

'No, there's nothing like that.'

'But it is possible you'll be able to give us a positive identification, if it does turn out to be Melanie?'

'I'm . . . I'm willing to give it a try,' Lucas said uncertainly. 'But first I'll have to ring Betty Hutton, to tell her where I'll be.'

'All right,' Paniatowski agreed.

'And if she wants to talk, I'll have to let her. I can't just hang up on a woman whose husband is dying before her very eyes.'

No, Paniatowski thought, he probably couldn't.

'I'll wait in the car,' she said.

Chief Inspector Barrington looked out of his office window at the car park below. There had been a long line of volunteers queuing up there the previous morning, but now there was not a soul to be seen.

Why would there be? he asked himself. They would all have heard the news on the radio, and assumed that Melanie Danbury had been found.

He looked up at the clock. Soon, the Manchester police helicopters that he had requested for that day's search would be setting off from their base. The choppers would start costing the Mid Lancs police money the moment they were in the air, and at the end of the day, the chief constable would find himself presented with a whacking bill.

Barrington could all too easily imagine Pickering furiously demanding to know why the helicopters had been called in when they'd already found the body.

And what would he say in his own defence?

That the body had not been formally identified at the time?

That they still hadn't been sure that it was Melanie that Alfie Clayton had found?

But it had to be Melanie – it simply *had to* be.

He picked up the phone.

'Get me the Manchester police,' he told the switchboard.

* * *

Dr Shastri had gone to Preston, where she was appearing as an expert witness in a major trial, and it was one of her assistants who pulled back the sheet covering the large, adult-sized trolley, to reveal the tiny dead infant beneath.

'Oh, my God!' Dr Lucas choked.

Paniatowski said nothing, but exactly the same words bounced around her brain like a demented squash ball.

Oh, my God . . . oh, my God . . . oh, my God . . .

This could have been one of my children, she thought – this could *easily* have been one of my children.

'Is it Melanie?' someone asked, in a calm, professional voice – and Paniatowski realised, much to her amazement, that the words had come from her own mouth.

Dr Lucas stared down at the dead child.

'Could you turn her over?' he asked the mortuary assistant.

Gently – as if he were handling a live baby – the assistant picked up the corpse and held it, face down, a few inches above the trolley.

'Well?' Paniatowski asked.

'I don't know. I think it's her, but I'm not sure.'

'Close your eyes for a moment,' Paniatowski said.

'Why?'

'It's a technique we use to bring back people's memories. Please just do as I ask.'

Lucas closed his eyes.

'You've been called to the Danbury house because Melanie isn't feeling too well. All right?'

'Yes.'

'You've just parked your car in the driveway. I want you to picture what you can see as you get out of it. You walk over to the front door. Can you see the front door?'

'Yes.'

'You ring the bell. Who answers it?'

'Jane.'

'She leads you upstairs. You both enter the baby's room. She's lying in her cot. You pick her up. Can you picture picking her up?'

'Yes.'

'What do you do next?'

'I put her on the changing table, which is next to the cot, so I can get a better look at her.'

'Is there anything wrong with her?'

'She has a rash, but it's a perfectly normal baby rash and there's nothing to worry about.'

'Open your eyes,' Paniatowski commanded. 'Do it quickly. Is this Melanie, Dr Lucas?'

Lucas gazed at the body for a few seconds, then said, 'I'm afraid you'll have to get someone else to make the identification.'

'Jesus Christ, there *is* no one else!' Paniatowski said, exasperatedly. 'Don't you understand that?'

'There must surely be someone . . .'

'There isn't! So tell me – is it Melanie or isn't it?'

'If I said it was her, you'd call off the search, wouldn't you?'

'Yes,' Paniatowski admitted. 'We would.'

'But supposing I was wrong,' Lucas said, in an agonised voice. 'Supposing it was some other infant instead? Then Melanie would still be out there somewhere, but nobody would be looking for her.'

'If I was holding a gun to your head, and you had to answer yes or no, what would your answer be?' Paniatowski demanded.

'On balance, I'd say it probably was her,' Lucas replied, with some reluctance.

Paniatowski sighed. It wasn't a good answer, but it was probably the best answer she was going to get.

Archie Danbury had been waiting outside the Fox and Hounds when it opened its doors at ten o'clock, and now – though it was still only a quarter to eleven – he was already on his third pint.

What went on between a man and his wife was nobody's business but theirs, and that bobby had had no right to threaten him – no right at all – he thought angrily, as he sank another inch of beer.

'But he scared you, didn't he?' asked a nagging, unfamiliar voice in the back of his mind. 'He really put the shits up you.'

'No, he didn't scare me,' Danbury muttered.

'So why didn't you give Ethel a good pasting last night? You know she was asking for it.'

The voice – this stranger in his head – was right, Archie thought as he ordered another pint. He was no longer in the mood to give Ethel a thrashing, but when he got back home, he would do it anyway – because that was what he *needed* to do in order to get his manhood back.

William Danbury glared at Paniatowski across the interview table.

'For the hundredth time, I did not kill my wife and I did not kidnap my own child,' he said.

'I'm not here to question you,' Paniatowski told him. 'I'm here to give you some information.'

'And what information might that be?'

'We can't be certain until we've run the blood tests, but we think we may have found Melanie's body.'

The anger drained from Danbury's eyes, but before they had time to change to another natural expression, he brought his mental shutters down, and it was like staring at a blank wall.

'You *think* you've found her?' he said. 'You need to run some tests? Surely, it should be obvious whether it's her or not.'

'The body had been subjected to certain stresses which have made identification rather difficult,' Paniatowski said carefully.

'It can't have been decay,' Danbury said. 'She hasn't been missing for that long.'

'No, it wasn't decay.'

'Then what was it?'

'You don't want to know.'

Now why had she said that? Paniatowski wondered.

Why should she choose to spare the feelings of man who she was convinced had cold-bloodedly murdered his own child?

Could it be that she was having some doubts about his guilt?

Of course not! All the evidence pointed to him. There was no one else in the frame.

'You didn't ask me *where* we found the body, Mr Danbury,' she said.

'Does that matter?'

No – not if you already knew, Paniatowski thought. He'd never asked exactly how his wife had been murdered, either – because he'd known that, too.

'Melanie is dead,' Danbury said. 'I have been mentally

preparing myself for the news, and now it's happened. The details are unimportant. They won't bring her back.'

'We still don't know for certain that it's her,' Paniatowski cautioned.

'Of course it's her!' Danbury said. 'If another child of her age had gone missing, don't you think the parents would have reported it straight away?'

'I'm very sorry,' she said.

'But nowhere near as sorry as you'll be when you realise you've made a mistake and have to let me go,' Danbury said. 'Because when that happens, I'll have your job for what you've put me through. You can bank on it.'

The only reason Archie Danbury had stopped drinking was because he had run out of money, but by that time he had already sunk seven pints and convinced himself that not only had his wife earned a good thrashing, but that if that bobby came around to his house again, he would break the bugger's nose for him.

He had his keys in his pocket, but he could not be bothered to fish them out, and when he reached his front door, he simply banged on it with his big fist.

He expected to hear the sound of his wife scuttling down the corridor, but instead there was only silence.

He banged again, harder this time.

Still nothing.

'Ethel, are you there?' he shouted, knowing his words would penetrate the thin wooden door. 'Let me in, Ethel, before I lose my temper with you.'

Half a minute passed, and that grew into a minute, and then two.

He couldn't believe what was happening.

He really couldn't bloody believe it!

Finally he gave up, fumbled in his pocket for his keys, and, after a couple of attempts, managed to insert the key in the lock.

As he entered the house, he turned around and saw that several of the neighbours were watching him from the other side of the street. They were laughing at him, he thought – laughing at a man who couldn't even control his own wife. Well, Ethel would pay for this – by God she would.

He slammed the front door behind him and stormed down the corridor. Then he reached the living room door, and came to an abrupt halt.

Ethel was standing at the far end of the room. She had his double-barrelled shotgun in her hands, and she was pointing it directly at him.

'What the bloody hell do you think you're doing, woman?' he demanded.

'Don't come any closer,' Ethel said.

'Put that gun down before you do some damage,' he said.

'No.'

'It'll be much worse for you if you don't do as I say right now.'

'I'm not putting it down.'

'You'd never use it on me. You know you wouldn't,' Archie said, stepping into the living room with some caution, but clearly intent on crossing to where his wife was standing.

He's right, Ethel thought, as she watched him approach. I will never use it on him. I've made just one more mistake in a life that feels as if it's been nothing *but* mistakes.

And then she thought of Jane, lying there in the lounge of her big house – the house that Archie would never allow her to visit – with her head smashed in.

Still moving slowly, Archie was almost halfway across the room. He was smiling now. It was a triumphant smile – a vicious smile.

Ethel closed her eyes and squeezed the trigger.

Paniatowski could recognise an ambush when she saw one, and there was no question in her mind that the three men who were sitting in the chief constable's office were just that.

Individually, the three men were a local estate agent-cum-town councillor, one of Whitebridge's most senior magistrates, and the managing director of the ironworks. Collectively, they were members of the police authority.

The chief constable was also present. Pickering was trying to look as if this whole situation was as much a surprise to him as it was to Paniatowski – and maybe, she thought in fairness, it was.

'These gentlemen requested an informal meeting with you, and I agreed to it,' the chief constable said. 'Do you have any objection to such a meeting, DCI Paniatowski?'

'No, none at all,' Paniatowski replied.

She couldn't blame Pickering, she supposed. He was still not confirmed in his post, and it would be foolish of him to offend people with influence. So the important thing now was not that he had allowed the meeting to happen, but whether he backed whatever she said *during* that meeting.

It would be the ironmaster, Alderman Horace Cudlip, who took the lead, she thought.

Cudlip was approaching seventy. He was a heavy man with a walrus moustache, who wore thick tweed suits whatever the weather, and smoked a pipe. When he spoke, it was slowly and ponderously, like the mill owners in the 1930s black-and-white films. He could almost have been regarded as a comical figure, but he had a sharp mind and a great deal of influence, so it would have been a mistake to underestimate him.

'You are probably aware, chief inspector, that as the police authority, it is not our function to intervene in the day-to-day policing activities,' Cudlip said.

'Yes, I am aware of that,' Paniatowski replied neutrally.

'Nevertheless, we do not consider it beyond our remit to offer advice when we consider that such advice might be necessary.'

What was it that Dr Lucas had said about William Danbury's admirers?

'These men who admire him would have done everything they could to block any prosecution mounted against William, and since some of them are in the police force, and several are members of the judiciary, the prosecution would have faltered and died before it even reached the first hurdle.'

Yes, that was it.

'Advice,' she said aloud. 'Well, I'm certainly willing to listen to some *advice*.'

'We recognise that you are quite within your rights to treat William Danbury as a suspect in this matter . . .' Cudlip began.

'It's not about rights, Alderman Cudlip,' Paniatowski interrupted him. 'It's about duty. It's about seeing justice prevail.'

'Er . . . quite so. But isn't there scope for a little compassion, here? After all, William has recently lost both his wife and his daughter, so while we are not asking you to change your attitude to him for the present, wouldn't it be possible, while the investigation proceeds, to release him on police bail?'

'On compassionate grounds?'

'Exactly so.'

Isn't that a bit like the story of the barrister defending a man who'd killed both his parents, and asking the jury to feel sorry for his client because he was an orphan? Paniatowski wondered.

Less than an hour earlier, India Road had been the same nondescript mill town street it had been for generations. But that had all changed after the shooting. Now, there were police barricades in place five doors up from the Danbury house, and five doors down from it. Now, there was a line of police vehicles parked directly in front of the Danbury house, and behind the off-side of those vehicles squatted highly trained officers with pistols.

Nor was police activity confined simply to street level. At the bedroom window of every house from which it was theoretically possible to take a shot at the Danburys' front door, there was a police marksman, armed with a high-powered rifle and more than willing to show just how good he was.

From behind one of the police barricades, Chief Superintendent Briscoe – a mountain of a man, who had a chest broad enough to display almost all the medals he had won as a Royal Marine – surveyed his deployment pattern with calm satisfaction. There were many aspects of police work that he quite enjoyed, he thought, but it was from operations like this one that he got the most pleasure.

An unmarked car pulled up just beyond the barricade, and a man in his thirties got out.

'That's him, sir,' said Sergeant Cox, Briscoe's bagman. 'That's DI Beresford.'

'Is it, by God,' Briscoe said. 'Well, let's see if we can find out what makes *him* so special.'

'Do you know Mrs Ethel Danbury well, Detective Inspector?' Briscoe asked Beresford.

'No, sir, I don't. As a matter of fact, I met her for the very first time yesterday.'

'Hmm,' Briscoe said pensively. 'Well, you certainly seem to have made an impression on her.'

'In what way, sir?' Beresford asked.

'We'll get to that later,' Briscoe said, 'but first I'd like to fill in a little of the background. According to the neighbours – who seem to have developed nosiness into an art form – Danbury left the front door open when he came home. He went inside, and there was the sound of shots. Then Mrs Danbury appeared in the hallway and closed the door – and she had a double-barrelled shotgun in her hand. From which we can assume that she shot her husband, don't you think?'

'If she hadn't, she wouldn't have been in any state to close the front door – in fact, she'd probably have been lying on the living room floor, unconscious,' Beresford said.

'Are you sure it was only *yesterday* that you met the family?' Briscoe asked, suspiciously.

'Yes, sir, but it didn't take long to work out what their home life was like.'

'That bad, was it?' Briscoe asked.

'That bad,' Beresford confirmed.

'At any rate, we arrive on the scene, and I get my negotiator – who can normally charm the birds out of the trees – to ring Mrs Danbury. And what do you think she said to him?'

'I've no idea, sir.'

'Take a guess,' Briscoe said – and it was more an order than a suggestion.

'She said she wanted to talk to me,' Beresford hazarded.

Briscoe nodded. 'She said she wanted to talk to you – and *only* to you. Now why was that?'

'Don't take your frustration with me out on your missus, because I'll be coming back to talk to her tomorrow, and if there's a mark on her, there'll be consequences,' Beresford tells Danbury.

'What, you'll have me arrested?' Danbury sneers.

'No,' Beresford replies. 'I'll beat the shit out of you.'

Mrs Danbury hadn't been there, Beresford thought, because her husband had exiled her to the kitchen. But she must have heard the exchange through the door, and now she saw him as her defender – her champion.

'Well, *can* you explain it?' Briscoe asked.

'Maybe she fancies me, sir,' Beresford suggested – because there was no way that he was going to admit to a superior officer that he'd threatened to beat up a member of the public, however odious that member of the public might have been.

The chief superintendent frowned. 'Maybe that's it,' he said, unconvinced. 'At any rate, we have three possible courses of action open to us. The first is that we could storm the house – and if I thought there was anyone inside in immediate danger, that is what we would do. But Mrs Danbury assures us that her husband is dead, and since all the neighbours have reported hearing *four* gunshots, I think it very likely that he is.'

'I agree, sir.'

'The second course is that we lay siege to the place until she simply gets tired of it, gives up and comes out. I'm almost inclined to go for that one, but the danger is that, given time, she'll decide to turn the gun on herself. What do you think?'

'I think it's more than likely.'

'That leaves me with the third option,' Briscoe said.

He paused. It might be a good idea, before embarking on the third option, to get the chief constable to agree – preferably in writing – that it was the right course of action to take, he thought, but Pickering was in an important meeting, and had left strict instructions that he wasn't to be disturbed.

Of course, given the seriousness of the situation, he could always insist on being put through, but he was not sure he actually *wanted* the chief constable's guidance, because Pickering was one step removed from the sharp end of policing now, and rapidly becoming what all chief constables became eventually – a bureaucrat rather than a bobby, whose decision would be coloured more by public relations considerations than the requirements of good practice.

'That leaves me with the third option,' he repeated, 'which, as you will already have worked out, is that you should talk to her.'

'Shall I ring her now?' Beresford asked.

'I'd like nothing better than for you to ring her now,' Briscoe replied, 'but unfortunately, she's ripped the phone out of the wall, so any talking you do will have to be face-to-face.'

Well, shit! Beresford thought.

'Listen, Colin . . .' Briscoe said. He paused. 'I am right? It *is* Colin, isn't it?'

'Yes, sir, it is.'

'I'm not going to order you to go in there, Colin. In fact, I'd put it in even stronger terms than that – no one involved in this entire operation will blame you if you *don't* go in there.'

'I want to go,' Beresford said.

And he did, not because his words may have led to Archie Danbury's death – if any man ever deserved to be killed, it was Archie – but because those same words might have determined Ethel's future.

'Well, if that's your decision – made independently, without any outside pressure – I'll get Sergeant Cox to issue you with a bullet-proof vest,' Chief Superintendent Briscoe said.

'I don't want a bullet-proof vest,' Beresford told him. 'If I go in wearing that, Ethel will see me as the enemy – and that's the last thing I need.'

'That may be a good point, but I can't allow you in there without one,' Briscoe replied, 'especially given that we've no idea what sort of mental state the woman is in. She might see you as a friend one minute, and an enemy the next. And she's armed with a double-barrelled shotgun, remember, so if she starts to see you as an enemy, then God help you.'

'She won't see me as an enemy,' Beresford said firmly.

'You can't know that for sure. By your own admission, you only met the woman yesterday.'

'I'll be all right,' Beresford said.

Briscoe sighed. 'Have you ever had to face someone wielding a gun?' he asked.

'No, sir.'

'The first time, you're so scared that you're absolutely convinced you're going to crap yourself. And it doesn't get any better – you think the same thing the *twentieth* time it happens. Believe me, I know.'

'I'm not saying I won't be scared . . .' Beresford began.

'Take the vest, son – because I'm not letting you go in there without one,' Briscoe said firmly.

'All right,' Beresford agreed, with more irritation in his voice than was prudent when addressing a chief superintendent. 'I'll wear the bloody thing.'

The bullet-proof vest was deep constabulary blue and had 'Mid Lancs Police' written across it in bright white capitals.

It slipped over the head, and was then tightened up by Velcro strips on each side.

'They call it a bullet-proof vest, but it isn't really bullet-proof at all,' Sergeant Cox said, as he checked the fasteners. 'I much prefer the other name for it, which is bullet-*resistant*.'

'Well, you are a proper little ray of sunshine, aren't you?' Beresford said drily.

Cox chuckled. 'I sometimes get carried away with the technical side of things,' he said, 'but don't worry, it stops bullets, all right. It's got a special layered synthetic fibre inside, which is five times as strong as steel. But if you do get hit, you'll still feel the impact all right, and for days after you'll have bruises the size and colour of syphilitic testicles.'

Briscoe and Cox watched as Beresford left the protective safety of the parked police cars and walked across the road to the Danburys' front door.

'He's got a key, has he?' the chief superintendent asked.

'Yes, sir, it's the spare one that Mrs Danbury left with one of the neighbours.'

Beresford came to a halt at the front door, but made no move to open it. Instead, he started fiddling with his bullet-proof vest, as if to assure himself it was still there.

'Do you think he's decided to bottle out?' CS Briscoe asked.

'Possibly,' the sergeant replied. 'I gave him a bit of a pep talk while I was helping him on with the vest, and he seemed all right then, but maybe now he's on his own, he's starting to have second thoughts.'

'We'll give him another half minute to make up his mind, then we'll pull him back,' Briscoe said.

Beresford suddenly took hold of the vest at the shoulders, and lifted it over his head.

'What the bloody hell is he doing?' Briscoe exploded. He clicked his radio over broadcast. 'Team B, get in there. Stop that maniac *now*!'

But it was too late to do anything about Beresford now, because even before the jacket hit the ground, he was opening the door.

Once he had closed the door behind him, Beresford had, in effect, locked one world out and imprisoned himself in other.

Outside, there was a variety of sounds – the whispered conversations, the intermittent crackle of police radios, the heavy footfalls as officers ran – almost bent double – from one protected position to another.

There was a variety of smells out there, too – car exhaust fumes, cigarettes, sweat, and, when the breeze suddenly changed direction, the fresh tang of roasted hops from the brewery.

Inside, the only sound came from the free-standing hall clock, as its pendulum made the journey from left to right, and then back again from right to left – tick-tock, tick-tock, tick-tock . . .

Inside, the air was dominated by the stink of cordite.

Beresford could see the open door to the lounge, but from where he was standing, he could not look far into the lounge itself.

'It's me, Mrs Danbury!' he called out, taking a step forward. 'Colin Beresford! There's nobody else with me. I've come alone.'

There was no answer from the lounge.

'I'm coming down the hallway,' he said, taking a second step. 'Is that all right?'

Still no sound, other than the ticking of the clock.

Tick-tock, tick-tock, tick-tock . . .

He stayed where he was.

'Before I come any further, I really need you to tell me it's all right, Mrs Danbury.'

Nothing!

Why wasn't she saying anything? he wondered.

Surely, she'd asked for him because she thought he was on her side – because she wanted to talk to him, and him alone.

And that meant that *she* was on *his* side, too, didn't it?

But what if he'd misread the situation?

What if she now regretted killing her husband, and blamed him for putting the idea into her head in the first place?

He hadn't put the idea into her head at all, of course, but if she was now feeling guilty, and looking for a scapegoat . . .

He was sweating, he realised. Though it was not particularly warm in the hall, the sweat was pouring from him, clogging up his armpits and streaming in rivulets down his face.

He could turn around now, quietly retrace his steps, and be at the front door before she knew what was happening.

And if, once she *did* realise, she followed him out onto the street, intent on doing to him what she had already done to her husband, the snipers would soon take care of her.

He had his whole life ahead of him, he thought, whereas Mrs Danbury's life was ruined, whatever the outcome of the morning's events.

So why take the risk?

'It can't go on like this, Ethel,' he said loudly. 'One of us has got to do something.'

And then he took another decisive step towards the lounge.

NINE

The three wise men from the police authority were still droning on endlessly, like wasps around a picnic table.

'. . . when you consider William's very valuable contribution to the community . . . it isn't doing his two little boys any good to be separated from their father, you know . . . perhaps, if you were to lay down some strict conditions, say, for example, that Danbury was required to report at the police station twice a day . . .'

Blah, blah, blah.

Their problem was that they just couldn't bring themselves to see Danbury as a serious suspect, Paniatowski thought.

It simply wasn't *possible* that good old Bill Danbury – who played golf with them and told some very amusing dirty jokes in the clubhouse, who had raised thousands and thousands of pounds for charity, who was a stalwart supporter of Whitebridge RFC and had been a brilliant prop forward in his day, who you could always rely on to help you out when you needed access to a line of credit or a domestic alibi – had actually murdered his wife and kidnapped his own child.

But it had gone beyond concern for William Danbury's comfort. Now, it was as much about them as it was about him.

They saw themselves as men of influence in the community – men whose opinions were deferred to. Yet here was this woman – a mere chief inspector, who, not so long ago, had been no more than Charlie Woodend's bag carrier – refusing to be swayed by the sensible advice they were offering.

So far, the chief constable had remained silent – had been, to all intents and purposes, no more than a spectator – but unless the meeting was to grumble on until the end of time, he was going to have to come down on one side or the other.

It was time to gamble on him coming down on the *right* side, Paniatowski decided.

'Do I have your permission to give these gentlemen some of the operational details of this case, sir?' she asked Pickering.

From the look in the chief constable's eyes, it was clear that he recognised the question for what it actually was – a request for permission to go on the attack.

He blinked twice, then said, 'I don't see why not. They are all members of the police authority, and I'm sure we can rely on them not to reveal to anyone else anything they are told in this room.'

He was still playing it cagily, she thought – speaking in a tone of voice which suggested he had taken the request at face value, so that later, if needs be, he could claim that what was about to follow had come as much a surprise to him as it had to them.

'Then let's start with the victim,' Paniatowski suggested. 'How often did any of you see Jane Danbury?'

Immediately, the wise men began to look uncomfortable.

'Not very often, as a matter of fact,' Alderman Cudlip admitted. 'William usually comes to functions and social gatherings alone. He says that his wife prefers to be at home with the children.'

'Jane Danbury virtually *never* left the house,' Paniatowski said.

'Sometimes that was because she was physically unable to – but we'll come back to that point later. She had no friends to speak of, and – even more crucially – no opportunities to make enemies.'

Cudlip laughed awkwardly. 'You seem to have read us all wrong, chief inspector,' he said. 'We never thought for a moment that she'd been killed by an enemy. What we assumed was that the murderer was a stranger who had broken in, with the intention of robbing the Danburys, and . . .'

'And was caught in the act by Mrs Danbury?'

'Well, yes.'

'And having disturbed him, you'd expect her to run as far away from him as she possibly could, wouldn't you?'

'I suppose so.'

'But she doesn't do that at all. She stays right there in the living room. And to make it easier for the burglar – a man she's never seen before – to attack her, she turns her back on him.'

'Perhaps she didn't know he was there.'

'As for the burglar himself, he doesn't just knock her unconscious – he keeps hitting her until her head is nothing but pulp.'

'He may have panicked.'

'Panicked, you say. A man in a panic would get out of the house as soon as possible. But he doesn't do that. He doesn't even take any of the valuables, which, according to your theory, is why he's there in the first place. What he does do is to abduct the baby.'

Alderman Cudlip looked at the other two wise men, as if he were expecting them to come to his rescue, but it was clear he had drawn a blank.

'Perhaps the baby was what he wanted all along,' Cudlip suggested. 'There are, after all, such things as baby traffickers. I was reading about one in the papers, just the other day.' He took a slow puff of his pipe, and was immediately surrounded by a cloud of blue smoke. 'I will admit that the case I read about happened down south,' he continued, 'but anything bad that starts down south does *eventually* find its way up north.'

'Have you ever examined baby trafficking from a business perspective?' Paniatowski asked.

'Certainly not! That's a horrible – grotesque – suggestion.'

'But that's the way the traffickers look at it. They work in the shadows, preying on the poor and helpless. The last thing that they want is the blaze of publicity that a murder would bring them.' Paniatowski paused. 'Now let's consider William Danbury himself. He is a man who is entirely dependent on his wife. Without her, he would have no job.'

'That surely can't be right,' Cudlip protested. 'William is a highly respected businessman . . .'

'A highly respected businessman who earns only what his wife chooses to pay him, and has no shares in the company he works for. His wife must have walked all over him, mustn't she?'

The three wise men looked neither at her nor at each other.

And that's because they know, she thought – that's because they *bloody well* know!

'Were you aware that William Danbury regularly beat up his wife, Jane – sometimes quite badly?' Paniatowski demanded.

'Did he, by God?' Alderman Cudlip said.

'He did.'

'Then no, we were not aware of it.'

'Really?' Paniatowski asked sceptically. 'Are you certain of that?'

'Sometimes, when we were out for the night, William might express the view that a woman needs a good slapping now and again,' Cudlip said, 'but we all say silly things when we've had a few brandies, and no one took it seriously.'

He was lying, Paniatowski thought. Maybe they didn't know the full extent of what was going on, but they knew, all right. They knew, and they had accepted it because they liked Danbury's company and they enjoyed his influence, and if his wife did get beaten up now and again, well, they hardly knew her.

'He had a mistress, too – the family au pair,' Paniatowski continued. 'She was in love with him and expected him to marry her – and that could have ruined everything, couldn't it?'

'Then surely, if he was going to kill anyone, it would have been more sensible to kill the au pair,' Cudlip said – and the moment the words were out of his mouth, it was obvious that he regretted ever uttering them.

'So you're admitting that he *is* capable of killing, are you?' Paniatowski challenged.

'No, of course not. I was speaking theoretically.'

'The house's security system is top of the range, and hadn't been tampered with,' Paniatowski said, hammering home her points. 'Only three people had keys – Jane, William and the au pair. We know that Jane knew her murderer, and we know that if she had found out about her husband's affair – which she was almost bound to – she would very likely have cut him off without a penny. Can you seriously doubt that it was William Danbury – and not some nameless intruder – who killed Jane Danbury?'

She waited for one of the three wise men to say something, but even Alderman Cudlip seemed unwilling to speak.

'And do you know what the worst thing about this tragedy is?' Paniatowski continued. 'The worst thing is that it could so easily have been prevented – because if one of Danbury's close friends had forced him to get help for his problem, the murder might never have occurred.'

'I'm not sure I approve of it, but I have to admire the way you twisted things around to make them feel guilty about what happened,' Pickering said to Paniatowski, when the three wise men had left.

'I didn't *twist things around.*' Paniatowski said. 'I didn't need to. They feel guilty because they *are* guilty. Anyone who tolerates violence to others must bear part of the guilt for the violence.'

'You're sure William Danbury did it, are you?' Pickering asked.

'Yes.'

'Well, I hope to God that you're right, because you've just made yourself three real enemies there . . .'

'My aim was never to make friends and influence people – it was to ensure that William Danbury stayed safely behind bars.'

'. . . and if Danbury does turn out to be innocent after all, they'll want your head on a platter.'

'He did it,' Paniatowski said firmly. 'I know he did it.'

The phone rang, and the chief constable reached across his desk for it.

'Yes?' he said. 'He's done what? . . . But why wasn't I told? . . . I know I said I wasn't to be disturbed, but this is . . . Yes, all right.'

When he put down the phone again, there was a grave – almost funereal – expression on his face.

'There's been a serious incident,' he told Paniatowski, 'and one of your people is involved.'

Ethel Danbury was sitting on an upright chair at the far end of the living room, with the shotgun cradled on her lap.

Archie Danbury was lying on the floor. His chest was pitted with shotgun pellets, and his head was a mushy mixture of blood, bone and brains.

'Is that gun loaded, Ethel?' Beresford asked, as he felt his heart beat furiously against his ribcage.

'Yes,' Mrs Danbury replied, in a distant voice.

'And would it be all right if I took it off you?'

'No!' Ethel said – much more harshly, more determinedly.

'If you won't give it to me, will you at least put it down? It doesn't look safe where it is.'

'It's safe enough. I was brought up on a farm. I started shooting as soon as I was big enough to hold a gun. I was a crack shot, and I still am – it's something you never forget.'

'Did Archie know you were good with guns?' Beresford asked.

'No, I knew he wouldn't like it, so I pretended that they frightened me,' Ethel said. She sighed. 'I let him think he was God. That was my first mistake – and I've made *so many* since.'

He should try and disarm her, Beresford thought, but he knew that he'd never make it – knew that, before he was halfway across the room, she'd have swung the shotgun into position, cocked it, and let him have it with both barrels.

'Would you like to talk?' he suggested.

'About what?'

'I don't know,' Beresford said – groping his way as he went. 'About your husband, perhaps?'

'He was a terrible man,' Ethel said. 'A cruel man. I accidentally singed one of his shirts once – and he did this.'

She held up her arms, and Beresford could see the imprint of an iron clearly burned into her skin.

'Why did he do it?' Ethel asked. 'And why did I let him do it? Can you explain that to me?'

So that was why he was there, Beresford thought – to explain her life to her, to make some sense of the terrible situation she found herself in.

He felt as if he were drowning in a sea of his own inadequacy, and knew that if he didn't learn to swim soon, there was a good chance that neither of them would walk out of this living room alive.

'I can't explain it,' he admitted. 'All I do know is that you're not alone. There are thousands – perhaps millions – of women who have found themselves in your situation, and have reacted just like you have.'

'I used to think it must be my fault. If I hadn't singed his shirt, he wouldn't have burned my arm. If I hadn't . . .'

'It's not your fault,' Beresford said softly. 'It was *never* your fault.'

'I feel so guilty – so ashamed,' Ethel said.

She was crying now, but she still had a firm grip on the shotgun.

'You shouldn't feel guilty,' Beresford said, glancing down at Archie Danbury's body.

'Not about Archie!' Ethel said.

There was a sudden anger in her voice, and it was directed against him, Beresford realised. And the *reason* she was angry was that he had failed her – she had expected him to understand, and it was obvious that he hadn't.

'So what *do* you feel guilty about?' he asked – doing his best not to look at the shotgun, fighting back thoughts of what it would be like to have dozens of small burning craters in his chest.

'I feel guilty about her!' Ethel said.

'Her?'

'I should have left Archie when William was a little boy. Either that, or I should have done then what I've finally done today. But I didn't. I stayed, and I suffered. And William saw it happening. William grew up believing that was how life was – how life *should be*.'

He'd got it now, he thought – he was tuned into her wavelength.

'You're talking about Jane, aren't you?' he said.

'Of course I'm talking about Jane. She was such a sweet girl – such an earnest girl. All she ever wanted out of life was a happy family. She reminded me so much of myself, when I was young. I should have warned her that my son was a monster, but that's not an admission any mother wants to make. So, instead, I lied to myself. I forced myself to believe that Jane would change William for the better. But deep inside me, I knew that would never happen – because he's fashioned from the same poisoned tree that his father was.' The tears were streaming down her cheeks, and her finger seemed – to Beresford, at least – to be tightening on the trigger of the shotgun. 'And because I said nothing to her, Jane – lovely, sweet Jane – is dead! And it's all my fault!' She wiped a tear from her eye. 'I want you to leave now.'

She had decided to end it all, Beresford realised, but she knew that he could be across the room, disarming her, before she'd had time to turn the gun on herself – and that was why she wanted him to go.

'I'm staying right here,' he said.

'Go, while you still have the chance,' she begged him.

He thought of his mother. She had had Alzheimer's disease. He had looked after her for years – had tried so hard to fix her – but it had been a battle which had been lost from the start, and, by the end, he had been left with the feeling that all his efforts had been wasted. Yet here was a woman – about the same age as his mother had been when she got ill – who he *could* help.

The problem was that she didn't want to be helped – she wanted to die, and saw him as standing in her way.

There had to be something he could do or say to ease the situation, he told himself.

There simply *had to* be.

But as hard as he tried, he couldn't think of anything.

Paniatowski stood behind the police barricade, staring at the front of the house in the old terraced street.

'He's going to die in there,' she told herself.

She could already picture him lying on the floor – his body punctured by dozens of pellets, his life's blood slowly oozing away.

She had remembered everything they had been to each other over the years, and though William Danbury claimed that people were only devastated because they *allowed* themselves to be devastated, she knew that Colin's death would leave a deep hole in her soul.

What right had he to take a risk like this? And how bloody stupid did you have to be – how bloody *irresponsible* – to walk into that kind of situation without a bullet-proof vest?

Didn't he know that there were people out here in the street who cared for him?

But that was the way Colin was, she thought – stubborn, foolish, kind and brave – and if he hadn't been like that, she probably wouldn't have loved him quite so much.

Any second now, Ethel would raise the shotgun and fire both barrels at him, Beresford thought. She didn't want to do it, but she had her own pain to deal with, and she couldn't deal with it while he was still around.

'Go,' she begged him.

'There's something you should know,' Beresford said. 'We don't think William was the person who killed Jane.'

'You don't think . . .'

'I wasn't going to tell you at first, because the investigation's still ongoing, and we're not allowed to rule anyone out, but William says he was with his mistress when Jane died – and it's looking like he was telling the truth.'

'You wouldn't lie to me, would you?' Ethel Danbury asked. 'I trust you, you know. You're the only person in the world I *do* trust any longer, and I couldn't bear it if you were lying to me.'

'I'm not lying,' Beresford said.

'Then who did kill Jane?'

'We don't know, but whoever it was, it has nothing to do with anything you've ever said or done.'

'Oh God,' Ethel said.

'I'm going to come across to where you're sitting, and take the gun off you,' Beresford said. 'I can do that, can't I?'

'Yes,' Ethel replied, suddenly weary, suddenly weighed down by the exhaustion brought on by forty years of misery and desperation.

Beresford crossed the room, took the shotgun off her, broke it open and removed the shells.

'They're going to lock me up for a long time – perhaps forever – aren't they?' Ethel asked. 'I don't mind.'

'You won't get a long sentence,' Beresford told her. 'Perhaps you won't go to jail at all. A great deal will depend on what you tell them.'

'I don't know what you mean.'

'Was it you who loaded the shotgun?'

'Yes.'

'*Why* did you load the shotgun?'

'To protect myself against Archie.'

'And you *needed* to protect yourself, because you thought he was going to kill you.'

'No, not kill me, hurt me – and I'm so very, very tired of being hurt.'

'You thought he was going to kill you,' Beresford repeated. 'He said when he went out that he was going to kill you when he got back. Promise me that when you're asked, that's what you'll say. Do it for me.'

Ethel nodded. 'All right.'

'What happened next?'

'He came in – he was drunk. I could see he was going to hurt me. I told him not to come any closer, and when he did, I shot him.'

'Good,' Beresford said. 'Then what happened?'

'He was thrown backwards. He was lying on the floor, and he wasn't moving. I wanted to make sure he was dead. I reloaded, and shot the next two barrels into his head.'

'I don't think you're remembering it properly,' Beresford said. 'What actually happened was that he went down, but then started to get up again. You were in fear for your life. You couldn't get out of the room, because he was blocking the doorway. In a panic, you reloaded and fired blindly. It was just by chance that you hit his head. Do you understand?'

'Yes.'

'Then tell me now exactly what you'll be telling the people who question you later.'

'Before he went out, Archie said he would kill me when he got back,' Ethel said. 'I loaded the gun. When I saw he was going to kill me, I fired it. He started to get up from where he'd fallen. I knew he'd kill me if he could. I reloaded the gun and fired again.'

It wasn't a great story, Beresford thought, and under serious interrogation it would fall apart almost immediately. But he was hoping that she would never be subjected to serious interrogation once the investigating officers had seen the iron branded on her arm – that they would believe her story not because it was a credible one, but because they *wanted* to believe it.

'It's time to go outside,' he said. 'Are you ready?'

'Will you stay with me?' she asked.

'For as long as I'm allowed to,' he promised.

He helped her to her feet. She was as light as a feather. She was crying again, and he was surprised to discover that he was too.

The snipers were still in position, the armed officers crouched behind the cars still had their pistols drawn, but when Beresford opened the door of the Danbury house and stepped outside carrying Ethel Danbury in his arms, it was plain to everyone on the scene that none of that was necessary.

Beresford looked around him, and saw an ambulance parked by the police barricade. No one tried to stop him as he walked over to it, and it was only when he had handed Ethel over to the paramedics that he even became aware that Chief Superintendent Briscoe must have been just behind him all the way.

'You disobeyed my orders,' Briscoe said angrily. 'I specifically told you that you could not go into that house unless you were wearing a bullet-proof vest.'

'I know, sir,' Beresford said. 'I'm sorry, sir.'

'I'm seriously considering hauling you up before a disciplinary board,' Briscoe told him.

Which would be a shitty thing to happen to his career, Beresford thought, but he had just saved a life, and he was finding it almost impossible to care about disciplinary boards at that moment.

'You're well within your rights to do that, sir, and you'll get no complaints from me,' he said.

Briscoe looked into his eyes. 'I'm never going to be able to make you regret what you've just done, am I?' he asked.

'No, sir, you're not,' Beresford told him.

Briscoe shrugged. 'In that case, I suppose I might as well recommend you for a commendation.'

Then he turned and was gone, only to be replaced, a second later, by Paniatowski, who looked about as furious as Beresford could ever remember seeing her.

'You stupid, stupid bastard!' she screamed at him.

'Listen, Monika . . .' Beresford began.

Paniatowski slapped him hard across the face, and when he made no attempt to evade her, she slapped him again.

And then she flung her arms around him, and hugged him as tightly as she could.

It was as she was walking back to her car that Paniatowski noticed that Chief Inspector Barrington's vehicle was parked next to it, and that Barrington himself was pacing up and down like a man who had a lot on his mind.

There was no reason for Barrington to be there, Paniatowski thought, no reason at all.

Unless . . .

'It wasn't Melanie Danbury who was buried in the woods,' Barrington said, as she drew level with him.

'Then who is it?'

'We don't know. We've really no idea. But it's the wrong blood group, and anyway, the poor little mite that Alfie Clayton found had already been dead for at least a day longer than Melanie has been missing.'

Well, shit!

'So what do we do now?' Paniatowski asked.

'I've called a press conference for five o'clock,' Barrington told her. 'I'd appreciate it if you'd be there.'

'Of course,' Paniatowski agreed.

Most of the press conferences held by the Whitebridge police – even the ones dealing with murders – were only attended by the local hacks, because, when all was said and done, crimes committed in a backwater like Whitebridge were only really interesting to those people who lived in and around that backwater.

A missing child was another matter entirely. A missing child was of national – and perhaps even international – interest, and the press room that day was packed with both hot-shot reporters from London and camera crews from all the major channels.

Barrington, about to make his opening remarks, looked out across the sea of sensation seekers spread out before him, and cleared his throat.

'Good afternoon, ladies and gentlemen. I am Chief Inspector Clive Barrington and this is my colleague, DCI Monika Paniatowski,' he said. 'I wish to make a statement, and then I will be willing to answer a few questions.' He cleared his throat for a second. 'The child whose body was recovered this morning was not Melanie Danbury, though she was of roughly the same age. A medical examination has already been conducted on this child, and foul play is not suspected.'

'She was buried in the woods!' someone called out. 'If she wasn't murdered, why was she buried in the woods?'

'Burial in an unauthorised location is an illegal act in itself, but it has been clearly established that the girl died from natural causes,' Barrington said. 'However, we are eager to talk to the parents of the dead child, and would ask them to contact us. We would also appeal to the general public to ring us if they have noticed that any small girls, who they have been accustomed to seeing round and about, have been notable by their absence for the last few days. Thank you for your attention. I will now take questions.'

'What about Melanie Danbury?' someone asked.

'The search for Melanie will, of course, continue.'

'What do you mean – *continue*?' asked a male reporter from the *Daily Dispatch*.

'I mean exactly what I say.'

'But you haven't been searching for Melanie, have you? Not since you found that other little girl?'

'That is not true, we have never stopped looking,' Barrington said shakily.

'Oh really?' the reporter asked sceptically. 'Isn't it normal to bring in the helicopters on the second day of a search for a missing child?'

'That is sometimes the case, yes,'

Paniatowski groaned inwardly. That was the worst possible way to have answered the question, she thought, because when the reporter asked his follow-up question – and he *would* ask it – it would reveal just how evasive Barrington had been trying to be.

'Had you planned to bring in helicopters for the second day of *this* search?' the reporter asked.

Barrington hesitated for a second, then said, 'Yes.'

'So what happened to them?'

'We . . . er . . . we cancelled them.'

'You cancelled the helicopters,' the reporter ploughed on relentlessly. 'That would be to save money, wouldn't it? And what about the volunteers? They weren't costing you anything at all – but you didn't use them, either. You just assumed – with no justification at all, as it turns out – that you'd found Melanie, and you simply gave up the search!'

Barrington was visibly shaking, and any moment now he was going to break down and beg forgiveness, first from the reporters and then from the world in general, Paniatowski thought.

She stood up. 'I'm glad you raised the issue of the volunteers,' she said. 'As a matter of fact, there *were* no volunteers today. And why was that?'

She paused, to give one of the assembled journalists the opportunity to provide her with an answer.

None of them did.

None of them was even looking at her.

'There were no volunteers because they all thought that Melanie had been found,' she continued. 'And *why* did they think that? Was it because we – the Mid Lancs police – told them she'd been found?'

She paused for a second time. All the reporters were either pretending to take notes or examining their hands.

'No, we didn't tell them. What happened was that one of you people learned from a contact he had in Whitebridge General that a girl's body had been found. Now what that reporter *should have* done was ring us, and if he'd done that, we'd have told him that no positive identification had been made, and it would be better if the story didn't go out. That would have been the responsible thing to do. Instead, it was broadcast, and the volunteers heard it. So don't go blaming the police because the search was scaled back today – blame one of your own!'

'We will be relaunching the search tomorrow,' said Barrington, who had made *something* of a recovery, 'and we would appeal to all those volunteers who have already helped us – and those who wish to help now – to report to this building at eight o'clock tomorrow morning. That's all. Thank you for coming.'

Barrington kept his eyes fixed on the door until all the reporters had gone, then turned to Paniatowski and said, 'Thanks, Monika, you just saved my bacon.'

She hadn't saved anyone's bacon, she thought. All she'd succeeded in doing was muddying the waters, and shifting a little of the blame for the abandonment of the search over to the reporters. And if Barrington thought she'd done any more, then the man was an idiot.

It had been a mixed day, she told herself, as she walked back down the corridor towards her office. On the one hand, her best friend had come out of a dangerous situation in one piece – which was wonderful. But on the other hand, there'd been the meeting with the members of the police authority and the press conference – both of which had been disasters.

But disasters usually came in threes, she thought, as she reached the CID suite, so when would the next one arrive?

And then she saw the look on DS Meadows' face – and realised it probably already had.

'It's bad news, isn't it?' she asked.

'It's *very* bad news,' Meadows replied.

TEN

The bearer of bad tidings was waiting for Paniatowski and Meadows in Interview Room A. He was around thirty-five years old, and was wearing a smart blue blazer, grey slacks, a pale shirt and a yellow and black striped tie.

'This is Mr Edward Boyle,' Meadows said. 'He's the assistant manager of the Ribble Valley Hotel.'

He *looked* like an assistant hotel manager, Paniatowski thought. He had one of those regular, slightly android faces which is pleasant enough, but only really seems at home behind a hotel reception desk – the sort of face you would remember if you booked into the same hotel regularly, but probably wouldn't recognise if you saw it on the street.

'The hotel is just outside Whalley,' Meadows supplied.

'I know it,' Paniatowski said.

Oh yes, she knew it, all right. Once, long ago, when she and Bob Rutter – Louisa's father – had been in the throes of their passionate, all-consuming affair, the Ribble Valley Hotel had been a regular rendezvous. She'd been a *lapsed* Catholic back then, but every time she'd crossed the hotel lobby, heading for the room they'd booked, she'd felt weighed down with guilt. She wondered how she'd feel about doing the same thing again, now she was a lapsed atheist.

'What the hell are you doing, Monika?' she asked herself angrily. 'Why are you thinking about the past *now*?'

But she already had the answer. The past, though painful, was behind her, while the interview with Mr Boyle still lay ahead – and though Meadows had already given her the gist of what he was about to say, she was dreading hearing it from his lips.

'Tell the chief inspector what you told me,' Meadows said to the assistant manager.

'I was on duty, at half-past seven on Wednesday night, when this chap in a Jaguar turned up and asked for a room,' Boyle said.

'What was his name?' Meadows asked.

'He signed in as Mr Smith. In the old days, that just showed a lack of imagination, but now it's more of a way of challenging us,' Boyle said.

'What do you mean?' Paniatowski asked.

'It's a way of saying, "We're not married, and what are you going to do about it?" to which the answer is, "It's the nineteen seventies, we're in the business of renting out rooms, and we couldn't care less if the lady you're with is your sister, as long as you pay the bill."'

'Did you know what the man's real name was?' Meadows asked.

'Not at the time.'

'But you know now, don't you?'

'Yes, I believe his name is William Danbury.'

'And that belief is based on what?'

'You showed me a photograph, and . . .'

'But you knew his name even before I showed you the photograph, didn't you?'

'Yes.'

'How did you know it?'

'One of the waitresses at the hotel recognised him.'

'From where?'

'The Freemasons. She's been on the catering team for several of their social evenings.'

'Go on,' Meadows said.

'Mr Smith . . .' Boyle paused, '. . . or should I call him Mr Danbury . . .?'

'It would be simpler if you called him Mr Danbury.'

'Mr Danbury booked a double room for the night. He said that he was expecting his wife to arrive at some point in the evening. Once he'd checked in, he went to the bar.'

'And what time would that be?' Paniatowski asked.

'Seven forty? Seven forty-five?'

'And how long was he there?'

'Until around nine forty-five. That was when he got the phone call.'

'What phone call?'

'A man rang up and asked to speak to Mr Smith.'

'You're sure it was a man?'

'I'm not, no, because I didn't take the call. But the barmaid swears it was a man.'

'So what happened next?'

'Mr Danbury left – straight away.'

'Without paying his bill?'

'He'd paid for the room in advance – in cash. That's what a lot of customers of his ilk do.'

'And what ilk might that be?' Paniatowski wondered.

'The ones who never bother to take any luggage upstairs, and who pay for the night, but are never in the room for more than a couple of hours.'

Ah yes, the Paniatowski-Rutter ilk, Monika thought.

'You're sure about this?' she asked. 'It was definitely William Danbury?'

'Mr Boyle, his assistant and two barmaids have all picked him out from a selection of photographs of different men of roughly the same age and build,' Meadows said.

'And you're also sure he checked in at seven forty and left at nine forty-five?' Paniatowski asked.

'Give or take a few minutes either way,' Boyle said.

So Danbury had arrived at the Ribble Valley Hotel well *before* the murder, and had left just in time to reach his own home at ten minutes past ten.

'Thank you, Mr Boyle, you've been very helpful,' Paniatowski said.

But what she actually meant was, 'Sod you, Mr Doyle, for smashing a hole a mile wide in the case I've been building up.'

Paniatowski had lit up two cigarettes, no more than a minute apart. Now, one of them was burning itself out in the ashtray, while the other was held tightly – almost crushingly – between her index and middle finger, as she strode continuously from one end of her office to the other.

Meadows, sitting in one of the visitors' chairs, watched her and worried. Paniatowski had gone out on a limb in this case, she thought, and now, totally unexpectedly, that limb had been sawn off – and the only way to go was down.

Paniatowski came to a sudden halt.

'How's this for a theory?' she asked. 'Danbury employs a hit-man to kill his wife. He gives the man his key, so that access to the house will be no problem, then books into the Ribble Valley Hotel, where he knows he'd bound to be noticed by several of the staff.'

Meadows shook her head, perhaps a little sadly.

'You're clutching at straws, boss,' she said. 'If Danbury had wanted to set up an alibi for himself, he'd have arranged a drinking session with some of his pals on the police authority.'

'Maybe he didn't want to involve them, and . . .'

'What he *wouldn't* have done is book an extra night in the Ambassador Hotel in Newcastle upon Tyne, then change his mind, drive back down to Lancashire, and book a room in the Ribble Valley Hotel at the last minute.'

'You're right,' Paniatowski said despondently.

'We simply have to accept the fact that most of the things that

Danbury did on Wednesday were not based on any kind of calculation on his part, but were simply a reaction to circumstances,' Meadows said.

'What circumstances?'

'You've got me there,' Meadows admitted. 'I have no idea what the circumstances might be.' She paused, reluctant to add another brick to the pile which was already weighing Paniatowski down. But it was no good – it simply had to be said. 'There's something else we have to ask ourselves, boss – if Danbury had an alibi which he must have known would stand up to rigorous examination, why didn't he come up with it right at the start of the investigation?'

'Perhaps he kept quiet because was trying to protect Gretchen Müller,' Paniatowski said.

'Would that be the same Gretchen Müller who he suggested to us might have killed his wife?' Meadows wondered.

Paniatowski groaned. 'There are so many things that we don't have an answer to,' she said.

'That's true,' Meadows agreed. 'In fact, the only thing we do know for certain is that William Danbury didn't kill his wife.'

Gretchen Müller was sitting at the table in Interview Room A, next to the solicitor called Fairfax, who she had felt no need of until the question of Danbury hitting her had arisen. The evidence of that blow – the bruise on her jaw – was starting to fade, but the defiance in her eyes blazed as strongly as it ever had.

'I have done absolutely nothing wrong,' she said to Paniatowski and Meadows, 'and I demand that you release me immediately.'

'Your darling Billy is far from sure you've done nothing wrong,' Meadows taunted.

'What do you mean?'

'Billy went so far as to suggest that you might be the person who actually killed Jane.'

'You are a liar!' Gretchen screamed. 'He would never have said that to you. He . . . he . . .'

'Loves you?' Meadows suggested.

'He is a nice man, who likes me very much,' Gretchen said, making an obvious effort to calm down. 'He would never believe that I could murder anyone – not even her.'

'You certainly hated her, though, didn't you?' Meadows said.

'You don't have to answer that,' the solicitor cautioned.

'She was not good enough for him,' Gretchen said. 'He is a handsome man in his prime. And what was she? Nothing but a fat little *hausfrau*!'

The late Jane Danbury hadn't been fat, Meadows thought, though she had certainly had more curves than the boyish Gretchen.

'Where did you go on Wednesday?' she asked the au pair.

'I got on my motorbike, and I drove until I saw signs for Dundee. Then I turned around and . . .'

'You went to Newcastle upon Tyne to see William,' Meadows interrupted her. 'Your plan was to go up to his room in the Ambassador Hotel, and once you were there, to make the beast with two backs.'

'What does that mean?' Gretchen asked. She turned to her solicitor. 'I do not know what that means.'

'Really, sergeant, you have to make some allowance for the fact that English is not my client's native tongue,' Fairfax said.

'I'm sorry,' Meadows said – and genuinely did sound contrite. 'I'll make a real effort, from now on, to only use words I'm sure Gretchen will understand.' She leant forward, so her own face was slightly closer to the German girl's. 'What I should have said, so that you would understand me, Gretchen, was that once you were in his hotel room, you planned to let him screw the arse off you.'

Fairfax grimaced, and Gretchen said, 'No, that is not true.'

'Listen, Gretchen, we have more than enough evidence to charge you with Jane Danbury's murder,' Paniatowski said. 'For a start, you were William Danbury's mistress . . .'

'I was not.'

'Then why did he buy you an expensive motorbike?'

'It was a reward, for all the hard work I had done.'

'If that's the reward for being an au pair, he must have bought his gardener a bloody Rolls-Royce,' Meadows said.

'Is that a question?' the solicitor asked sternly.

'You say that when you arrived back at the Danbury house, Jane was already dead,' Paniatowski said.

'It is true.'

'Why should we believe you? The way we see it, you arrived

at the house an hour earlier than you now claim you did. You murdered Jane Danbury in cold blood, because you wanted to have her husband all to yourself. Then you went upstairs and killed the baby . . .'

'Why . . . why would I kill Melanie?' Gretchen asked, and now – for the first time – she was starting to look scared.

'We don't *know* why you killed her, Gretchen,' Paniatowski said dismissively, 'but I've no doubt you'll give us your reasons in your own good time. Now where was I?'

'Gretchen kills the baby,' Meadows prompted.

'That's right. You kill the baby, stuff her into a rucksack, get on your bike again, and drive off. You head for somewhere you think she won't be found – probably the moors – and dump her poor little body, and then return to the house. And only then – only *then*, Gretchen – do you call the police!'

'My client is obviously becoming distressed, and I would like to request a break,' the solicitor said.

'Is that what you want, Gretchen?' Paniatowski asked. 'Would you like a break? Or are you finally willing to tell us the truth?'

'It would have been impossible for me to reach the house any earlier than I did,' Gretchen gabbled. 'Even if I had driven very fast, I could not have got back from . . . from . . .'

'From where?' Paniatowski asked.

'I don't know. From anywhere.'

'From Newcastle,' Paniatowski said firmly. 'Given the time you left Newcastle – the time you left William Danbury, your lover – it would have been impossible for you to get to Milliners' Row any earlier than you did. Is that what you're saying?'

'Yes,' Gretchen admitted, defeated.

'Then tell us what actually happened.'

'Billy had booked the hotel room in Newcastle for an extra night,' Gretchen said, looking down at the table. 'We planned to stay there until about eight o'clock. Then we would come back to Whitebridge. Billy would tell Jane he had been working late, and I would say I had been out with my friends.'

'So what went wrong?'

'I had forgotten to take my contraceptive device . . . is it called a Dutch cap in English?'

'Yes, that's what we call it.'

'I had forgotten to take my Dutch cap with me to Newcastle. Billy was very angry with me.'

'Is that when he hit you?' Meadows asked.

Gretchen continued to stare at the table. 'Yes, that is when he hit me,' she admitted.

'What happened next?'

'He said that I had spoiled everything for him, and we would have to come back to Whitebridge.'

'Why didn't he simply go to the chemist's shop, and buy some contraceptive sheaths?'

'Billy will not wear rubbers. He says it is just like washing your feet when you are wearing wellington boots, and no real man would ever do that.'

'What was the plan for when you got back to Whitebridge?'

'He would book a room at the Ribble Valley Hotel, and wait for me there. I would go back to the house to pick up my Dutch cap. But when I got to the house, I . . . I found Mrs Jane. She was dead.'

'We simply have to accept the fact that most of the things that Danbury did on Wednesday were not based on any kind of calculation on his part, but were simply a reaction to circumstances,' Meadows had said, in Paniatowski's office.

And much as she didn't want to accept it, it seemed to Paniatowski that Meadows had been spot on.

Interview Room B was on a different corridor from Interview Room A – a deliberate positioning to ensure that no one who was being interrogated in one of them would ever accidentally come face-to-face with anyone being questioned in the other – and by the time Paniatowski and Meadows had walked from A to B, William Danbury and his solicitor, George Fullbright, had already been ushered into the latter.

Danbury was sitting at the table with his head in his hands, but he looked up when the two detectives entered the room.

He was a real mess. His eyes were red, his skin was blotchy and his chin trembled.

'Why can't you leave me alone?' he said, in a voice which was half a whine and half a mumble. 'Don't you know I'm in mourning?'

'In mourning?' Paniatowski repeated. 'Who are you in mourning *for*? Could it be your wife? No, you said you were far too strong to allow yourself to be devastated over her death. Your daughter, then – who is most likely dead, too? No, you're perfectly capable of controlling your grief for her. So it must be your father, mustn't it?'

'He was a great man,' Danbury said. 'I wanted him to be proud of me, but I could never quite . . . I could never quite . . .'

'He wasn't a great man,' Paniatowski told him. 'He was a bully – and a coward.'

'You have no right to judge him,' Danbury said, with a hint of his old spirit. 'You would never have understood him, because you're just a woman.'

'Yes, I suppose that pretty much does rule me out of understanding anything at all,' Paniatowski agreed.

'Who put her up to it?' Danbury demanded, his voice firmer now, as if he had somehow managed to find some reserves of strength within himself.

'Who put who up to what?' Paniatowski replied.

'Who put that bitch – my so-called *mother* – up to killing my dad?'

'Nobody put her up to it.'

'But of course they did. She would never have done it on her own. She loved and respected him.'

'She *feared* him.'

'Yes, she feared him, too, and that's just as it should be.' Danbury raised his hand off the table, and pointed his index finger directly at Paniatowski's forehead. 'You women *know* that you were put on this earth to serve us men. And you *want* to serve us – you really do. But sometimes you're weak – and sometimes you're treacherous – and you need to be kept in line. Don't pretend that you don't welcome the discipline – don't pretend that you don't see that we only do what we have to do for your own good.'

'You're sick,' Paniatowski said.

'You'd better keep that bitch in jail forever,' Danbury told her, 'because if you let her out, I swear I'll kill her.'

'Well, that should teach her a lesson she won't forget in a hurry,' Meadows said.

'You might want to kill your father's wife, but you didn't kill your own, did you, William?' Paniatowski asked.

'No, I didn't. I told you right from the start that I didn't.'

'And you didn't pay to have someone else kill her, either.'

'No.'

'So why are you here?'

'I'm here because some idiot decided to put a woman in charge of the investigation.'

'No, you're not,' Paniatowski contradicted him. 'You're here because you refused to give me an alibi.'

'At the time my wife was killed, I was in my car, driving back from Newcastle . . .'

'At the time your wife was killed, you were drinking in the bar of the Ribble Valley Hotel.'

'What?' George Fullbright exclaimed.

'He has an alibi, Mr Fullbright – he just didn't bother to tell you about it,' Paniatowski explained.

'Then why is my client still . . .'

'Why is he still here? Because he didn't bother to tell us about it, either, and it wasn't until an hour ago that we found out from quite another source.'

'What, in God's name, were you thinking of, William?' Fullbright asked, so shocked by what he'd just learned that he didn't even seem to realise he was breaching professional etiquette.

'I was thinking of friendship,' Danbury said.

'Would you like to explain to us exactly what you mean by that?' Paniatowski asked.

'I'll explain – though I don't imagine for a minute that you'll understand what I'm saying,' Danbury told her. 'Friendship – male friendship – is the most valuable thing in the whole world, and the only true measure of a man is whether he will defend his friend whatever the cost to himself.'

'*A man rang up, and asked to speak to Mr Smith,*' the assistant manager from the Ribble Valley Hotel had told Paniatowski.

'*You're sure it was a man?*'

'*I'm not, no, because I didn't take the call. But the barmaid swears it was a man.*'

'You're protecting the man who rang you at the hotel, aren't you?' Paniatowski demanded. 'The man who told you not only that your wife was dead, but *how* she died.'

'No comment,' Danbury said.

'No comment necessary,' Paniatowski told him.

'Since there seems to be no grounds for detaining my client any longer, I assume you will be releasing him within the next few minutes,' George Fullbright said. 'Is that a correct assumption on my part?'

'Yes,' Paniatowski said wearily. 'Yes, it is.'

Rain had been threatening all day, and as Paniatowski drove through the centre of town, there was an ominous rumble of thunder overhead.

By the time she reached Dr Lucas' house, the storm had broken, and the lightning, searing its way across the sky, was bathing what she already thought of as the Gothic Mansion in its pale, eerie glow.

She parked, and waited for the rain – which was beating out a rapid drum solo on her roof – to abate a little. She could see the light in Lucas' living room, and wondered what he was doing – and whether he had heard the news yet.

Then she noticed the curtain twitch – just briefly – and the light went off immediately after that.

'Oh, for God's sake!' she said exasperatedly.

The rain was still pouring down, but she couldn't wait any longer.

Using her RAC Road Atlas as a hat, she climbed out of the car and sprinted over to Lucas' front door, splashing her legs in several newly formed puddles on the way.

There was a bell-push set in the wall, but she ignored it and instead hammered on the door itself with an angry fist.

'It's no good pretending you're not in there, Dr Lucas, because I know you are,' she shouted.

The light came on in the living room again, then the hallway light lit up, and she could hear the sound of reluctant footsteps moving towards the front door.

Lucas opened the door. He looked very frightened – and Paniatowski was sure it was not the thunderstorm that was scaring him.

'What do you want?' he asked.

'Do you mind if I come in?' Paniatowski asked, then barged past him without waiting for an answer.

'Have you got a warrant?' Lucas asked, following her – almost *scampering after her* – down the corridor.

'I shouldn't have thought that, given your own precarious legal position, you'd be over-bothered by legal niceties,' Paniatowski said, over her shoulder.

A large suitcase lay on the table in the middle of Lucas' living room. It already contained two jackets and a collection of shirts.

'Are you going away?' Paniatowski asked.

'Yes,' Lucas said, 'my nerves are rather frayed. I thought a short holiday by the sea would do me some good.'

'Nice work if you can get it,' Paniatowski said, looking into the case, and noting that Lucas had packed the edges with socks and underwear. 'What's the name of your locum?'

'My locum?' Lucas repeated, as if he had absolutely no idea what she was talking about.

'It's a Latin word,' Paniatowski explained. 'It means substitute. It's what, in the medical world, they call a doctor who fills in for another doctor. So who's your locum, Dr Lucas? Who'll be looking after your patients while you're down by the sea, resting your nerves?'

'I . . . I don't have a locum,' Lucas mumbled. 'I haven't had time to arrange one.'

There was another crash of thunder above them and, for a second, the lights flickered.

'You're not really *going* away at all,' Paniatowski said. 'What you're actually doing is *running* away. Isn't that right?'

'I don't want to go to jail for perverting the course of justice, chief inspector,' Lucas said, dropping all pretence. 'I just *can't* go to jail.'

'So what were you planning to do once you were clear of Whitebridge?' Paniatowski wondered. 'Get a job on some isolated farm? Join the circus? Keep running forever?'

'I . . . I hadn't thought that far ahead.'

No, he wouldn't have.

'I take it that what brought about all this panic was that you had a phone call from your good friend, William,' Paniatowski said.

'Yes,' Lucas admitted. 'He said he hadn't told you anything, but he thought you might have guessed.' He began to pace up and down. 'Can you even begin to grasp how truly heroic he's been? To protect me, he hid the truth from you. He understood the consequences of his actions. He could have been found guilty of murdering Jane. He could have gone to prison for a long, long time. Yet he kept quiet – because that's the kind of man he is.'

'Would you have let him go to jail?' Paniatowski asked. 'Would you have allowed William to serve a long sentence in order to avoid serving a short one yourself?'

'Of course not,' Lucas said. 'If he had been found guilty, I think I would have come forward.'

'You only *think*?'

'I *would have* come forward,' Lucas said – but even with the emphasis, his words lacked conviction.

'What exactly happened on the night of Jane Danbury's murder?' Paniatowski asked.

'If I tell you all I know, will you promise me there'll be no charges laid against me?' Lucas asked.

'Why should I want to do that?' Paniatowski wondered. 'What makes you so special?'

'I'm a good doctor – a caring doctor – and I'm trying my very hardest to be a good man, too,' Lucas said. 'Isn't that enough for you?'

He probably was a good and caring doctor, Paniatowski thought – certainly Inspector Flowers, who was no fool, believed that he was.

But he was also the man who had sabotaged her investigation, and thus caused her to manoeuvre herself into a position from which she was not sure her career would ever recover.

'I am prepared to promise you something – and it's this,' she said. 'If you don't tell me everything I want to know right now, I'll work tirelessly to make sure both that you are charged and that you serve the longest possible sentence.'

'Please . . .' Lucas begged.

The storm was now directly overhead, and the thunder seemed to shake the whole house.

'That's the deal,' Paniatowski said. 'Take it or leave it.'

'Before I got in the police car, all I knew was what you'd told me . . .' Lucas began.

Gretchen is sitting in the back of a police patrol car, wrapped in a blanket. Lucas slides in beside her.

'They said you asked for me particularly,' he says. 'Would you like me to give you something to help calm you down?'

'I don't want any of your medicines, but there's something you must do,' Gretchen whispers urgently.

'What?'

'You must warn Billy about what has happened. You must tell him to get away from there as soon as he can.'

'Get away from where?'

'The Ribble Valley Hotel. If the police find him there, they will want to know why *he is there. And when he tells them he was waiting for me, they will suspect him of Mrs Jane's murder.'*

'So you did exactly what she wanted you to do?' Paniatowski asked.

'I didn't see I had any choice. What Gretchen had said made perfect sense. William hadn't killed Jane, but if you ever found out he had a mistress, he would become your prime suspect. And when you *did* find out, that's exactly what he became.'

'You didn't *just* tell him that his wife had been murdered, did you?'

'No.'

No, he certainly hadn't.

Once Inspector Flowers had proved that it was not one of her team who had told Danbury the exact nature of his wife's injuries, Paniatowski had assumed that the only way Danbury could have known would have been if he was the killer himself.

It just had to be him – because no else had known the details.

Except that someone else had.

'I'm sure it was an accident,' Lucas had told her in a rush, standing in the hallway. *'I'm sure he didn't mean it. He just doesn't know his own . . .'*

'Go on.'

'I think I've said more than enough.'

'Are you saying that you know who might have hurt Mrs Danbury?'

'*No, of course not. How could I know that?*'

'*So you've no idea who could have smashed in her skull with a bronze statuette?*'

'Why did you give Danbury all the details?' Paniatowski demanded.

'I didn't want to, but . . .'

'Why did you give him *the details?*'

'Because he insisted that I told him.'

'And you couldn't say no?'

'I could never say no to William.'

'Is there anything else that you should tell me?'

Lucas hesitated. 'I think . . . I think that Jane may have had a lover.'

'What!'

'I was always going over to the Danburys' house. I was the boys' doctor, and every time one of them got a minor cut or scrape, Jane would call me. I was little Melanie's doctor, too, and she really was quite delicate. And then, of course, Jane had her health issues . . .'

'Mainly because your mate, good old William, kept beating the crap out of her and expecting you to patch her up.'

'The point is, I did spend quite a lot of time there, and so, naturally, I saw quite a lot of Jane.'

'Go on.'

'Most of the time she cut a sad – almost tragic – figure . . .'

'Now I wonder why that might have been.'

'But there were some days – especially the ones on which William was going to be away overnight – when she seemed much happier.'

'That was probably because she knew she didn't have a beating to look forward to.'

'No, it was more than that. Much more. She would wear one of her favourite dresses, and have taken special care over her hair. And you could tell from the way she moved that she was looking forward to something.'

'Is that all?'

'Not quite. Once, when I'd gone up to see Melanie, I came downstairs again while she was on the phone. She was laughing and talking in the sort of voice women sometimes use when they're talking to a special man. Then she saw me, and hung up immediately. She said it was a wrong number, but you don't call someone who's rung up by mistake "darling".'

'If all this is true, why wait until now to tell me about it?' Paniatowski demanded.

Lucas looked down at the floor. 'I'd rather not say.'

'How do you think you'd manage in prison?' Paniatowski asked, mercilessly.

'I don't know.'

'I suppose you might just about get by in a nice, soft, white-collar open prison, but if you were locked up in one of the others – the ones that the real hardened criminals are sent to – you'd be eaten alive. And if you persist in holding anything back from me . . .'

She left the threat dangling. She knew that to get what she wanted, that was all she *needed* to do.

'If I'd told you about it the first time you interviewed me, it would soon have become common knowledge that Jane had been unfaithful to William.'

'Yes, it probably would – especially if we'd tracked down the man she was having the affair with.'

'Yes, especially then. There would have been articles in newspapers, then a trial, and sooner or later, William's father would have heard about it, and he would have despised his son for failing to control his woman properly. That would simply have killed William.'

'Let me see if I've got this straight,' Paniatowski said, hardly able to believe what she'd heard – and still nurturing a vague hope that she'd misinterpreted it. 'You decided that it was better that Jane's murderer should go free than that William's father should learn she'd been unfaithful. Is that right?'

'It's the choice that I'm sure William would have made himself. Jane was dead, and there was nothing he could do about that – but to lose his father's respect would be devastating.'

'But now his father's dead.'

'Yes.'

'And William won't mind that lots of other people will know Jane was unfaithful?'

'He'll mind, but their opinion won't matter a tenth as much

– a hundredth as much – as his father's would have done. And anyway, he's taking the boys to Canada to start a new life out there. So perhaps now that the situation's changed, it *will be* possible to get a little justice for Jane.'

'And what about Melanie?' Paniatowski asked angrily. 'If you'd told us all this before, it might have been possible to track down her kidnapper before he killed her.'

She was shocked to hear herself say those words. It was the first time she had talked about the little girl's death without adding some hopeful qualification.

'I thought about it,' Dr Lucas said. 'I really did. But by the time I learned she'd gone, she'd already been missing for over two hours. And we both know that means she was dead before you even started looking, don't we?'

The thunder was more muted now. The raging storm had passed by.

'Yes,' Paniatowski agreed, because in nearly all cases of this kind, hope was illusory. 'Yes, we both know she was dead by then.'

Paniatowski was so tired that twice, on the way home, she almost fell asleep at the wheel.

When she had returned to work, she had promised herself that she would never put in more than a ten-hour day. She'd known at the time that the promise was not worth the mental space it was imprinted on, but she had hoped that she would manage to have at least a few hours a day with Louisa and the twins.

But what had happened during her first week back on the job?

She had spent no more than a couple of hours at home in the previous thirty-six. She had slept at her desk for perhaps three disjointed hours more.

And it had all been for nothing!

She had been forced to release her prime suspect, who had never been one of her biggest fans, but who now probably hated her with a vengeance. And who could blame him for that?

She had alienated at least three members of the police authority, and possibly Chief Constable Pickering, too.

And she was no further on in the investigation than she had been at the very start.

She could, she supposed, arrest Dr Lucas for perverting the course of justice, and – with a little luck – she might even manage to get him banged up for a fair stretch. But what would be the point of that? How would locking him away help either her investigation or her reputation?

She pulled up in front of her home. She could see a bright light burning in Louisa's bedroom, and the more muted, orange glow of the night-light in the room she shared with the twins.

Home – the promise of a normality she was desperate to embrace, but too exhausted to appreciate.

She took a deep breath and prepared herself to meet her family and grovel to her housekeeper.

She loved her job – it could be tiresome, frustrating and sometimes even heart-breaking, but she loved it – and she was not sure she could go on doing it any more.

ELEVEN

Saturday, 8th October 1977

I t had stopped raining sometime in the middle of the night, but it was a truce, rather than an armistice, and just before dawn the clouds opened again with a vigour and ferocity which led the sheep out on the moors to huddle more closely together, and caused the town cats – out on their early morning patrols – to dash for the nearest available cover.

It was still raining when the volunteers turned up at Whitebridge police headquarters to resume the search for little Melanie Danbury.

Watching them line up through his office window – men of all shapes and sizes, some in oilskins, some in plastic mackintoshes, some even wearing rain-hats they had obviously scrounged from their wives – Chief Inspector Barrington was surprised to discover that he was becoming emotional.

These men – his fellow Lancastrians – had come out in filthy weather, he thought, to take part in a search which could only be counted a success if it ended in tragedy – and he was proud of them.

'Another call from somebody who claims to know who the dead girl is, boss,' said his sergeant from the other side of the room.

Barrington turned round to face him.

'It's probably just another crank,' he said.

'It could be,' the sergeant agreed, 'but not only is this one making sense, she sounds a bit upset.'

Barrington sighed. 'I suppose I'd better talk to her,' he said.

Tiny vertical rivers of rain ran energetically down Paniatowski's office window, only to come to an abrupt halt when they hit the frame at the bottom.

The investigation had been like that, she thought, gazing through the window at the watery world outside – they had seemed to be making steady progress, and then, suddenly, they had hit what seemed an insurmountable barrier, and spattered.

She turned around to face her team.

'I take it everyone who had any contact at all with the Danbury house has already been interviewed?' she asked her inspector.

'Yes, they have,' Beresford replied. 'But those interviews were given low priority, because we were pouring most of our effort into following our strongest lead – which was Danbury.'

'So who's on the list?'

Beresford flicked through the reports. 'There's the gardener and his assistant. They work for Danbury four days a week, but the gardener's sixty-two and the assistant's only seventeen.'

'Their ages make it unlikely that either of them was Jane's lover, but it certainly doesn't rule them out,' Paniatowski said. 'Who else is there?'

'All the heavy housework is done by the contract cleaning team, who come in three times a week. The composition of that team changes regularly. According to the officers who conducted the interviews, seventeen different members of staff have worked on the Danbury contract over the last year – all of them women.'

'That doesn't rule them out, either,' Paniatowski said. 'Jane's lover doesn't have to have been a man. In fact, given her experiences with men – or rather, with one man in particular – it's

more than possible that if she was looking for love, she'd look
for it in the arms of a woman.'

'All the groceries come from Lomax and Sons, which is the
posh supermarket in the shopping precinct,' Beresford continued.
'William Danbury phones in the order personally. They make
three deliveries a week, using one of four drivers, all of them in
their late thirties to early forties.'

'Who else is there?'

'No one. That's it.'

Dear God, Paniatowski thought, what a life Jane Danbury had
had, locked up in that luxury prison, and only seeing tradesmen.
Would it have been any wonder if she had fallen for the first
person to smile at her?

'Can I ask a question, boss?' Meadows said.

'Yes.'

'How do we know Jane even *had* a lover?'

'Dr Lucas said . . .'

'I know what he said, but he could have misread the signs –
God knows, he's only a man.'

'Even if he hadn't pointed us in that direction, we'd have come
to it eventually ourselves, Paniatowski argued. 'Jane Danbury
virtually never left the house, and was killed in an excessively
violent manner. It has to be a lover. That's the only possible
logical inference.'

'With respect, boss, that might be what you're saying today,
but yesterday we all thought that the only possible logical inference was that her husband, William, had done it.'

'Have you got any other ideas, sergeant?' Paniatowski snapped.

'No, boss.'

'Then that's the one we run with. I want all the cleaners,
gardeners and deliverymen re-interviewed – and this time, I want
it done in-depth. Additionally, check on any other tradesmen who
might have visited the Danbury house in the last year or so –
people like plumbers, electricians and painters. You'll have to
get that information from Danbury himself.'

'That may not be too easy, boss,' Beresford pointed out. 'At
the moment, Danbury hates the police.'

'He doesn't hate the police – he hates me,' Paniatowski countered. 'Send round a detective constable who plays rugby – God

knows, one of them shouldn't be too hard to find – and I think you'll find he'll cooperate. After all, it is *his* wife who's been murdered and *his* daughter who's gone missing, and even though he doesn't seem to have cared a great deal for either of them, he'll still want whoever did it brought to justice.'

'That's true enough,' Beresford agreed.

'I also want a fresh round of door-to-doors on Milliners' Row.'

'They didn't turn up anything very useful last time, which given the sorts of lives the people on the Row live is hardly . . .'

'Last time, we were asking them questions about the day of the murder,' Paniatowski said. 'This time, I want to know if they've seen any men – or women – visiting the house in the last few months. If they have, try and pin them down to a date. Then get Danbury's appointment book from his secretary, and cross-reference whatever sightings and dates you've got from the neighbours with the days William Danbury was away from home.'

'How do we know that, if this lover actually exists, Jane didn't go and visit him or her, rather than have him or her visiting her?' Beresford asked.

'Two reasons,' Paniatowski told him. 'One: she didn't trust Gretchen to look after the kids. And two: even if she had decided it was safe to leave the au pair in charge, she'd have been worried that Gretchen would have told William about her little excursions.'

'If she was killed by her lover,' Meadows said, 'why did he or she . . .' She paused. 'I'm finding this annoying. Is it all right if I call the supposed lover "him" for the present?'

'Yes, as long as that doesn't mean you fixate on it being a man,' Paniatowski said.

'I won't,' Meadows promised. 'So if she was killed by her lover, why did the lover take Melanie with him?'

'For the same reason that we thought Danbury had taken her, when he was our number one suspect – to move the focus away from the murder and onto the disappearance. And the lover would have had even less compunction about killing her than Danbury – because she wasn't his child.'

There was a knock on the office door, and Chief Inspector Barrington walked in.

'I'm sorry to disturb you, DCI Paniatowski, but I think I'm

about to tie up a loose end in this investigation,' he said, 'and if you can spare the time, I'd really like you to come with me.'

Paniatowski looked questioningly at her team.

'We know what we've got to do,' Beresford said.

William Danbury had slept in his own bed for the first time in nearly a week, but it had been a far from peaceful sleep.

A tall, stern man had haunted his unconscious hours – a shouting, contemptuous man, whose disapproval was more crushing than the angry blow of a sledgehammer.

'You're tired, you say? But you've only walked six miles. What kind of man are you going to be when you grow up?'

'You want to know where the cat is? The cat's dead. It got run over. You're not crying, are you? I'd better not catch you crying.'

'How old are you now? Fourteen? A fourteen-year-old should be able to drink five pints of best bitter without spewing up his ring. You make me ashamed to be your father.'

'I'm sorry, Dad,' he'd mumbled over and over again, in a voice that sounded like his much younger self. 'I'm so sorry.'

Yet for all his suffering in the night, he discovered, when he finally awoke mid-morning, that he felt surprisingly fresh. He felt, in fact, as if a heavy weight had been lifted from him.

He walked over to the window, and looked out onto the garden. It had stopped raining, and Gretchen and the boys were playing football on the all-weather pitch he had had specially installed.

Gretchen did not have a maternal bone in her body, he thought, and she hated playing with the boys, but she was doing it because she knew that was what he wanted. He smiled. That really was most satisfying.

Gretchen made him a late breakfast, and when he'd finished it, he said, 'I think I'll go down to the rugby club, and sink a few pints.'

Gretchen frowned. 'Are you sure that's a good idea?'

'Why wouldn't it be a good idea?'

'Well, because . . .'

'Are you questioning me?' he demanded.

'No, of course not,' the girl said hastily. 'Things have been very difficult for you. It is only right that you should have some relaxation.'

As he drove to the rugby club, he was thinking of his dead wife.

He had wanted her to persuade her father to change his will, and she had failed him in that, a fact he often reminded her of, sometimes punctuating each reminder with a kick to her prone and terrified body. But she'd been a good wife in other ways – she had borne him two fine sons and then conveniently got herself murdered, thus freeing him from the bother of having to take her to Canada with him. Yes, on the whole, he had no complaints about her.

The rugby club car park was quite full. That was good, because it meant that when he made his entry, he would have a large audience.

As he walked across the car park, there was a spring in his step. He had been the strongest and most ferocious prop forward the club had ever known, and was something of a hero to the men in the bar, he reminded himself. He was in no doubt at all about the kind of reception he would get.

The street that Paniatowski and Barrington were driving down was lined with highly respectable semi-detached houses. It was the sort of street on which husbands religiously washed their cars every Sunday, and where wives made cakes for the parent-teacher association raffles.

They parked in front of No. 26, walked down the neat path to the front door and rang the bell. Their ring was answered by a skinny man with thinning hair, who was probably only in his thirties, but was starting to look much older.

The man gazed with horror at Barrington's uniform, then said, 'Yes?' in a voice which quivered with fear.

'Mr Holloway?' Paniatowski asked. 'Mr Reginald Holloway?'

'Yes.'

'Can we come in, do you think, Mr Holloway?'

'Why would you want to do that?'

'We have some questions we'd like to ask you.'

'The thing is, you see, I've got to get the kids fed before I drop them off at the childminder's.'

'We really do need to come in,' Paniatowski said firmly.

Holloway gave her a defeated shrug, and said, 'I suppose you'd better follow me, then.'

He led them into the living room. Four children, aged between five and ten, were sitting around the table, eating an early lunch.

'What's that bobby doing here, Dad?' the eldest one – a boy – asked, pointing at Barrington. 'And who's the lady?'

'They're *both* bobbies, and they just want a bit of a chat, like,' Holloway said. 'You kids go up to your rooms and get ready, and then I'll take you to Mrs Finnigan's house.'

'But I haven't finished eating, Dad,' a girl of around eight said.

'Then take it up to your bedroom, Lucy.'

'You said we couldn't eat food in our bedrooms. You said . . .'

'Well, now I'm telling you that you can,' Holloway snapped. 'Be a good girl,' he continued, softening, 'and we'll have fish and chips for tea.'

'*Bought* fish and chips?' asked Lucy, who was clearly a natural negotiator. 'From the chip shop?'

'From the chip shop,' the father agreed tiredly.

The children, recognising a good offer when they heard one, quickly left the room.

'Well, I suppose you'd better sit down,' Holloway said.

They sat.

'So what's this about?' Holloway asked.

They all of them knew where this conversation would end, Paniatowski thought, but there was a ritual that must be gone through first.

'We'd like your wife to sit in on this conversation, too, Mr Holloway,' she said.

'She isn't here.'

'What time will she be back?'

Holloway hesitated. He seemed to be contemplating telling a lie, then realising just how pointless that would be.

'She won't be back,' he said. 'She's gone away.'

And not alone, according to the neighbours. She had, in fact, taken a car mechanic called Sam with her, to change her tyres, when necessary, and keep her company in the night.

'So you look after all your children on your own,' Paniatowski said. 'That must be hard work, especially if you also have a job.'

'I've got two jobs – one in the day to put the food on the table, and the other at night to pay for the childminder,' Holloway told her. 'The only reason you find me here now, is because it's a Saturday. And yes, you're right, it is hard – but the kids make it all worthwhile.'

'We've been talking to the neighbours, and they say they haven't seen your youngest child – Ruth, is it? – for several days.'

'It's nothing to do with them,' Holloway said. 'They want to learn to mind their own business.'

'Apparently, you always take her out in her trolley as soon as you get home from work – regular as clockwork, they say – but sometime last week you stopped doing that.'

'It's been too cold to take her out.'

'Really, I'd have said it's been unseasonably warm for the time of year,' Paniatowski said. 'Can we see her, Mr Holloway?'

'No, you can't – because she isn't here, either.'

'Then where is she?'

'Her mum came and took her away.'

'She took Ruth, but left the other children?'

'She likes babies – it's only when they get a bit bigger that she can't be bothered with them.'

'So could you please give us her address?'

'She didn't leave an address.'

'You obviously care very much about your children, Mr Holloway,' Paniatowski said softly.

'I do. I love them all to pieces.'

'So are you seriously trying to tell us that you'd hand Ruth over to your wife, without even asking where she was taking her?'

Holloway started to cry. 'She was in her cot – just lying there,' he said. 'I thought at first she was sleeping, then I realised that she wasn't breathing at all. It was nothing I did to her. I swear that it was nothing I did to her.'

'We know that already,' Paniatowski said. 'She died of an aneurysm. It's been like a time-bomb ticking away in her head since the moment she was born. She could have gone at any time.'

'I wrapped her up in her shawl, and I drove her to the woods,' Holloway said. 'I found a tree I thought she would have liked, and I buried her in front of it. It was the hardest thing I've ever had to do in my whole life.'

'Why *did* you do it, Mr Holloway?' Paniatowski asked, although she thought she knew the answer already.

'I thought they'd blame me for her death,' Holloway sobbed. 'I thought social services would take the rest of my kids off me.'

He was a good man, Paniatowski thought – a very good man.

She felt as if she had been swimming in a pit of slime – the natural home of a man like William Danbury – for days, and now, at last, she had reached fresh, clean water.

'What happens now?' Holloway asked.

Chief Inspector Barrington sucked in air, and squared his shoulders.

Paniatowski recognised the signs. He was adopting a formal stance as a prelude to a formal act.

'Could you come outside with me for a moment, Chief Inspector Barrington?' she asked.

'Now?' Barrington asked, clearly annoyed by the unexpected interruption to the small drama he'd been about to play out.

'Now!' Paniatowski insisted.

They stepped out of the front door, and walked back down the path towards the garden gate.

'You're going to charge him, aren't you?' Paniatowski asked.

'Yes, of course I am,' Barrington replied. 'He's failed to report a death and he's buried a body in a place not authorised for that purpose, both of which are criminal acts.'

'And once you've charged him, you'll take him down to head-quarters for processing.'

'Yes.'

'And then you'll lock him up in the custody suite until Monday morning, when he'll appear before the magistrate.'

'That is how things are done.'

'And what will happen to the children?'

'Social services will have to make arrangements for looking after them.'

'You could easily put off charging him until Monday morning,' Paniatowski suggested.

'No, I couldn't. Once I'm aware that a crime has been committed, I'm duty bound to act on that information.'

'You could leave it until Monday,' Paniatowski repeated. 'He'll still be here. It's not as if he's about to abandon his kids and do a runner, now is it?'

'There is a clear procedure to follow in cases like this one, and I intend to follow it.'

'I'm going to ask you one last time,' Paniatowski said. 'In fact, I'm not going to *ask* – I'm going to *plead* with you.'

'I'm sorry, I'd like to do it, but I simply can't go making exceptions,' Barrington said. 'Once you put one foot on that particular slippery slope, there's no telling where it might end.' He paused. 'After yesterday, we're both on shaky ground, Monika. Let's not do anything to make our situation any worse than it already is.'

The anger which had been bubbling up inside Paniatowski finally came to the surface.

'Sooner or later, you're going to need another favour from me,' she said, 'but when you come to ask for it, don't be in the least bit surprised if all I do is spit in your face.'

Edgar Bunting, the gardener who worked for William Danbury four days a week, lived in what had once been a derelict farmhouse on the edge of the moors. He had bought it thirty years earlier, when he married Mary Hinchcliffe, and had been working on improving it ever since.

The farmhouse had been built out of stone, and had a blue slate roof. Carefully managed ivy grew up the walls, and the path to the front door ran through the centre of a rose garden.

The place had an almost chocolate-box beauty about it, Jack Crane thought, as he walked up the path. It was the sort of cottage that Wordsworth might have lived in. It was hard to imagine that the man who *did* live there had brutally bludgeoned Jane Danbury to death in her own living room, but somebody had done, and the only way to catch the killer was by a process of elimination.

He rang the bell, and the door was opened by a grey-haired woman in her early sixties, who said she was Mrs Bunting.

'I'm looking for *Mr* Bunting,' Crane explained, when he'd shown her his warrant card. 'I tried ringing, but all I got was an annoying beeping sound.'

'The phone line's down again,' Mrs Bunting replied cheerfully. 'When you live in the back of beyond, you get used to it.'

'So if you could just tell me where your husband's working today . . .' Crane began.

'He's not working. He's inside. Would you like to see him?'

'Yes, please.'

'Mind your head on the beams,' Mrs Bunting said, as she led

him down the corridor. 'This house wasn't built for a big lad like you.' She halted by a door at the end of the corridor. 'He's in there. You go and introduce yourself, and I'll just nip into the kitchen and make a pot of tea. You'd like a piece of cake, wouldn't you? It's homemade.'

'I'd love a piece of cake,' Crane said.

Crane hesitated for a moment on the threshold, and reminded himself that having a nice house and nice wife didn't necessarily prevent a man from being a cold-blooded murderer. Then he knocked and entered.

Mr Bunting was sitting in an armchair, and had his right foot resting on a straight chair in front of him. His right leg was encased in plaster from the ankle to the knee.

'When did that happen?' Crane asked.

'A week yesterday,' Bunting told him. 'I got careless.'

The team was working against the clock, and he had just wasted over an hour, Crane thought despondently.

On the other hand, he told himself, there would be cake.

When Dr Lucas opened the front door and found William Danbury standing there, his stomach did a nervous somersault.

'I'd never have just sat back and watched you go to prison,' he said hastily, before Danbury had a chance to speak. 'I'd have come forward in the end. You know I would.'

'Of course I do, old friend,' Danbury replied. 'Would you mind if I came inside?'

His voice had changed, Lucas thought. Its customary certainty – which some people thought of as arrogance – was quite absent. His face had changed, too. He normally had a ruddy, healthy complexion, but now his skin was almost grey, and showed signs of sagging.

'*Can* I come inside?' Danbury repeated, almost plaintively.

'Of course,' Lucas said. 'Of course you can come in.'

He led Danbury into his living room, sat him down, and poured him a glass of whisky.

'Would you like to talk?' he asked.

'Yes, I would, as a matter of fact,' Danbury replied, and now his voice had a musing, mystified quality. 'I've just been to the rugby club. I've always loved it down there.'

'I know you have.'

'It's one of the few remaining places that men can call their own – a refuge from the so-called "liberal values" that seem to be swallowing up everything that we hold dear.'

'What happened?' Lucas asked, with a hint of concern in his voice, because something unpleasant clearly *had* happened.

'I expected a bit of manly sympathy,' Danbury said. 'After all, my wife's been murdered, my daughter's missing, I was in police custody for nearly two days, and now my father's dead. Surely, I thought, everybody will want to rally round and do their best to cheer me up.'

'And didn't they?'

'No, they didn't. Oh, they all went through the motions – very sorry to hear about what's happened . . . if there's anything I can do . . . et cetera, et cetera – but as soon as they'd said their pieces, they drifted away. The bar was positively heaving when I arrived, but after fifteen minutes, the only people left were me and the bar steward. Now why was that?'

'Maybe some of the lads thought you shouldn't have been out enjoying yourself while your daughter's still missing,' Lucas suggested tentatively.

'Oh, for God's sake, they can't be upset about that!' Danbury said. 'I worry about Melanie, you know. I honestly do. But a real man doesn't sit whimpering in a corner when things go wrong – a real man gets on with life. And they all understood that. I'm sure they did.'

'Then again, maybe they've heard, because of the police investigation, that you beat your wife,' Lucas suggested.

'It can't be that, either,' Danbury said dismissively. 'I've never made a secret of the fact that I gave her the odd backhander when I thought she deserved it.'

'We both know it was more than the odd backhander, William,' Lucas said, 'and now, from what you've just described to me, it seems as if they do too.'

The magistrate's name was Winston Crouch, and when Paniatowski finally tracked him down, he was having a drink – possibly not his first – in the members' bar of the Whitebridge Golf Club.

Crouch had heavy side-whiskers, which reminded Paniatowski of the jovial Mr Pickwick – one of her old boss, Charlie Woodend's, favourite Dickensian characters – but from the expression on his face as she explained what had happened to Reginald Holloway, she quickly decided that his heart was more in tune with Mr Bumble, the beadle at the orphanage in which Oliver Twist was incarcerated.

'So let me see if I've got this straight, chief inspector,' Crouch said, when she'd finished her story. 'What you'd like me to do is convene a special session of the magistrate's court and grant this Hollington chap . . .'

'That's Holloway, sir.'

'. . . and grant this *Holloway* chap bail?'

'That's right.'

Crouch took a sip of his gin and tonic. 'No chance,' he said. 'I'm booked on the green in half an hour. Social services can look after the kids over the weekend. God knows, the idle sods do little enough to earn the huge salaries we pay them.'

'It's not really Mr Holloway and his children I'm worried about, sir,' Paniatowski said. 'My main concern is you.'

'Me? But you don't even know me.'

'I'm not talking about you personally,' Paniatowski explained. 'I'm referring to you as a holder of the office of magistrate.'

'Go on,' Crouch said.

'You've heard of a reporter, Pete Dolan, who works for the *Whitebridge Chronicle*, haven't you?'

'Yes, I've heard of him,' Crouch said. 'The man's more a muckraker than a journalist. He seems to have absolutely no respect for authority at all.'

'None,' Paniatowski agreed, 'and if his editor had any decency about him, he'd have sacked Dolan long ago.'

'What a sensible young woman you seem to be,' Crouch said, clearly surprised to find her in agreement with him.

'Thank you, sir,' Paniatowski said. 'The thing is, I've just heard that Dolan has been tipped off about this story, and is very keen to run with it. You can just imagine the kind of headline a man like him – a man with no principles and no respect for his betters – might write, can't you?'

'No, I'm not sure I . . .'

'Because I certainly can! "Broken-hearted children taken into care while magistrate plays golf!" is the first possibility that comes to mind.'

'That's likely, is it?' Crouch asked, sounding increasingly troubled.

'Of course, I wouldn't blame you if you refused to bow to such intimidation,' Paniatowski continued. 'Although I suppose you might argue that if your friends and neighbours lose their respect for you, they'll be also, in a way, losing their respect for the law, and that it's your duty to prevent that.'

'You're sure that Dolan is interested in the story?' Crouch asked.

'Positive,' Paniatowski said. 'In fact, I believe that he's working on it right now.'

That was not strictly true, she thought, but if Crouch didn't do what she wanted him to, Pete Dolan would certainly be informed that he *should* be working on it.

'Taking everything into account, I think it might be best if I did convene a special session of the court,' Crouch said. 'Thank you for bringing this to me, chief inspector.'

'My pleasure, sir,' Paniatowski replied. 'After all, we are both on the same side.'

As she walked back to the car park, Paniatowski ran the implications of what she'd just done through her mind.

If it ever became common knowledge around Whitebridge police headquarters that she'd taken time off – in the middle of a murder enquiry – in order to persuade a magistrate to do what any decent man would have done without prompting, then she'd be in deep trouble with everyone from her own team right up to the chief constable.

But she didn't care, she realised.

Jane Danbury was dead, and Melanie Danbury almost certainly was, too. There was nothing she could do for them any more – but she could still make a difference for the Holloways.

There had to be one good thing that could come out of this whole sorry mess – just one point at which decency and goodness triumphed.

There just *had* to be.

'I'll fight for you, Mr Holloway,' she said aloud. 'I'll fight for you tooth and claw. And I'll get you a suspended sentence if it kills me.'

Maggie Thorne was wearing jeans, and the sort of check shirt made famous by lumberjacks.

The last time she'd been interviewed, the man on the other side of the desk had been a DC Green, and his notes on that interview covered less than half a sheet of foolscap. Meadows didn't know Green, but had already decided that he wasn't very good at his job, because though she'd only just met Maggie herself, she was prepared to bet that she already knew – or had guessed – enough to fill a complete sheet of foolscap.

'Tell me, what do you like to do in your free time, Maggie?' she asked.

'What the bloody hell has that got to do with this murder up on Milliners' Row?' Thorne asked.

She was either nervous or afraid, Meadows decided – but which was it?

Lots of people were nervous when they were questioned by the police, but Maggie didn't strike her as the sort of woman to be cowed by authority. And nervous people didn't usually swear in the presence of a bobby, either.

Afraid, then – afraid *and* defensive.

But why would someone with nothing to hide be either of those things?

Meadows smiled. 'The question hasn't got anything to do with the murder, really. I was just curious.'

'I spend a lot of time in the gym,' Thorne said. 'I like to keep fit.'

Meadows clapped her hands delightedly. 'I knew it,' she said. 'The moment you walked in here, I could see you were a woman who took care of herself. And, if you don't mind me saying so, you're in great shape.'

'You're not in bad shape yourself,' Thorne said, softening.

'Why, thank you.'

'I don't suppose you'd fancy coming out for a drink with me one night?' Maggie said.

There was a smile on her face, but her eyes were cold and

predatory, Meadows thought. It was like being stalked by a wolf.

'I'm afraid I can't go out with you,' she said, 'not while I'm part of this investigation – and you're still a suspect.'

Thorne rocked in her chair. 'I'm still a *what*?'

Meadows laughed. 'I'm only joking. Of course you're not a suspect, and of course I'd love to go out for a drink with you.'

'I'd love it, too.'

Meadows ticked off a mental box in her head, then reached into her purse and produced a photograph of a baby, which she'd borrowed from one of the constables in the canteen.

'I'd like to show you this,' she said. 'It's my niece, Monika.' She passed the photograph across the table. 'Isn't she just adorable?'

'Very nice,' Thorne said, hardly glancing at the picture before handing it back.

Meadows sighed regretfully. 'Well, as enjoyable as it is to sit here chatting, I suppose we'd better get down to business. You were one of the cleaning team that worked at the Danbury house, weren't you?'

'Yes,' Maggie Thorne said, suddenly stiffening again.

'I never met Mrs Danbury, but I've seen photographs of her, and she looks rather dishy. What was she like in the flesh?'

'She was all right,' Maggie Thorne said, turning away to look at the corner of the room beyond Meadows' shoulder.

'Did you see much of her while you were working there?'

'Not a lot. She kept pretty much to herself.'

'But you must have talked to her occasionally.'

Maggie shifted uncomfortably in her chair, as if her buttocks had suddenly started to ache. 'I suppose so.'

'And what did you talk *about*?'

'Not much. The weather, and things like that.'

'Funny, you don't look like the kind of woman who talks about the weather,' Meadows said.

'Well, you know . . .'

'No, I don't think I do.'

'She'd . . . she'd ask me about my life – what I did, and where I went. I think she was a bit lonely.'

'Did you ever see her outside working hours?'

'What do you mean?'

'Did you ever go to the Danbury house just for a chat, rather than as a cleaner?'

'No.'

That's a lie, Meadows thought. That's a dirty great whopper.

'Have you ever been in trouble with the police?' she asked, and now the tone of her voice had slipped from playful into rock-crushing mode.

'No,' Maggie Thorne said, completely knocked off balance.

'Are you sure?' Meadows demanded.

'Yes, I . . .'

'Before this particular investigation began, had you ever been *questioned* by the police?'

'I . . . I was, once.'

'And why, exactly, did the police consider that it was *necessary* to interview you?'

'There was this girl,' Maggie Thorpe mumbled. 'She got hurt.'

'Now that *is* interesting,' Meadows said.

Gretchen was waiting for Danbury in the lounge, and had put on a dress which she knew was one of his favourites.

'Welcome back, my darling,' she said. 'Did you have a good time at the rugby club?'

'No, I didn't,' Danbury replied, in a throaty growl. 'They all treated me as if I was some kind of leper.'

Gretchen's face took on a pained expression. 'Perhaps it was a mistake to go to the club while they are still looking for Melanie.'

'That's what Lucas said.'

'Was he there?'

'No, I went round to see him later. I thought it might make me feel better, but it didn't.'

'Never mind, darling,' Gretchen said. 'We don't need any of them as long as we have each other. And guess what. I have cooked you a pork stew. It is the same stew that my mother and I used to make for my father, and he said it was the most delicious meal in the world.'

'I'm not hungry,' Danbury said.

Gretchen pouted. 'But darling, I've spent hours preparing it.'

'I don't want it.'

'Just try a little,' Gretchen wheedled. 'Try the tiniest, tiniest portion, just to please me.'

Jane would have read the signs by now, but Gretchen hadn't quite mastered the art yet – and it came as a complete shock to her when Danbury smashed her in the face.

The team was waiting for her in her office, and the moment she entered the room, Paniatowski could sense the excitement in the air.

'We've not had time to check out all our lines of enquiry yet, but those we have checked out have led nowhere. Except for one – and that one is a real beauty,' Beresford said. He turned to Meadows. 'Tell the boss about her, sergeant.'

'I interviewed a woman called Maggie Thorne,' Meadows said. 'She was one of the cleaning team that worked up at the Danbury house, and there are several reasons we should consider her a serious prospect. One: she's a lesbian, a fact that the DC who interviewed her the first time round seems to have missed completely. Two: she got very cagey when I started asking her about Jane Danbury. Three: she said she'd never been to the house except in her capacity as a cleaner, and I'm sure she was lying.'

'But four is the clincher,' Beresford said.

'Yes, it is,' Meadows agreed. 'She's got a history of violence.'

'Why am I only being told about this now?' Paniatowski demanded angrily. 'Why didn't somebody pull her criminal record out at the very start of the investigation?'

'Because she doesn't have a criminal record,' Meadows said. 'Do you happen to know Sergeant Conley, boss?'

'Yes, I know him,' Paniatowski replied. 'He's a good bobby – very dogged and determined.'

'That's the impression I got,' Meadows said. 'Anyway, he told me this story about what happened to a girl called Anne Hoole, a couple of years ago.'

'I'm listening,' Paniatowski said.

'Apparently, Anne was found in one of the alleys behind the brewery, in a pretty bad way. Not to put too fine a point on it, she'd had the crap kicked out of her. She said she didn't know who'd attacked her, but Conley wasn't convinced she was telling the truth, so he did a little snooping around.'

'And what did he find out?'

'Anne Hoole was Maggie Thorpe's girlfriend, but she'd also been seeing another woman. The sergeant's theory was that Maggie found out about it, and beat her up.'

'And was this theory based on anything?' Paniatowski asked.

'If you had a boyfriend, and he was beaten up so badly that he had to be hospitalised, what would you do?' Meadows asked.

'Go to the hospital to see how he was?' Paniatowski guessed.

'Exactly, but Maggie never went near the place. She didn't even ring up. The sergeant thinks that the reason Anne kept quiet about who attacked her was because she was worried that, if she didn't, she'd get an even worse beating next time. And despite the fact that she's a Whitebridge girl, born and bred, Anne left the town as soon as she was discharged from hospital, and hasn't been seen since.'

'And there's a five,' Beresford reminded the sergeant.

'That's right,' Meadows agreed. 'We'd reached a point in the interview when she really thought she was going to get me into her bed . . .'

'What made her think that?' Paniatowski asked.

'Me. I led her on. Anyway, at that point, I showed her a picture of a kid. I said was my niece, and since it obviously mattered to me, she must have known that one way to get on my good side was to put on a show of enthusiasm. And she couldn't do it! She has absolutely no empathy with children at all. So if you were to ask me if she could kill Melanie in order to cover her own tracks, I'd say she'd do it without a second thought.'

Meadows had done brilliantly, Paniatowski thought. She'd handed them a suspect with a violent nature who had had both the means and the opportunity to kill Jane Danbury.

And what about motive?

If Jane had rejected her, she might have flown into a rage, as she'd done with her previous girlfriend, only, this time, she'd gone even further.

Yes, she was the perfect suspect.

But then Danbury had been the perfect suspect, too.

*   *   *

He picked up the phone and dialled Whitebridge police headquarters.

'My name's William Danbury, and I want to speak to the chief constable,' he said.

'Connecting you to Mr Pickering's office now,' the girl on the switchboard told him.

A new voice came on the line – another bloody woman.

'This is Mr Pickering's secretary, sir. If you'd like an appointment with the chief constable . . .'

'I don't want an appointment with him – I want to speak to him,' Danbury said.

'I'm afraid that might not be . . .'

'If I was in your shoes, I wouldn't want to get on my bad side, because that's a very uncomfortable place to be,' Danbury said menacingly. 'If I was you, I'd tell Keith Pickering that I want to speak to him *now*.'

'Hold the line for a moment, sir,' the secretary said, clearly shaken.

Danbury heard a whimpering behind him. He put his hand over the phone and turned round to face the battered and bleeding girl huddled in the corner.

'And you can shut up – or you'll get more of the same!' he screamed.

The chief constable did not look a happy man.

'I've had William Danbury on the phone,' he said. 'He told me that he'd been cold-shouldered at the rugby club, and that he blames it on you. He also told me I should force you to resign.'

'Were those his exact words?' Paniatowski asked.

'No, they weren't. What he actually said was, "I want you to get rid of that bloody Polak bitch."'

'And what did you say to him?'

'I told him that while I had a great deal sympathy for him after the ordeal that he'd been through, I really didn't appreciate him telling me how to run my police force.'

Paniatowski smiled. 'Then *he* said, "Oh, my God, I've overstepped the mark. I realise that now, and I'm so sorry." Is that how it went?'

'No, not exactly. He said he would be taking the matter up

with our ultimate boss, the Home Secretary, who just happens to be a friend of his.'

'Do you think that's true?'

'That he's the Home Secretary's mate? I certainly wouldn't dismiss it as a possibility. The man's constituency is just over the Pennines, and I know for a fact that he's a keen rugby fan. But even if he doesn't know the Home Secretary, and even though he's been shunned by the rugby club, he's still got enough influence in this town to make waves when he feels like it. The rich and powerful of Whitebridge aren't going to cross William Danbury just to save you, Monika.'

'So are you asking me to resign, as a sort of pre-emptive strike?' Paniatowski asked.

'No, I most certainly am not, and there are two good reasons for that. The first is that he was in custody because you'd built up a very convincing case against him, and if he chose to keep quiet about his alibi, then that was his choice, and he only has himself to blame.'

'And what's the second reason?'

'I very much want to be confirmed in this post, Monika, and I realise that to get that confirmation, I'm going to have to kiss a few arses along the way. But if getting the job is dependent on kissing the arses of men like William Danbury, then it's not worth having.'

'Thank you, sir, for being so frank with me,' Paniatowski said.

'How's the investigation going?' Pickering asked hopefully.

'We've got a new prime suspect, sir. We really think we may have got it right this time.'

I'm saying it, but I'm not sure I truly believe it, Paniatowski thought. There's still a nagging feeling in my gut which tells me we're looking the wrong way again.

'Catch the killer, Monika,' Pickering said. 'Catch him in the next couple of days – because, if you don't, the question of whether you resign or not may well be taken out of my hands.'

The rain had finally stopped, but its effect was still all too evident in the Whitebridge Mortuary car park, and to reach the main building, Paniatowski was forced to navigate a zigzag course between the dozens of deep puddles which had established themselves in dips in the car park's decaying surface.

The building itself, now thoroughly soaked, looked even more depressing than usual.

Or maybe it's just me, Paniatowski thought – maybe I'm just more depressed than usual.

Dr Shastri was seated in her bright, antiseptic office, catching up on her paperwork.

'I am so very busy,' she told Paniatowski. 'It seems that even though I am no more than a humble Indian doctor – little more, in fact, than a barefoot medicine woman – there are many people in my field who wish to hear my views on quite complicated medical matters, and I have been asked to assist in a number of cases far beyond the bounds of our small town. It is all most tiring.'

'And you're as chuffed as little apples about it, aren't you?' Paniatowski said, with a grin.

Shastri smiled. 'Indeed,' she agreed. 'Though striving for recognition is perhaps something of a vanity, we still all like to bask in the glow of our colleagues' approval.'

Yes, I remember that feeling, Paniatowski thought.

'I have a question, Doc,' she said aloud.

'But of course you do,' Shastri replied. 'The only time I see you is when you wish to tax my poor brain with unanswerable conundrums. What is it this time?'

'I need to know if Jane Danbury could have been killed by a woman,' Paniatowski said.

'Would that be because you have a prime suspect who is a woman?' Shastri guessed.

'Yes,' Paniatowski agreed.

Though she was forced to admit to herself that the only thing that made Maggie Thorne a *prime* suspect was the lack of any alternative.

'I am tempted to say that if a woman had struck the blows, she must have been a very strong one,' Shastri said, in measured tones. 'But as I have often told you in the past, rage can make even the weakest of us very powerful for a short time, and there is no doubt that whoever killed Jane Danbury was more than a little annoyed. Is that any help?'

'Well, you certainly haven't ruled out my suspect,' Paniatowski said. 'Thanks anyway, Doc.'

'You are always rushing off,' Shastri said. 'Won't you stop for a drink? I have a bottle of your favourite vodka in the cupboard.'

Yes, she was always rushing off, Paniatowski thought. Shastri was her dear friend, and yet as soon as she'd got the information she needed, she was gone. Building up her case against Maggie Thorpe could be put on hold for fifteen minutes, she decided.

'I will stop for a drink, but only the one,' she said.

'You will only be *offered* the one,' Shastri said severely. 'After all, you are driving.'

Maggie Thorpe was walking along the canal bank, flanked, on either side, by the decaying ghosts of old cotton mills. She was holding a small cloth bag in her right hand, and she had still not decided what to do with it.

When Jane Danbury had invited her to visit the big house on Milliners' Row – 'Come on Wednesday, my husband's away and it's the au pair's day off,' – she had, naturally enough, assumed that Jane fancied her.

When nothing had happened on that first visit, she had not been overly disappointed. Jane was – in her terms – a virgin, and virgins sometimes needed gentle coaxing.

But then nothing had happened on the second and third visits, either, and Maggie had decided that if she wasn't getting any sex out of it, then she might as well get something else.

On the fourth visit, Jane had said, 'After you left last week, I noticed that some of my jewellery was missing, Maggie.'

'Are you accusing me of being a thief?' Maggie had demanded, her hands automatically balling up into fists.

'No, no! It's just that I remember Melanie started to cry, and I went to comfort her, and when I came out of Melanie's room, I found you in my bedroom, very close to where I kept it hidden.'

'I didn't steal anything,' Maggie had said.

Even though that was exactly what she had done.

'It means a lot to me,' Jane had told her. 'My father gave it to me.'

'Maybe your husband took it.'

'He doesn't know about it. He . . . he doesn't like me having things he hasn't bought for me himself.'

In that case, there's no danger you'll report it to the police, is there? Maggie thought.

'I didn't steal anything,' she'd said, for a second time.

'I . . . I don't really mind that you took it,' Jane had said, with tears in her eyes. 'I enjoy your company so much, and if you want to keep the jewellery, that's all right. Just as long as you come back again.'

She had never gone back, and she still wasn't sure why. People always seemed to think that lesbians didn't like pretty things, but she did – and she'd virtually been given a licence to steal them.

Perhaps it was that Jane Danbury's intensity – Jane Danbury's *need* for her – had frightened her.

None of that mattered now. What did matter was the bobby who had talked to her that afternoon. The bobby knew she'd been to the house, and was probably already thinking about getting a warrant to search her flat.

She reached into the bag, and took out a necklace. She wanted to look at it one last time, but it was too dark on the canal bank to see anything more than a vague shape.

She sighed, put the necklace back in the bag, and threw the bag quickly into the canal, before she had a chance to change her mind.

They had chatted about Louisa and India, and Paniatowski's vodka glass was empty.

'I really have to go,' she said, standing up.

'Of course,' Shastri agreed. 'By the way, Monika, will you be seeing Dr Lucas soon?'

'I might be. Why do you ask?'

'There were quite serious mistakes in the medical records that he sent me,' Shastri said. 'I intend, of course, to inform him of them myself, but as I said, I am very busy at the moment, and if you could do it . . .'

'What kind of mistakes?'

'He has made an error in the blood typing of both Melanie Danbury and William Danbury.'

'And how do you know this?' Paniatowski asked, as she felt a shiver run down her spine.

'You remember that you took a sample of Mr Danbury's blood when he was in custody?'

'Yes.'

'And do you also remember that I told you it would not be necessary, because Dr Lucas had already sent me the records?'

'Yes,' Paniatowski said, more impatiently this time.

'The sample had already gone to the lab by then, and they sent me the results this afternoon. And that is when I noticed Dr Lucas' error. The blood type that he sent me and the blood type from the sample are not the same at all, and this could have very serious consequences, because if Mr Danbury ever needed a blood transfusion, and they gave him the blood that his medical record indicated he needed, he would probably die.'

'But how do you know he got Melanie's blood typing wrong, as well?' Paniatowski asked.

'Ah, that is because of the inconsistencies. Whilst it is perfectly possible, going by the medical record, to say that Mr Danbury could be Melanie's father, the blood sample says he could not. And since he *is* Melanie's father, it is only logical to infer that Dr Lucas has got Melanie's blood type wrong too.' Shastri frowned. 'I must admit, I am quite disappointed in Dr Lucas. He has previously struck me as a very good doctor, but he has proved to be very slipshod in this case.'

He was a careful man, Paniatowski thought, and if he had made mistakes, they had been deliberate mistakes.

'Shit!' she said. 'He's been playing me – he's been playing me all along!'

The woman who opened the front door of Dr Lucas' house looked both surprised and relieved to find Paniatowski standing there.

'My goodness, that was quick,' she said. 'I only rang the police station five minutes ago.'

'And why did you ring?' Paniatowski asked. 'Was it because Dr Lucas has gone missing?'

'That's right.'

'When did you first notice he wasn't here?'

'I didn't. A friend of mine, Betty Hutton, rang me up at home, to say he's missed his last three surgeries, and that's most unusual, because he's never missed even one before.'

Missed his last three surgeries!

Betty Hutton!

Rang me up at home!

'Is Mrs Hutton's husband dying?' Paniatowski asked.

'No,' Mrs Dale replied. 'Whatever gave you that idea? Pete Hutton is as fit as a fiddle.'

'And you're not a live-in housekeeper, are you?' Paniatowski asked.

Mrs Dale laughed. 'Bless you, no. Mr Dale would never stand for that. When he gets home from a hard day's work, he expects to find his tea waiting for him on the table.'

'So how often *do* you come here?'

'Only three times a week – Tuesday, Thursday and Friday – but this week, for some reason, he gave me Friday off.'

'I'd be totally lost without my housekeeper. I simply wouldn't be able to keep the whole show afloat,' Lucas had said to Paniatowski on her first visit to his gothic pile.

'Would you like a cup of tea or coffee?' he asked, the second time she'd visited him. *'It may take some time, because Mrs Dale isn't up yet, and I don't know where she keeps everything. Still, I expect I can manage.'*

He had chosen his words carefully – she now saw that he had *always* chosen his words carefully – in order to convey the impression that Mrs Dale was a full-time employee.

And the purpose behind that had been to send a message – 'There can't have been anything odd or unusual going on in this house, because if there had been, Mrs Dale, *who is here all the time*, would have noticed it.'

The dying patient had been another strand he'd woven in to his tissue of lies, because that said, 'And anyway, I wouldn't have had the time to get up to anything odd or unusual myself – because I've been spending most of my time with Betty and Pete Hutton.'

'I need to search the house,' Paniatowski said.

Mrs Dale looked dubious. 'I don't know. I'm not sure how Dr Lucas would feel about . . .'

But Paniatowski was already heading up the stairs.

Lucas' bedroom was almost excessively neat, tidy and orderly.

It certainly wasn't the bedroom of a man who would make a mistake over not just one, but two, medical records, Paniatowski thought.

The wardrobe was fairly full, but there were some significant gaps on the rail, suggesting that several sets of clothes had been removed. One of the drawers in the chest of drawers – which Paniatowski guessed was the sock drawer – was empty. And there was no sign of the large suitcase she had seen on her last visit.

She checked the bathroom next – no shaving brush, no razor, no toothbrush.

A search of the ground floor of the house revealed nothing, until she reached the kitchen, where she noticed a door in the wall opposite the cooker.

'Where does that lead?' she asked Mrs Dale, who had been following worriedly in her wake since the start of the search.

'It goes down to the wine cellar,' the other woman said. 'But it hasn't been used for years. Dr Lucas doesn't drink very much, and when he does, it's usually whisky.'

The wine cellar would have both thick walls and ventilation, which would make it perfect for Lucas' purposes, Paniatowski thought.

She tried the door, and discovered it wasn't locked. But why would it be locked, when the horse had already bolted?

Beyond the door were steep stairs, leading down to the bowels of the house. Paniatowski found the light switch, and descended.

She was not in the least surprised by what she found beyond the foot of the stairs.

There was an electric fire, which Lucas had not even bothered to turn off when he left, because, however high the next electricity bill turned out to be, that was no concern of his any more.

There was a small table of the sort that is wheeled up to a patient's bed in hospital, and on it were a number of mild sedatives, which, without checking, Paniatowski knew would be suitable for children.

And there was a cot, just about large enough for the two-year-old Melanie Danbury.

TWELVE

Sunday, 9th October 1977

The gulls were out in force that morning. Some, framed against a battleship-grey sky, seemed content to glide lazily on the air currents, and emitted only the occasional shriek to make the world aware of their existence. Others had landed on the quay, where, chests puffed out and necks craned forward, they strutted up and down, angrily disputing the ownership of the remains of a sandwich that one of the dock workers had thrown to them.

Paniatowski walked quickly along the dock, the collar of her coat turned up against the cold wind blowing in from the sea. She had hardly spoken to DC Jack Crane on the drive down from Whitebridge, and even now, as they approached the prefab that served as a temporary station for the Port of Liverpool police, she did not really feel like talking.

The problem with the evidence they had was that it was all circumstantial, she told herself. There was no difficulty in proving that Dr Lucas had been in the Danbury house on the night of the murder, nor that he had taken Melanie away with him. But proving that he had struck the blows which killed Jane Danbury was quite another matter.

A good defence lawyer could argue convincingly that it had all been a burglary gone wrong, and however much the prosecution talked about locks and security systems, the jury might just look at weak, amiable Dr Lucas, sitting there in the dock, and find it very hard to believe that he had taken the life of another human being.

So she needed a confession – and she was not at all sure that Lucas *would* confess.

One of the gulls on the quay – a big brute, a William Danbury

of a seabird – had succeeded in grabbing most of the prize, and
as he flew off with the sandwich in his beak, the others screamed
their curses after him.

That could happen to me, Paniatowski thought. I could lose
this one – I really could lose it!

The walls in the biggest room of the temporary police station were
covered with nautical charts, shipping schedules and tide time-
tables. There were two smaller rooms which led off the main
one – a holding cell and an interview room. Dr Lucas had been
in the former before Paniatowski and Crane arrived, but now he
had been transferred to the latter, and was looking at them across
the table.

Lucas seemed remarkably calm, given the circumstances he
found himself in. His hands, cupped in front of him, showed no
signs of a tremble, nor did he twitch while the standard police
protocol was being recited for the benefit of the tape recorder.

Perhaps the fact that he'd acted decisively for once in his life
had given him new confidence, Paniatowski thought.

'Are you sure that you don't want a lawyer present, Dr Lucas?'
she asked.

'Why would I want a lawyer?'

'I need you to tell me, specifically, and in your own words,
that you don't want one.'

'I don't want a lawyer. Is that good enough for you?'

'Thank you.'

'Where's Melanie?' Lucas asked.

'The Liverpool Social Services Department is taking care of
her for the moment,' Paniatowski said.

She took out her cigarettes, and offered the packet to Lucas.

The doctor shook his head.

'I've given up,' he said. 'I've done it for Melanie. Nobody
should smoke around children.'

He was sending her a message, Paniatowski thought. He had
weighed up the probabilities, just as she had. He had realised
that making a run for it had been a mistake, and now he was
saying, 'If you charge me with murder, I can beat it, and if I
want custody of Melanie, I can have it!'

She lit up her own cigarette.

'Right,' she said, 'let's get started. You were caught trying to bribe a crew member to smuggle you aboard a merchant ship heading for Panama, weren't you?'

'Yes. So what? It's a very minor crime, and I'm sure I'll get away with a slap on the wrist.'

'I agree with you,' Paniatowski said. 'It *is* a minor crime. However, murder and kidnapping are not.'

'And are you *going* to charge me with murder and kidnapping?' Lucas challenged.

'Not for the moment. Just now, all I want to do is talk.'

'And what if I don't *want* to talk?'

'Well, I suppose if you're too frightened to talk, then you'll just have to listen to me wittering on to Detective Constable Crane,' Paniatowski told him.

'I'm not afraid to talk,' Lucas said. 'What would you like to talk *about*, Chief Inspector Paniatowski?'

'Let's start with William Danbury. He was never *really* your friend at all, was he?'

'Of course he was my friend.'

'I don't see how any kind of real friendship was possible between two men with such a big gap dividing them.'

'What do you mean – a big gap?'

'He was the great dramatic hero, striding across the centre of the stage of life, with everyone's eyes on him. And you followed in his wake – no more than the humble spear carrier. And you resented it. God, you resented it! But you did it anyway – because without William, you wouldn't have been on the stage at all.'

'I *did not* feel inferior to William Danbury,' Lucas said.

'Of course you did. You were bound to. He had everything, and you had nothing.'

'And perhaps the main reason I did not feel inferior to him was that *I* was not ambivalent about my sexuality.'

'And he was? Is that what you're trying to tell me now?'

'Was? He still is! Haven't you noticed what a boyish figure Gretchen Müller has? And she wasn't his first.'

'His first what?'

'His first mistress. She's merely the latest in a long line – and they all looked like her. I can give you some of their names, if you like, so you can judge for yourself.'

Paniatowski turned to Crane.

'Do you fancy Gretchen Müller, DC Crane?' she asked.

'Yes, ma'am, I do.'

'Just a little? Or quite a lot?'

'Quite a lot.'

'And are you homosexual, DC Crane?'

'No, ma'am. Definitely not.'

'We're not convinced,' Paniatowski said to Lucas. 'Neither of us can really accept this picture of William Danbury that you're trying to foist onto us.'

'William is a man born out of his time,' Lucas said, sounding more agitated now. 'He should have been an ancient Greek. They married only because they wanted children. But women were always regarded as inferior creatures – scarcely even human. For love, they chose boys. And for company, they chose men – men to drink with, and wrestle naked with.'

'I think what Dr Lucas is trying to tell us is that he had an affair with William Danbury,' Paniatowski said to Crane.

'No, I'm not,' Lucas protested. 'Don't you understand anything of what I've just said? I'm a perfectly normal heterosexual. I would have found the whole idea of an affair with William totally repulsive.'

'Maybe, but I'm sure you would have agreed to it if that had been what William wanted. You'd have been too weak to refuse,' Paniatowski taunted. 'If he'd asked you to, you'd have lain face down on the bed, gagging yourself with the pillow, and let him do whatever he wanted to you.'

'He never would have asked me,' Lucas said. 'He would never have asked *any* man, because he'd have been too afraid that that brute of a father of his might find out and want nothing more to do with him. But he still has the yearning. Look at the charities he's involved in. Virtually all of them deal with young men.'

'So you're telling me that because you know about this weakness of his, you feel as superior to him as he must feel to you, and that's how you make the friendship work?'

'Isn't that how all friendships work?' Lucas asked. 'Could you ever have a real friendship if there wasn't some way in which you were top dog?'

'I'm not buying any of this "I feel superior" shit!' Paniatowski said. 'You crap yourself at even the *thought* of displeasing William. Take the night of the murder, for example. Gretchen asked you to ring William at the Ribble Valley Hotel. You didn't want to do it. You knew it could get you into trouble. But you did it anyway – because you were afraid of what William might do to you if you didn't warn him.'

'That's not why I did it. I did it because . . .'

Lucas suddenly clamped his mouth closed.

'Because?' Paniatowski prodded.

'. . . because he was my friend.'

'You did it because you knew he'd react exactly in the way he did react. You wanted us to make him our prime suspect, not because you thought the charge would stick – you knew it wouldn't – but because it would stop the focus of the investigation coming anywhere near you. Isn't that right?'

'No comment.'

'Tell me about Jane,' Paniatowski suggested.

'What would you like to know?'

'I can understand why she agreed to sleep with you – she was like a frightened, wounded animal, and she would have slept with anyone who offered her comfort. But why did *you* want to sleep with *her*? Was it to get revenge on William – even though you knew you'd never have the balls to let him know you were taking that revenge?'

'I had no need to take revenge.'

'Then why?'

'I loved her.'

'Then why kill her? And why do it in such a vicious manner? Why crush her skull to a pulp?'

'I did not kill Jane.'

'I think you did.'

'Then prove it.'

She couldn't prove it conclusively, not without hard evidence – and he knew that as well as she did.

'You don't deny that you were in the Danbury house on the night she died, do you?' she asked.

'How could I?'

Indeed, how could he? That, at least, was easy to prove.

'How did you get in? Did Jane let you in?'

A smile crossed Lucas' face, and then was gone. He thought he was back in control again – and perhaps he was.

'How could Jane have let me in?' he asked. 'She was already dead when I arrived.'

'So how *did* you get in?'

'Jane had a key made for me.'

'Can you show me the key?'

'No.'

'Why not?'

'After the murder, I threw it into the canal.'

'Why?'

'Why do you think? It had nothing to do with Jane's murder, but I knew that if you found it, you'd make it *seem* as if it had.'

There'd been no key, of course. Jane had let him into the house herself. And possibly the prosecution could make something out of that – could point out to the jury that such specialist keys were numbered, and difficult to duplicate. But then the defence would produce four or five locksmiths who would testify that they could easily have replicated it, and the jury would be so confused that the point would be lost.

'So tell me what happened that night,' Paniatowski said.

'William was away and it was Gretchen's day off, so Jane had asked me to come up to the house. There was always a chance that William would turn up unexpectedly, of course, but even if he did, there was no problem, because I had the perfect excuse for being there.'

'You were the family doctor.'

'I was the family doctor. The gate was locked, and I undid it with the key I've since thrown away, but the main door to the house was wide open, as if someone had left in such a hurry that they'd forgotten to close it.'

He was already laying the ground for the burglar theory, Paniatowski thought.

'Go on,' she said.

'Jane was lying on the rug – dead.'

'Did you touch her?'

He had only to say no, and she'd got him – because if he hadn't touched her, how had the blood got on Melanie's pillow?

'Yes, I touched her,' Lucas said. 'I knelt down beside her, and I touched her head.'

'Why did you do that when, by your own admission, she was obviously dead?'

'I don't know. It was instinctive. Maybe it was because I loved her.'

Oh, he was good, Paniatowski thought – he was *very* good.

'And then you went upstairs, lifted Melanie from her bed, and took her back to your house?' she asked.

'Yes.'

'Why did you do that?'

'It was for her own protection. I knew that once your investigation really got underway, William would learn that he was not Melanie's real father, and I was frightened that when he did, he might hurt her.'

It was all sounding so plausible, Paniatowski thought, and she could almost see the jury nodding in agreement with him as he gave his evidence.

She decided she was going to have to go for his weak spot – his fragile sense of his own superiority. It was risky, and if she blew it this time she would never get another chance, but there really was no other way.

'You know what the people who know you will say when all this comes out in the newspapers, don't you?' she asked.

'I don't care what anybody will say – especially the people I know.'

He had to be lying, she thought.

But what if he wasn't lying? What if his ego was now so inflated that he really didn't care what other people thought?

'They'll say – and I think I'll agree with them – that you did it for William. When they learn that it was Jane who actually controlled the purse strings, and that she was thinking of divorcing William because of his affair with Gretchen . . .'

'She wasn't thinking of divorcing him.'

'. . . they'll say that William put you up to it. Remember how the two of them were at school, they'll say. Remember how Roger followed William round like a faithful dog.'

'They'll never say that,' Lucas protested.

But the look on his face suggested that he thought they would.

'They'll say, "Did you know that Roger and William were supposed to have gone to bed together? I don't know whether it's true or not – but if it is true, you know which one will have been on top, don't you?"'

'They won't say that, they won't say that, they won't say that . . .' Lucas chanted, as if he was trying to hypnotise himself.

'And when William asked Roger to kill his wife . . .' Paniatowski said, raising her voice in order to penetrate his wail of denial, '. . . when William asked Roger to kill his wife, Roger agreed immediately – even though he was supposed to be in love with her – because William still had the power over him.'

'That's not why I killed her!' Lucas screamed.

'What was that you just said?' Paniatowski asked.

'That's not why I killed her,' Lucas repeated, more softly this time.

'So why *did* you kill her?'

Lucas isn't listening. More than just not listening, he isn't really there in that police station, with those officers, any more. He has travelled back in both time and distance, and now he is in the Danburys' living room, facing Jane across an expensive Persian rug.

'I don't want you to go to Canada,' he says.

'And do you think I want to go?' Jane asks.

'If you don't want to go, why are you going?'

Jane shrugs helplessly. 'It's what William wants – and William always gets his own way in the end.'

'But he doesn't have to – not this time. You can say that you refuse to go, and move in with me.'

'The children . . .'

'You'll get custody of them, and I'll raise all *of them as if they were my own. I promise you that.'*

She laughs. 'That's easy for you to say here and now, with William away in Newcastle, but you'd never go through with it if he was here. You're as frightened of him as I am.'

'I'm not,' he says – and wishes he sounded more convincing.

'Besides, I need him,' Jane says. 'I couldn't imagine life without him.'

'But that's just part of the syndrome,' he tells her. 'Battered

*wives always think they can't manage without their husbands
– but once they've escaped the man's clutches, they see things
as they really are.' He pauses. 'You say you still need him. Do
you still* love *him, too?'*

'I think so.'

*He knows he shouldn't ask the next question, but he asks it
anyway. 'And how do you feel about me?'*

'I'm fond of you,' she says. 'You're very sweet and very kind.'

'But you don't love me?'

*'I know that's what you want, and I've tried to love you, Roger,
I really have, but I just can't bring myself to do it.'*

*'Why? What's wrong with me?' he says, knowing that this is
another question he should never have asked.*

*He can see her searching for the right words – the words he
will find acceptable. And then he sees her decide it is a hopeless
task, and give up.*

'You're so weak, Roger.'

It feels as if she has driven a burning hot spear through his heart.

*'And what is it that makes me weak?' he asks. 'Is it the fact
that I don't knock you around like he does?'*

She shrugs helplessly.

'No, it's just . . . it's just that you are.'

*'I won't allow William to take Melanie to Canada,' he says,
drawing what he thinks of as his line in the sand.*

*'How will you stop him?' she asks. 'By telling him she's your
daughter, and not his? You know you'd never be brave enough
to do that.'*

She turns her back on him.

Why?

Is she crying?

Or is she merely showing her contempt for him?

*His mind takes another leap backwards, and though he is still
in the Danburys' living room, he is also back in the school
playground.*

*He is sitting in the narrow strip of dirt between the end of the
asphalt and the fence which separates the school from the street.
He has his head pressed down on his knees, and he is softly
sobbing to himself. He cannot have been there long, but to him,
it feels like a lifetime.*

Someone touches him on the shoulder. He looks up, and sees William standing there.

'What's the matter?' William asks.

'Phil Briggs has been picking on me again. He's always hitting me.'

'Then I'll go and put a stop to it. I'll hit him so hard he won't dare go near you again.'

'But he's a lot bigger than you.'

'That doesn't matter.'

'Thank you,' Roger says.

'That's what friends are for,' William tells him, 'but before I do that, you'll have to do something for me.'

'What?'

William looks around, and sees a beetle rummaging in the dirt. He scoops it up in his hand.

'Eat this,' he said, holding the panicking insect level with Roger's mouth.

'Why?'

'To prove you're my friend, just like I'll be proving I'm your friend by beating up Phil.'

'Couldn't I do something else?'

'No, you have to eat the beetle.'

'Can I kill it first?'

'No, you have to eat it alive.'

He takes the beetle from William, and puts it in his mouth. He can feel it wriggling as it searches for a way to escape this damp cavern which has suddenly enclosed it.

He bites into the beetle, and it stops struggling, but now his mouth is filled with a bitter, foul juice.

He swallows. The beetle goes down, but he knows it will not stay down, because he is about to be sick.

'Don't throw up,' William warns him. 'If you throw up, it doesn't count.'

Somehow, he manages to avoid vomiting, and after a minute or so, all is left of the experience is a vile taste which will linger for days.

William nods his head, satisfied.

'Right, now I'll give Phil Briggs a real good hammering,' he says.

He doesn't succeed on the first day – in fact, he gets a good hammering himself – nor on the second, but on the third, he does manage to knock Briggs down, and he has won this battle, as he will win many in the future.

The playground recedes, and Lucas is back in the Danburys' living room.

They both passed the test of friendship that day, he thinks, but the difference was that William did it by being heroic, whereas he had done it by humiliating himself.

Jane still has her back to him. She was right when she said he would never dare tell William that Melanie was his daughter, he realises.

But why did she have to say it out loud?

They had both known – deep inside themselves – that he would be too frightened, but until she had put it into words, he, at least, had been able to pretend that he wouldn't.

He feels as humiliated as he did back in that playground, all those years ago – he can almost taste the beetle in his mouth – and it is all Jane's fault.

He sees the statue on the mantelpiece, and almost before he knows what is happening, it is in his hand.

'I asked you why you killed her,' says a voice which has no place in his own personal tragedy, and which drags him back to the present.

'Why did I kill her?' Lucas asked Paniatowski. 'I killed her out of kindness. For years, I've been protecting her from William as far as I was able, but once she was in Canada, she'd have been on her own. It was better for her to die then than to endure more years of misery.'

Paniatowski didn't believe it. He didn't believe it himself, she thought, but give it a little time and he would persuade himself it was true. Give it a little time, and he would finally see himself as a hero.

'If you hadn't made one careless mistake, you might just have got away with it,' she said.

Then she sat back and waited.

Almost a minute passed before Lucas said, 'And what mistake was that?'

'You needed us to think Melanie was William's child, so you changed the blood group on his medical record.'

'Yes, I did. So what?'

'Once we'd had William's blood sample analysed, we knew that the medical record had been changed.'

'I always knew there was a risk you'd take a sample of his blood and make the comparison, but what choice did I have?'

'You could have left his record alone, and changed Melanie's so it matched our sample.'

'I thought I was being so clever – but, you're right, that's what I should have done,' Lucas said, in a voice which mingled anger with disgust at his own stupidity.

Then, suddenly, he seemed to cheer up again.

'It will have to come out at the trial – or maybe even sooner – won't it?' he asked.

'*What* will have to come out?'

'The fact that Melanie isn't William's daughter at all, but mine.'

'Yes, that will have to come out,' Paniatowski agreed.

A broad smile – a look of pure happiness – came to Lucas' face.

'William won't like that,' he said. 'He won't like it at all.'

THIRTEEN

Tuesday, 11th October 1977

The wind had changed direction, and the purple heather, which had been waving towards Whitebridge for the previous hour, had turned its back on the old mill town and was now favouring the lands further north.

William Danbury, dressed in wellington boots, thick trousers and a heavy combat jacket, strode through the heather in search of small animals whose lives he could terminate.

He was carrying a Purdey shotgun. He had purchased it, second-hand, from a local aristocrat down on his luck, but even so, it had cost him an arm and a leg.

He hadn't bought the gun for himself, it had been intended as a gift for his father, but Archie Danbury would have none of it.

'It's not the gun in front of the man which matters,' he had said dismissively, 'it's the man behind the gun. So you keep it, and then maybe someday . . .'

Maybe someday you'll be as good as I am, he had meant.

He was always doing that, the old man – leaving thoughts unsaid, but nevertheless clear enough.

He had *never* been able to truly please his father, Danbury thought. However hard he'd tried, he had somehow always managed to fall short.

He could imagine what his father would have said if he'd known what he himself knew now.

'Cuckolded by a weed like Roger Lucas! You should be ashamed of yourself. Do you think your mother would ever have had an affair behind *my* back? No, she wouldn't have dared.'

'No, Dad, but she dared to blow you to pieces with your own shotgun,' he said into the wind.

Yet, in a way, that only proved his father's case. His mother had recognised that his father was so much of a man that there could be no half-measures – that if she was going to defy him in *any* way, she must also completely destroy him.

His own wife, on the other hand, had felt free to humiliate him – admittedly, only in secret, but it was still a humiliation – and that was more his failure than it was hers.

How they would laugh, those rugby players who had so admired him, those fresh-faced members of the Boys' Brigade who had wanted to be just like him when they grew up.

His wife had betrayed him with his dupe – his clown – and no one who knew him would ever forget it.

Worse yet, his own sons would be bound to learn about it eventually, and when they did, they would snigger behind his back.

His thoughts shifted to Ernest Hemingway. Now there was a real man, he told himself. Hemingway had driven an ambulance in the Spanish Civil War. Hemingway had caught big fish, and shot huge, strong creatures. Even his father had approved of Hemingway.

He turned to look back at the town in which he had once been a presence, and was now no more than a joke.

Well, what was good enough for Papa Hemingway was good enough for him, he thought.

His gun was already loaded and cocked. He put the barrel in his mouth, and pulled the trigger.

It was early evening, and in the public bar of the Drum and Monkey, Monika Paniatowski was having a quick drink with her team before going home to her children.

Not that she was likely to have a team for much longer, she thought, because she had made enemies on the police authority, and that was the kiss of death for most careers. They wouldn't sack her, of course – they had no grounds for that – but they would get her pushed into traffic or administration, so that instead of a quick execution, she would be forced to endure a living death.

The door opened, and Alderman Cudlip entered the bar. He looked around, located Paniatowski's table, and made a beeline for it.

'Trouble,' Meadows said.

'You're not wrong,' Paniatowski agreed.

Cudlip arrived at the table. 'I'd like a quiet word with DCI Paniatowski, if you don't mind,' he said to the rest of the team.

They didn't mind. When the chairman of the police authority asked you to clear off, it was wisest *not* to mind – even if you did.

Cudlip waited until Beresford, Meadows and Crane had gone over to the bar, then he sat down.

'Can I get you a drink?' Paniatowski asked.

'No, thank you, I'm not intending to be here long enough for that,' Cudlip said. 'You'll have heard what happened to William Danbury, won't you?'

And so it begins, Paniatowski thought. As far as Cudlip is concerned, I not only arrested Danbury for a crime he obviously hadn't committed, but also refused to release him even when the police authority practically begged me to. The strain that put on him was so great that he took his own life – and that makes it my fault.

'Yes, I've heard,' she said.

'I want you to know that when we came to see you, it was

because we were genuinely concerned about William's children. I'd like you to believe that.'

'I do believe it,' Paniatowski said, 'but you were also there because one of your own was not getting the privileged treatment you thought he was entitled to.'

'Aye, there may have been a bit of that behind it, as well,' Cudlip conceded. He paused. 'You were right about him, you know.'

'What!'

'I said you were right about him.'

'I was totally wrong – he *didn't* kill his wife.'

'That's as maybe, but you were right that he was a coward and a bully.'

'I never said that – at least, not to you.'

'You might not have said it, but I could read it in your every word and gesture,' Cudlip said. 'You'll hear a lot of people expressing a lot of sympathy for William Danbury in the next few days, but you won't hear any from me. A man who blows off his own head, and leaves his little children to fend for themselves, is no kind of man at all, in my book.'

Cudlip stood up.

'I'm a traditionalist, chief inspector. I don't like to see a woman doing a man's job, especially when that woman is as bloody-minded as you are, so I think it's more than likely that we'll lock horns again, and maybe next time I'll do my damnedest to see you get shifted into a job which is more suitable to your sex. But that's next time. This time, I'm here to tell you, you're off the hook as far as I'm concerned.' He gestured to the team that they could now return to the table. 'I'll see you around, Detective Chief Inspector Paniatowski,' he said.

'I'm sure you will, Alderman Cudlip,' Paniatowski agreed.

EPILOGUE

Monday 5th December 1977

I t had snowed overnight, and the speed of Beresford's journey from Whitebridge to Preston had been determined by the maddeningly slow snow plough he was following. But he had made it in the end, and now he sat in Preston Crown Court, listening to the closing stages of Regina v. Ethel Danbury.

Monika has been lucky with her crusade, he thought. Reginald Holloway, who had secretly buried one of his children in order to protect the other four, had been given the suspended sentence which his boss had argued was merited.

His own crusade had fared less well. Despite the story he had concocted for her, Ethel had been charged with her husband's murder, and now stood in the dock, soon to hear the verdict of her peers.

The Crown had presented a very good case, and perhaps the strongest evidence against Ethel had been delivered by the medical experts. It would have been impossible, they all agreed, for Archie Danbury to have moved more than minimally after he had been shot in the chest. Therefore, it followed that he no longer posed a threat to his wife. Therefore, her claim, that she only shot him in the head because she was in fear for her life, was simply not true. And finally, therefore, the jury had no alternative but to bring in a verdict of murder.

And as much as I like and pity her, if I was on that jury, that would be my verdict, too, Beresford thought miserably.

The counsel for the defence, Rodney Harding QC, was on his feet and was making his closing remarks to the jury.

'Ethel Danbury has suffered a lifetime of abuse,' Harding said. 'You have heard that her husband branded her with a hot iron when she singed his shirt. You have heard that he beat her – brutally and regularly. Is it any wonder, then, that she was in fear for her life?'

But none of that mattered, Beresford thought – because she wasn't in fear for her life when she shot him in the head.

'You have heard the prosecution's medical experts say he could not have posed any threat once he had been shot in the chest,' Harding continued, 'but what they should have said is that it was *unlikely* he could have posed such a threat. Every day, in the newspapers, we read of extraordinary physical feats which astound medical science. Frail women who find the strength to lift up cars in order to release their babies trapped underneath. Explorers, speared by hostile natives, who nevertheless manage to walk hundreds of miles through harsh jungles – with the spears still sticking in them. I could list countless other examples, but there is no need to. The point is that Archic Danbury *could* have started to get to his feet, and Ethel Danbury *could* have felt threatened. There is an element of doubt here, ladies and gentlemen of the jury – and where there is doubt, there can be no conviction.'

It was a noble effort, Beresford thought, but the jury simply weren't buying it. They wanted to let Ethel off – that was obvious from their faces – but unless Harding gave them something more, they could not, in all conscience, reach any verdict other than guilty. And the problem was that Harding had shot his bolt, and there was nothing more he *could* give.

'Finally, you must ask yourself whether Ethel Danbury *could* kill in cold blood,' the barrister continued. 'This is a woman who, as anyone who knows her will tell you, has a heart of gold. This is a woman who, if she were found not guilty, would gladly bring up her three grandchildren – one of whom is not even a blood relative – as her own, rather than see them abandoned to an orphanage . . .'

The prosecutor was on his feet, outraged, but his intervention was unnecessary, since the judge already had the matter in hand.

'Mr Harding!' he said sternly. 'Mr Harding! You are on the verge of contempt of court.'

Harding looked suitably contrite. 'I apologise, your honour,' he said, 'my last comment was totally inappropriate, and I withdraw it unreservedly.'

The judge turned to the jury.

'You have heard what Mr Harding just said. He withdraws his

comment unreservedly. And rightly so, because what Mrs
Danbury would, or would not, do if she was found not guilty of
the crime with which she is charged is totally irrelevant to these
proceedings. Therefore, I am instructing you to disregard the
comment, and to let it play no part in your deliberations.'

There was no chance of that, Beresford thought happily, just
as there wasn't a chance in hell now that this jury would ever
find Ethel Danbury guilty.

CPSIA information can be obtained
at www.ICGtesting.com
Printed in the USA
BVHW030214130720
583579BV00001B/77

9 781847 516701